The Dutchman

A Novel of Guilt and Redemption

WANDA DEHAVEN PYLE

Also by Wanda DeHaven Pyle

Windborne
The Stone House Legacy
The Steel Canyon Legacy
The Edgewater Legacy

https://rb.gy/d7jugr

The Dutchman

This is a work of fiction. All incidents and dialogue, all characters with the exception of some well-known historical and public figures, are products of the author's imagination and are not to be construed as real. Where real-life historical or public figures appear, the situations, incidents, and dialogues surrounding those persons are entirely fictional and are not intended to depict actual events or to change the entirely fictional nature of the work. In all other respects, any resemblances to persons living or dead are entirely coincidental.

DEDICATION

To the members of the DeHaven clan
who have labored to keep the legend alive
for over 200 years.

AUTHOR'S NOTE

The legend of Jacob DeHaven has been a part of our family history for as long as I can remember. According to the story, Jacob DeHaven provided George Washington with cash and supplies while the army was encamped at Valley Forge. Unfortunately, in the aftermath of the Revolution, any record of the loan was lost amid the chaos of the Continental Congress and the framing of a new nation. Numerous attempts have been made over the years to get the government to repay the loan or, at a minimum, recognize the contribution of our ancestor, but to no avail.

The following information was published in part in the *New York Times*, May 27, 1990.

213 YEARS AFTER LOAN, UNCLE SAM IS DUNNED

By Lisa Belkin, Special to the New York Times

More than 200 years ago, a wealthy Pennsylvania merchant named Jacob DeHaven lent $400,000 to the Continental Congress to rescue the troops at Valley Forge. That loan was apparently never repaid.

What Mr. DeHaven did was respond to a desperate plea in 1777 from George Washington, the commander in chief of the Continental Army, when it looked as if the Revolutionary War was about to be lost. One of nine children in a wealthy family of merchants and landowners, Mr. DeHaven was living in Pennsylvania on farmland adjoining the Valley Forge campgrounds in the winter of 1777-78. The soldiers there were short of food, clothing, shelter, and ammunition. General Washington sent a plea to the leadership of Pennsylvania asking for money saying: "Unless aid comes, our affairs must soon become desperate beyond the possibility of recovery. The Army must disband or starve." Mr. DeHaven was among those who responded.

He lent the Government $50,000 in gold and what his descendants estimate to be another $400,000 in supplies. The Continental Army survived the winter at Valley Forge, and when the war was over, Mr. DeHaven apparently tried several times to collect what was owed to him. Mr. DeHaven was offered Continental money for his loan certificate, but he refused and held out for gold.

The Continental dollars were notoriously worthless, leading to the expression at the time that something was "not worth a Continental."

Mr. DeHaven died penniless in 1812 and is believed to be buried in Swedeland, Pennsylvania in a family cemetery. He had no children; had he possessed anything tangible to bequeath, his siblings and their children would have been his legal heirs.

This is the inspiration for *The Dutchman*. I have not used the DeHaven name in my story to avoid confusion with the actual legend. I have also taken some liberties with the legend to enhance the plot. This is, after all, a work of fiction.

PART I

One of the hardest lessons in life is letting go.
Whether it is guilt, anger, love, loss, or betrayal,
Change is never easy.
We fight to hold on and we fight to let go.
—Anonymous

:

1

The harbor lay shrouded in yellow fog. Coal fires throughout the city of Rotterdam belched smoke and soot into the air where it became trapped beneath the cold air above the city, choking those of us who dared to venture out. I arrived at the wharf early to join the mobs of emigrants storming the docks to board the ships heading for America. I held on tightly my knapsack with the goatskin packet inside that Father had given to me when I left my home in Gelderland. It contained the only real link I had to my heritage in America.

The chaos in the harbor was overwhelming. Women and children cried, and dockworkers shouted orders. Many passengers had to toss their luggage on board from the quay, and clamber on board by the rigging. The men were able to jump on board with comparative ease; but most of the women were unable to accomplish the task without much screaming and hesitation. Here and there a woman became entangled with her skirts about her waist, and her legs still more sadly exposed to the loiterers on shore. She could be heard imploring aid from the sailors or passengers above, most of whom laughed or ignored her pleas. Many a package missed its mark and fell onto the dock, where it was rescued and handled up by a man in a small boat who followed in the wake of the mighty ship. I clutched my knapsack to my chest to protect it from thieves and pickpockets while I elbowed my way through the crush of passengers and dock workers.

Father had given me the goatskin packet on the morning of my departure from Gelderland. We had been seated at the rough-hewn wooden table he had built when he and mother were first married. A single candle cast early morning shadows across his lined face.

"What's this?" I asked when he pushed the goatskin packet across the table toward me. It was obviously old. The leather was cracked and brittle. I gazed at it in surprise, a little afraid to touch it. He had never given me a gift before.

His voice was uncharacteristically tender. "I know things have not gone as you had hoped, and I cannot take away the pain you must feel." He paused as if a long-buried memory had passed through his mind. "This is the only thing I have to give you that might be of some value on your journey. It has been passed down in our family for generations. I have kept it hidden away all these years because I was not sure what to do with it. But it seems that it should go to you as you begin a new life in America."

I pulled the packet toward me and carefully untied the bundle revealing a sheaf of letters and papers. They were yellowed with age, but I could make out the fact that they were letters written to my great-grandmother when she was just a teenage girl.

"Most of them are love letters," Father said, "but they hold a key to your heritage that may prove useful in America."

"Who wrote them?"

Father sighed and rose from his chair. "It's a long story. Perhaps it will help us pass the time on the way to the depot."

My decision to emigrate had been a long time coming. In 1861, Albertus Virderman had visited my father's parish from Fond du Lac County in Wisconsin. He extolled the virtues of land near the settlement of Alto. Virderman spoke so favorably of the place and surrounding region that, as an impressionable 16-year old, I felt a strong magnetic power drawing me to the area. It was all I could think about…until I met Lanie Van Huel.

Lainie's brother, Dirk, and I had been schoolmates, but we harbored a deep-seated animus toward each other that often led to fistfights. He was two years older than I and although not as tall, he was broad-shouldered and thickly built. What he lacked in stature, he compensated for with sheer meanness. At school, he had made it his mission to bully the younger students into submission. He was usually accompanied by a group of minor players who encouraged his attacks and often added to the abuse once the victim was subdued.

It was after one of these encounters that Lainie came upon me sitting in the road spitting up blood and dirt. She was a vision of loveliness. She wore a dark cotton dress covered by a lace-trimmed pinafore that just touched the top of her shoes. Her flaxen hair was plaited into braids and wound into a halo around her head, but stubborn tendrils had escaped and curled around her face and neck.

"What happened to you?" she asked.

I got to my feet and dusted myself off. "It's nothing. I just tripped."

A gentle breeze fluttered the pink ribbons in her hair. She stooped and helped me gather my school books. Her hand brushed mine as she handed them over to me. "I don't believe you," she said, smiling sweetly. "But I admire your courage. It was Dirk, wasn't it?" When I didn't answer, she continued, "My brother is a brute. He must think you are a threat to him, or he would leave you alone."

"Why would he think I'm a threat? I've done nothing to him."

She smiled again and dazzled me with the light of her spirit. "Because you are smart and handsome and strong…all those things he is not."

I felt the blood rush to my face in embarrassment. Lainie laughed and her voice rang in my ears like tiny bells.

Then she skipped away from me, taking my heart with her.

I clambered aboard the Dutch packet ship bound for New York and glanced back to take one last look at the land I was leaving behind. Mother and the rest of my family were still sleeping when Father and I left for the train depot in Zutphen that morning. We had said our goodbyes the night before among a flood of tears. The pain of leaving my family mixed with my own grief was too much to bear a second time.

Father and I began our journey in silence. The only sound was the steady clip-clop of the horse's hooves on the hard-packed earth. Dawn was just stretching her flaming fingers into the sky. Soon bright sunshine would flood the fields, encouraging the first blush of color from daffodils that had lain dormant through the winter. But winter did not give up so easily in the Netherlands. The early morning air still held her winter chill along with the scent of newly turned soil.

I held the knapsack with the goatskin packet in my lap and waited expectantly. Father stared straight ahead. I glanced at him from time to time, waiting for him to speak.

"You're wondering about the love letters," he said, glancing across at me. "They were written to my grandmother by a Dutch privateer named Jacob Van Pelt."

My eyes widened in amazement. "A pirate! I cannot imagine Grandmother falling for a pirate. She was always so prim and pious."

Father chuckled and the sound rippled up from deep in his throat. "People are not always what they seem." I waited for him to continue. "They met while his ship was in port in Rotterdam and fell madly in love, but grandmother's family were strict Calvinists and she had already been promised to your grandfather, Arie De Jong, a Gelderland farmer of the same faith. Her parents would not allow their 15-year old daughter to run off to America with a man of questionable character who was ten years her senior, even though he had received a large land grant from Governor William Penn to settle in America."

I felt a sudden compassion for this teenage girl. "I think I know how he might have felt."

"I thought you might," Father said, allowing himself the slightest of smiles. "Her father forbade her to see her lover, but before Van Pelt left for America, they had one night of passion together. That night produced a child. My father was that child." He paused and let the words hang between us like dead weight. "My grandmother never told anyone she was with child. Van Pelt returned to America and the arranged marriage to Arie De Jong proceeded as planned."

Realization slowly dawned on me. "So, are you saying that your father was the illegitimate child of this pirate, Jacob Van Pelt?"

Father nodded. "That is the story my grandmother told him when she handed over the packet to my father. No one ever questioned the legitimacy of my father's birth. He was christened Louis De Jong after the monarch, Louis I who ruled over the Netherlands from 1806-1810." Father said, proudly. "My grandfather never knew or guessed that the child he raised as his own was fathered by another man."

I was incredulous. "Why didn't you ever tell us?"

11

Father shrugged and continued to stare off into the distance. "It didn't seem important. My father was raised in a loving home and he raised a large family of his own. I am proud to be his son. A piece of paper and a few old letters change nothing."

"Then why are you telling me now?"

Father sighed and the sound came from deep within his chest like the wheeze of the bellows that he used to coax a flame from a spark of tinder. "When Jacob Van Pelt returned to America, the country was on the verge of revolution, but he continued to secretly write to my grandmother for several years. He told her of his efforts to support the Continental Army during the rebellion by providing money and supplies to Washington's army during the terrible winter at Valley Forge."

"I know that many of our countrymen supported the Colonists in their effort to gain independence from British rule, but I had no idea that our family was directly involved," I said.

"There was no need for anyone to know," Father continued. "Van Pelt's letters refer to the night of passion the two of them spent together and his hopes that they could be together again once the war was over." He paused to consider his thoughts. "There is no evidence that my grandmother ever responded to his letters or told him about the child he had fathered." Father paused again, as if trying to remember. "Finally, the letters stopped. Then, as he was dying, Van Pelt wrote to her again. He told her that he had made and lost a fortune after the Revolutionary War. He had never married, hoping against all odds that they could rekindle their relationship. But now, as his health was failing, he had nothing left to show for his life, no family, no wealth…only a promissory note from George Washington that pledged to repay the $450,000 in money and supplies Van Pelt had provided to keep the army from starving at Valley Forge. Although Van Pelt's efforts to collect on the debt all these years had come to naught, it was all he had left that might have any value. It wasn't much, but he wanted her to have it."

I struggled to process what he was telling me. "The promissory note…is it in this packet?"

He nodded, "I'm an old man. Your brothers will take over the farm and your sisters will soon marry and start families of their own. Their futures are set. Your future is still undetermined. If this note will help you in your new life in America, then you should have it."

He glanced sideways at me. "Just be careful. If the note is valid, there may be those who would be willing to do you harm to get their hands on it."

His warning echoed in my ears when an old seaman with a grizzly beard, tugged at my shoulder. "I'll be happy to hold yer valuables for safekeeping till we reach America," he said, eyeing my knapsack. Along with the goatskin packet, my knapsack contained a single change of clothes, a loaf of wheat bread and a small wheel of cheese. Except for the tiny pouch of gold coins from the sale of our best dairy cow that Mother had sewn into the lining of my coat, it was everything I owned.

"No thanks," I said, hugging it close. "I have nothing here of value, so I'll just keep it with me." The old sailor shrugged and moved on to accost the next passenger.

At last, amid a final rush to load the last of its human and material cargo, the ship signaled her readiness for departure. When the ship cleared the gate and floated out into the bay, I joined the other passengers against the railing to catch the last glimpse of land before the ship reached open sea. The spectators on shore took off their hats and cheered lustily. The cheer was repeated by the whole body of emigrants on deck, who raised a shout that must have been heard from a mile away in the noisy and busy thoroughfares of Rotterdam. They all seemed glad to leave their native land. We hardly got outside the harbor before fiddles and concertinas were produced and they began dancing away on the fore deck. However, the joy of the journey did not last long.

Most of the immigrants on board had never been at sea. They were haunted by the sea's mysterious powers and changing moods. They stared blankly into the distance or spoke to each other in languages I did not understand. My fellow passengers were remarkable only for their extreme plainness, nothing but wood in their constitutions. For many, the voyage across the Atlantic was just another dreary chapter in an existence made up of periods of strife and adversities.

"*Spreek je Nederlands?*" A young man with a pale round pock-marked face interrupted my thoughts. He was several years younger than I, dressed in traditional Dutch clothing with loose-fitting breeches, a white cotton shirt and suspenders under his long woolen cloak. A blue fisherman's cap perched on his head covered a mop of shaggy dust-colored hair. There was no mistaking the nervous anxiety in his eyes.

"*Ja,*" I nodded, trying not to sound encouraging.

He stepped to the rail beside me. "My name is Jelle Schippers. I'm from Zuid, Holland," he said, eagerly.

"Harke De Jong," I answered. "From Zutphen, Gelderland."

We stood together quietly watching the land slowly recede into watery nothingness. "This is my first crossing," he said at last. "I'm going to join my uncle's family in America. He has a place out west in Wisconsin."

I couldn't help but register my surprise. "That's where I'm headed as well!"

Jelle's face lit up with pleasure. "My uncle is a haberdasher by trade. He moved west to homestead." Jelle's round face clouded slightly. "He's a great shoemaker, but he's no good at farming or managing a business. That's why they sent for me. I'm going to help him manage his affairs. I studied for a year at the university and apprenticed as a clerk while I was there." Jelle's eyes brightened with hope. "Maybe we could travel there together. I'm a bit nervous about the crossing."

The thought of shepherding this scared young man across the ocean did not appeal to me. However, the trip ahead was long and arduous, and he was relatively clean and odor free. Given our common destination, he might also prove to be good company on the journey. "Of course," I answered. "I have no one waiting to meet me when I arrive. Perhaps your uncle could use an extra hand until I get settled."

Jelle's eyes brightened. "I'm sure he could. I understand that he has done little to prepare the land for spring planting. Do you know anything about agriculture?"

"My family owns a small farm near Arnhem. But with land prices what they are, there was no possibility of expansion. So, I decided to stake my own claim in America."

"It's brave of you to strike out on your own," Jelle said.

"Not so much brave, as a necessity," I answered.

Our family had farmed the same piece of land in the Netherlands for generations, yet we still only managed to eke out a marginal living. The best I could hope for by remaining was a future as a tenant farmer, turning over the fruits of my hard labor to the landowner. This was not the life I envisioned for myself. My only chance at independent land ownership lay in America where cheap land was still available for homesteading.

"I understand that the railroads are expanding at an alarming pace and opening the American west to new settlement," Jelle said.

"There is no time to waste for those of us wishing to establish a homestead," I said. "If I wait much longer, all the best land will already be taken."

Jelle nodded sympathetically, but he did not press for more information. Instead, he chose to fill the time chattering about the home and family he had left behind and his hopes for the future. I didn't mind. The one-sided conversation left me free to nod in occasional agreement without divulging much of my own story. I breathed in the damp sea air deeply through my nose and blew it out slowly through my mouth and stared out at the endless ocean. I blinked away the ghostly images that danced just behind my eyelids.

"You don't have to do this now, Harke," Father had said that morning. I felt his presence behind me as I stared out into the early morning darkness, but I still flinched when he placed his hand on my shoulder. It wasn't his voice that had startled me, it was his touch. Although he seldom raised his voice in anger, he was not inclined toward demonstrations of tenderness. "You can wait until you've had time to put all this behind you." His voice held a mixture of hope and despair.

"I believe it's for the best," I said, but I continued to stare out into the comfort of the darkness. "It's the only way I can redeem myself and shed this burden of guilt."

I knew that there was no use dwelling on the past. But the past is not so easily ignored. Still, I was determined to make a good show of it for his sake. "Besides, the longer I remain here, the more difficult life will be for you and the rest of the family." I turned away from the darkness and followed him back into the kitchen.

Father tried to sound reassuring. "You must understand that what has happened was God's will. You must trust in his wisdom in this matter."

His remark caused a resurgence of all the anger and resentment I had held inside for so long. Even now, at the age of 24, it was a beast that I fought constantly to control, and not always successfully.

"I have no illusions about the power of God's will!" I exclaimed. "Where was God when I needed him most?"

A brief flash of anger passed over Father's face. He believed that everything happened according to God's plan and that God would protect those who adhered strictly to his word. I knew I had hit a nerve, but he managed to keep his voice calm. "You mustn't blame God for what happened to Lainie," he said. "Her death was a terrible accident. If your faith is strong, God will help you overcome the pain and guilt you are feeling."

We had been over this argument many times, but I still found it impossible to hide my disdain. "If we Calvinists are the righteous ones, then why are we being punished?" I asked. "We worship in secret to avoid drawing the attention of those in power who adhere to the doctrine of the state church. Whole congregations have already emigrated to America to escape the persecution. Those who stay behind are mocked and scorned; some even suffer imprisonment!" My anger rose on its haunches and I snarled at him. "Our family is no exception! People turn aside when we pass and refuse to buy our produce in the open market, asking instead that we bring our wares to them under the cover of darkness. And things have only gotten worse since the deaths of Lainie and her father. We are blamed for their deaths. Now her brother has vowed revenge and mounted a campaign against us!"

Father stared hopelessly into his cup as if he were willing the answer to my dilemma to suddenly appear there. "It is my fervent hope that you can find some peace for your troubled soul in America," he said, sadly. An awkward silence settled between us before he sighed and spoke again. "You have the name of the leader of our congregation in Wisconsin. Once you connect with others of our faith, they will help you get settled."

I ran my fingers through the unruly mop of hair that continually fell over my eyes. Seeing him bent with sadness and regret, my anger subsided as quickly as it had risen. "I'm sorry that my actions have caused you such grief," I said. "I just hope my leaving will ease some of the tension you're under."

"Emotion and reason both have important roles in our lives," Father said, thoughtfully. "They both provide information and guide behavior. The key is to know when to trust one over the other."

Beside me on the ship's deck, Jelle had ceased his chattering and begun to make small gasping noises. "I'm not feeling well," he said, and indeed, his face had taken on a sickly shade of green.

"I think you had better get below deck," I said, turning to him. "You may feel less motion there."

I led him down the stairs and helped him get settled in his cot. Like most of the immigrants on board, we traveled in steerage. Our quarters had berths lining the walls and a long dining table in the middle. The daily routine in steerage began early with washing, dressing, and tidying up before breakfast. Then we began our daily chores: cleaning berths, scrubbing decks, and doing washing. I spent as much time as possible on deck away from the stench of sickness and unwashed bodies, watching the ship's wake as it made its way languidly across the ocean.

2

The storm came upon us without warning. One minute the ocean was quite calm, but in an instant, it became a raging monster. Without warning, gentle waves became deadly killers. Aboard ship all was bedlam as the ship pitched and rolled in the waves. Seasickness, groans, and cries of fright filled the night. The stench below decks became unbearable. Jelle spent most of his days bent over the bucket by his cot. "I hate the sea!" he wailed, during a moment of lucidness. "We can't reach land soon enough to suit me."

The storm continued for several days and burials at sea were all too commonplace. One woman lost her little one from fever, and the poor child had to be thrown overboard. The grief-stricken mother wept for her child and could not be comforted. "It is a sad thing to have to hide one's offspring in the grave on land," I said to Jelle, "but there is something about death and burial in the cold canvas winding-sheet at sea, in a fathomless grave, that is even harder and more galling."

When the storm finally abated, I made my way up to the poop deck. Travelers in first and second-class cabins enjoyed a far different experience from the cramped and crowded conditions we experienced. A cook and a steward prepared and served their meals. The assistance of a steward also meant cabin passengers had more time for social activities, games, reading and writing or lounging on the poop deck. There was even a committee to organize entertainments such as dances and theatrical or musical performances.

First class passengers could visit all accommodation areas on board, but those of us in steerage could only access these areas by invitation. Most passengers from steerage were confined to the main deck, but I soon discovered that these boundaries were only minimally enforced, and I occasionally wandered up to the poop deck in the evenings when the first class passengers had retreated to their cabins or were enjoying card games in the ladies and gentleman's rooms just below.

I leaned against the railing and filled my lungs with the clean salt air. The full moon cast soft shadows on the inky sea making it appear formless and unfathomable. The gentle motion of the ship as it rose and fell in the waves lulled me like a woman's sigh, tempting me to lie down in her soft embrace and drift into dark oblivion. The storm had resurrected painful memories that I had been trying hard to bury.

I was the one who found Lainie's body. She had gone to meet me at our special place down by the river. We shared our first kiss under the ancient oak tree anchored above the bank. We pledged our love to each other under its protective branches. I even carved our initials into the tree to claim it as ours. Afterward, I went back and cut it down.

I fell for Lainie Van Huel with catastrophic timing. We were blind to the sharp social divisions that would ultimately drive us apart. Lainie's father was a member of the wealthy social class who ruled the government of the Netherlands. He had made his fortune through investments in the Holland Land Company, and he had great hopes for the prosperous union of his only daughter to a man befitting his own social stature. My family were strict Calvinists whose religious beliefs were often at odds with those of the ruling class. As the youngest son in a family whose economic survival relied on a good harvest, the prospects for my future were limited. In the Netherlands, where land was scarce, and taxes were high, there was almost no opportunity for independent land ownership. My only chance for prosperity lay in emigration to America, where land was still plentiful and available to those willing to work hard and endure the hardships.

Lainie and I were filled with the passion and recklessness of youth. As we grew older, I tried to convince her to follow me to America, but she did not share my enthusiasm for emigration. Her father was in failing health and she refused to leave him and the life she had become accustomed to.

Years passed and the issue remained unresolved between us. We were trapped in a hopeless situation with no apparent way out. Even after she was promised in marriage to the Governor's nephew, I continued to hold out hope that things would somehow work out for us. When she became pregnant with our child, I increased my efforts to convince her to run away with me, but the arranged marriage would be socially and politically advantageous for her family. When I went to her father to seek his support for us, he threatened to bring ruin upon my family if I tried to interfere with the arrangement. We argued. He swung at me and I shoved him aside. He fell to the ground clutching his chest and gasping for air. Shocked at what I had done, I ran. I left him lying in the dust sputtering and trying to catch his breath, a quivering mound of overweight privilege and pomposity. It was an act I was later to regret.

On the day before Lainie was to be married to the Governor's nephew, I waited outside her house until she finally came out. I pleaded with her to meet me at our special spot down by the river and come away with me that night, but she refused. In desperation, I threatened to reveal our child's true birthright if she went through with the marriage.

I waited for her until the storm began and the river started to rise. Then I finally gave up hope. The next day, in the aftermath of the storm, I discovered that she was missing. I knew immediately what had happened. There was no other reason for her to be out in the storm. Her death left an empty spot in my heart to remind me of my guilt, where so many beautiful memories had once grown.

A humpback whale breached a few yards from the ship, mocking me with a snort of its spume before disappearing beneath the waves with a final slap of its tail. Within seconds the sea was calm again. A gentle English voice interrupted my thoughts.

"It's a perfect night for melancholy, isn't it?"

I turned to face a young woman wrapped in a dark woolen cloak. She had pale, wide-set eyes and straight, regal shoulders. Her face had a chiseled quality like fine marble. Her auburn hair, burnished by the moonlight, peeked out from the hood of her cloak, and soft tendrils blew gently around her face.

At that moment, the few English words and phrases I had learned from Lainie when she returned from London completely escaped me. "*Spreek geen Engels,*" I answered, sheepishly.

She smiled. "*Ik spree keen beetje Nederlands.*" Her Dutch was halting, but I could make out most of what she said. "You looked deep in thought just now. Were you thinking of someone you left behind?"

I nodded, sheepishly. "You might say that."

"It's never easy to leave an old life behind."

"Is that what you're doing?"

"You might say that." She repeated my response with a smile. It was a good smile, and it filled her lively eyes.

She held out a soft-gloved hand. "I'm Catherine. Catherine Weller."

"Harke De Jong," I answered, taking her hand. She had strong, long-fingered hands, but they appeared small in my large grasp. I held it a moment and then let it go.

The sky was clear, but a chill breeze stirred the air as the ship rocked gently in the waves. She moved to the railing and stared out into the vast emptiness of the ocean. There was a stillness about her that was striking because it carried with it an attitude of deep thoughtfulness. She shivered and pulled her cloak tightly around her. "You'd think I would be used to the cold and the damp coming from England."

"Winters can be cold and damp in Holland as well."

"Yes," she said. "We lived in Amsterdam for several years while my father was conducting business there."

I turned to face her. "Is that where you learned to speak the language?"

"I studied German while I was in school, so the Dutch language was not difficult to pick up," she said. "I thought if I mastered the languages of the countries my father was dealing with, it would be of benefit to him in his business."

"And was it?" I asked the question mildly, but there was nothing mild about the way she responded.

"Not the way I had hoped," she answered, curtly. "I had hoped that my opinions would be as valued as my language skills and that I might be viewed as his partner in business, rather than simply a translator. But that was not the case."

"I suppose it must be quite difficult for a lady of your station to be taken seriously in business matters," I said.

"And why is that, do you suppose?" she asked, and there was no mistaking the slight edge to her voice. "Do you think women lack the ability to be successful in business?"

"On the contrary," I stammered. "I only meant that most women of your station would not be interested in such matters."

She regarded me with soft gray eyes and a hint of mischief tugged at her smile. Polite society might have considered her look to be improperly suggestive, but I just found the contradiction between her casual tone and her searching eyes unexpectedly disconcerting. "Have you had occasion to speak with many ladies of my station? Wait. I suppose that someone with your rugged charm would have no trouble engaging ladies of my station in conversation."

I felt myself redden and I found myself strangely unnerved. I could bear her disdain, but not her mockery. I shifted uneasily under her gaze, suddenly aware of my unkempt appearance. "There was only one lady of your station who dared to give me a second look and I'm afraid my rugged charm was not enough for her." She took a step away from me. I had surprised and shocked her, and I was rather pleased about the fact.

"Is that the reason for your melancholy?" she asked, and the surprise on her face swiftly melted into one of curiosity.

I wasn't ready to let her off the hook that easily. "I'm leaving behind the only life I have ever known to start anew in a strange new land. I have nothing to offer but a broad back and a willingness to work hard to achieve my goals. Isn't that enough reason for melancholy?"

She ducked her head slightly at my rebuke and a tiny wrinkle formed between her eyes. "Perhaps," she answered, "but it takes more than hard work and desire to be successful." she said. "How do you plan to succeed in America if you don't speak English?"

"I speak a little," I said in English. "I'm hoping it's enough to get me by." I studied her face for a reaction, but she only nodded slightly.

"Americans can be quite brash and unforgiving to foreigners," she said, turning away from me.

"You sound as if you know the culture well. Have you been there often?" I asked.

"My parents are both American. We moved to England for father's business when I was quite young, but most of our family stayed behind in Philadelphia. That's where we're headed now."

I remembered the goatskin packet still tucked away in my knapsack below and I was tempted to tell her about my connection to the Van Pelt family in Pennsylvania. But warning bells clanged in my brain. Instead, I offered my own reasons for emigrating to America. "I am meeting some of my father's congregation in Alto, Wisconsin. I hope to homestead there."

"Are you a Seceder then?" she asked. "I would never have guessed you to be a religious zealot."

"My father is. I'm just hoping to contact people who can help me get started in America. It has long been a dream of mine to be an independent landowner."

Catherine turned to face me. "Homesteading requires hard work and fortitude," she said. "What makes you think you have what it takes?"

"It's not just a choice," I said, curtly. "It's my destiny."

She leaned toward me. Although there was still a good two feet between us, she felt unsettlingly close. She gazed at me for several moments without speaking. I had the feeling she was sizing me up, checking to see if I measured up somehow. "You carry an air about you, Mr. De Jong," she said at last. "Your speech indicates that you have had a decent education. Your manner is careful, but it is not that of a man who approaches the world with fear or temerity. You have a certain rough charm about you that is both intriguing and dangerous."

I had no response to this frank assessment, so I let the silence settle between us again. A loud burst of laughter reached us from the first-class cabins below. She moved away from me and I stole a sideways glance at her. She was tall and slender, and elegantly dressed. Her face had the chiseled quality of the marble statues in St. Walburgis Church near my home in Zutphen. She emanated an air of great confidence. She was obviously bright and ambitious, but there was an attitude of restless discontent about her.

"I must be getting back," she said, but there was no conviction in her voice. "Father will be looking for me."

"To be his translator?"

Catherine allowed a frown of dismay to cloud her gray eyes. "Not tonight," she answered. "I'm afraid ladies are not allowed in the Gentleman's Room. My role is to smile and be charming to their wives." There was a slight tinge of irritation in her voice as she said this.

"You sound as if you have no choice in the matter," I said.

I held myself still and watched Catherine make up her mind. It was a sight worth paying attention to. But then, there was a great deal about this woman to make a man wish to pay very close attention indeed.

"I believe we always have some choice in how we act and that we are free to choose our behavior," she said. "It's just that, as a woman, those choices are often more limited." She turned to face me, and determination was clear on her expressive features. I could not help thinking that here was a sight I would have been sorry to miss. "I believe you will be one of the few who actually make it in America," she said, firmly. "But if you are serious about making a success of it, I would suggest that you study American dress and customs and that you try to learn the language. I could help you with a few phrases to help you get through the immigration process if you like. It will help to pass the time before we reach New York."

"I would like that very much," I answered.

"Good," she replied. Her voice carried a note of finality, as if she was accustomed to having her requests fulfilled. "I like to take in the sunshine on deck after lunch while mother and father are resting. I will alert the Matron to allow you permission to come back to the upper deck." She held out her hand and I took it without speaking. "I'll see you tomorrow then," she said. She lingered for a second longer and her grey eyes held me spellbound. Then she turned away from me and disappeared down the stairs accompanied by another burst of loud laughter. The encounter left me shaken in a way I could not fully comprehend.

The next morning after breakfast I cleaned up as much as possible, shaved and changed into a cleaner shirt. I studied my reflection in the small mirror above the wash basin. I was taller than most, big boned and calloused. My clothes were patched and worn, reflecting my life as a Dutch farmer. My hair was bleached almost white by the sun, creating a sharp contrast to my dark eyes. I would certainly stand out amongst the first-class travelers up on the poop deck.

Jelle stirred on his cot and rose on one elbow. His color was finally returning, and he looked a little less green, but his clothes were rank with the smell of vomit and stale sweat. "Where are you off to?" he asked, weakly.

"I have found someone to tutor me in English," I answered, "She's going to help me with a few phrases that will help us get through the immigration process in New York."

Jelle flopped back on the bed. "We can't get there soon enough to suit me. I don't care if I ever see another boat in my lifetime."

"We should see land in a few more days." I said. "In the meantime, it wouldn't hurt you to clean up a little yourself." I threw him the bar of soap I had been using. "You reek of vomit and stale sweat."

He furrowed his brow with worry. "I hear that New York is big, busy and dangerous, especially for immigrants. There are masses of people all speaking different languages mixed up with the sound of carts and wagons going back and forth in all directions. They say the city is teaming with sharks and runners who pose as Dutch friends and steal your luggage at the first opportunity."

"I don't think you have to worry," I said. "We'll be disembarking at the Castle Garden on Manhattan Island. They say it is well-run and very protective of new arrivals."

I left him to meet with Catherine. It was a beautiful day. The sea was calm and met the sky in a thin blue line. The horizon seemed endless, stretching out toward eternity. For the first time since leaving my homeland, I felt a glimmer of hope.

I found Catherine on the upper deck as she had promised. She wore a large hat to protect her face from the sun and a pale silk shawl was draped around her shoulders. Catherine looked up from her book as I approached. "Ah, there you are," she said, motioning me to a seat beside her. "Are you ready to get to work?" I nodded and she wasted no time getting started. "Good. Then we will begin by speaking only in English. It will help me to know just how much of the language you already understand."

She approached our tutoring sessions with a sense of urgency and purpose. "We only have a few days before we dock," she said. "So, we must make the best use of our time. If I sense that you are not serious about this work, I will not waste any further time with you."

"I assure you that I am entirely serious," I answered in halting English.

"Excellent, then let's get right to work."

She asked me a few questions about my home and family, and I answered as best I could in English. I stumbled when she asked me why I was emigrating. I had to stop several times and ask for her help in translating my thoughts from Dutch into English. "A man came to our town who had lived for a time in a place called Alto in Wisconsin," I began. "He spoke so favorably of the place and surrounding region that I could think of nothing else. Even my father believed it was God's will that had brought this man to us at a time when my future in Gelderland was uncertain." It wasn't far from the truth and she accepted it without question. She listened intently but did not press me to expand my explanations beyond my ability to do so. Instead, she encouraged me to formulate questions for her to answer as well.

"Why are you going to America?" I asked, forming the words slowly and carefully.

"My mother's health is failing. Father has decided to move back to Philadelphia where we can be near family."

"What business is your father in?"

"He owns a bank in Philadelphia, specializing in the sale of American railroad bonds. He's been meeting with European banks to make connections abroad."

She spoke slowly and stopped often to explain words I did not understand. We spent an hour this way – asking and answering questions and expanding my one-word answers into complete sentences. The time passed quickly, but I found myself exhausted from the mental gymnastics of trying to comprehend and follow the conversation.

"I think this is enough for one day," she said, at last. "Why don't you try to get some rest. Tomorrow we can practice some phrases that you may encounter when we disembark in New York."

I continued to meet Catherine for English lessons every day. The words and phrases I had learned under Lainie's tutelage gradually came back to me and Catherine helped me to master a few key English phrases to speed me on my journey. But most of all, I looked forward to the time I spent with this intriguing young woman. In the short time we had together, she did her best to help me understand the culture of the New World so that I might assimilate more easily. In the end, she gave me a card with the address of her father's business in Philadelphia. "It's always good to have a reference from someone in America," she said. "You'd be surprised how many doors it can open for you."

A shock of recognition sent me reeling as I read the words: **Railroad Savings and Loan, Joseph Weller, President.** I had heard Lainie's father speak of Weller's efforts to build a transcontinental railroad through Minnesota into Canada. He had visited Gelderland once to encourage immigration and settlement to the area.

"I've heard of him," I said, unable to contain my amazement. "Hasn't he been promoting immigration along the Northwestern Pacific Railway through Minnesota."

She smiled. "Yes. We were just in Holland putting together another tour for a group of investors."

"Is it true that the climate in Minnesota is as mild and temperate as that of Virginia?"

She lowered her head as if the question embarrassed her. "It can be, at certain times of the year, I'm told."

"So, you've never been there?"

"Father discourages my involvement in these trips," she answered, and I detected a slight edge to her voice. "He says the West is still unsettled and is far too harsh a place for a lady."

"From what I hear, he is probably correct," I said, tucking the card into my vest. "Will I see you when we land?" I asked, trying not to sound too hopeful.

"I doubt it," she said, shaking her head. "I'm staying in New York for a few days with my brother, Charles and his wife, while my parents travel on to Philadelphia. I will meet them there later."

Trying to conceal my disappointment, I rose and offered her my hand. "I can't thank you enough for your help."

She covered my hand with her long slim fingers. "Good luck to you," she said, softly. For a moment, the air between us was charged with electricity. Then she released my hand. "You have my father's business card. If you are in Philadelphia, I hope you will call."

I watched her leave with a mixture of sadness and regret. Although I found this woman intriguing, there was a sadness about her that fed my own sense of guilt. My heart still belonged to Lainie. I had committed to her with all my heart and it had been broken to pieces with her death, leaving nothing but mountains of remorse. When I left my homeland, I resolved to direct all my energies toward making a life for myself in the New World. There was no room in my plan for anything else.

3

After twelve long days at sea, we rejoiced to see the bright autumn sun rising over the magnificent bay of New York City. The city awakened as if the sun were some celestial summons out of the dreamy darkness of the night. Bright sunshine flooded the sky, bay, clouds, and seaboard with streaks of gold and purple. We crowded the ship's rail for our first glimpse of the land that had filled us with such hope and promise.

The ship fired a salute and cast anchor amid the ringing cheers of passengers and crew. After days and nights of the same boundless blue and green of sky sea, with only now and then a ship in sight, or the wild wheeling sea gull on the vessel's track, we had finally come in view of the great city of New York. I found myself caught up in the excitement, hanging over the rail and cheering along with everyone else.

Finally, we were safely moored at the threshold of Castle Garden, grateful to set foot on land, and eager to rest our weary limbs and sea-worn souls. Castle Garden stood where New York City began, at the southern tip of Manhattan Island. It represented not only the city's growth, but the growth of a nation. The fortification had been transformed over the years to welcome theatergoers, immigrants, and now, millions of visitors to New York Harbor. Jelle and I stood with our mouths agape, taking in the sights. The river was filled with magnificent swift-moving steamers which fairly astonished the weak eyes and nerves of those of us accustomed only to the small streams and miniature landscapes of England and Europe.

The landing at Castle Garden was done in a stampede. The mix of languages and cultures along with a panicked selfishness only added to the disorder. People pushed, elbowed, and ran, their families following as best they could. Children fell and were picked up only to be rewarded by a rough slap about the ears. One child, who had gotten separated from her parents, screamed steadily and with increasing shrillness. An official kept her by him, but no one paid any attention or came to her aid.

"I plan to get out of the city as soon as possible," I said to Jelle, as we melted into the crowd of nationalities pushing and shoving their way toward the entrance. "I am anxious to reach our destination in the West." We elbowed our way through the throngs on the dock, passing women with swollen eyes, who had just parted with loved ones, perhaps never to meet again. I nearly tripped over an aged woman, sitting listless and sad, scarcely conscious of the bustle and confusion around her. She was totally oblivious to the sounds of mothers seeking to hush their wailing babies and the shouts of sailors and dock workers. The waterfront teemed with noise, combined together in an incomprehensible chorus. It was like nothing I had ever experienced before.

The passage to Castle Garden was blocked up with vehicles, peddlers of cheap cigars, apple-stands, and runners from the different boarding houses and intelligence offices nearby. However, despite having to fight through an outpouring stream of new arrivals, and then being nearly deafened by the repeated shouts of "D'ye want a conveyance?", "Hotel Stadt Hamburg!", and "This way, gents, this way!", we finally succeeded in getting through.

We encountered a runner carrying a huge bag in the left hand and a squalling baby in the right arm, which he vainly tried to pacify or smother, I do not know which; behind him came the mother with another baby in her arms, and a lot of children clinging to her petticoats; after her came her husband, smoking his Dutch porcelain pipe and carrying some bundles; and finally the grandparents made up the rear. Another fellow grasped my arm, and tried in half English, half German, to persuade me to go with him to some obscure hotel. I pushed him away and a moment later, I saw him accost some new arrivals with better success.

I felt Jelle's presence beside me. "*Jezus Christus!*" he muttered. "What do you think of Rotterdam Harbor after this?"

I looked for Catherine among the throng of those disembarking and caught a glimpse of her as she was leaving. She was greeted by a smartly dressed gentleman in a top hat and ushered into a carriage waiting at the quay. I watched for a few minutes as the carriage sped through the tangled streets lined with brothels and saloons. It careened through the streets as if its very presence there was distasteful.

The landing stage was alive with the officers of the Immigration Commissioners and the Customhouse. I presented my passport to the officer on guard at the entrance. He glanced quickly at the signature and repeated, "Hank De Jong". Before I could correct him, he wrote the name in his book and moved on to the next person in line behind me. We were ushered into the yard of the Garden, amidst a crowd of passengers, children, and baggage of all kinds. The different offices of the Garden rimmed the area, hemming us in. Jelle and I crouched beside our bags to await further instructions.

At last, we were directed to proceed up the corridor into the interior of the building. Our boxes and baggage had been removed to the luggage warehouses, and here they arranged themselves in order on the seats. In front of them, and in the center of the building, which was lit by a glass dome, stood a staff of some dozen gentlemen, all busily engaged in facilitating the movements and promoting the settlement of the newly arrived immigrants.

Each immigrant, man, woman, and child passed up in rotation to the Bureau, and gave his or her name, place of birth, age, occupation, and destination to the registrar. Remembering the officer at the entrance, I gave my name as Hank De Jong. The registrar checked his list and marked off my name.

One of the leading officers connected with the Bureau of Information then mounted a rostrum and addressed the immigrants. He was a thin man dressed in a style much different from most of the those assembled before him. He wore wide-legged trousers and a short jacket of a solid color. At his throat was a very narrow silk tie and the slim gold chain of his pocket watch could be seen on his vest. He glanced nervously at the crowd in front of him.

He spoke in English in a rather high-pitched voice that tended to squeak as he attempted to make himself heard. "May I have your attention, please." He waited for the crowd to quiet down, but then bravely continued, hoping to be heard above the noise. "If you have not made prior arrangements for accommodations, you can find shelter under the roof of the building." He gestured toward a building with a low overhang just to his left. "There you can find advice and information for tickets for railways and steamers to take you to your destination." He paused to catch his breath before continuing his instructions. "As to the best means of obtaining employment, a register is kept in the Intelligence Department of the Institution. You can also find information regarding the best and most expeditious routes to take if you are meeting up with friends or relatives. If you need to exchange currency, you may do so at the Bureau of Exchange."

He heaved a sigh of relief at having delivered the required information and stepped down off the rostrum. Due to Catherine's tutelage, I was able to understand most of what was said. After a few minutes of confusion, the assemblage began to move off in the direction of the building he had indicated. Long lines of immigrants were lined up to purchase tickets to the interior of the country where land was rumored to be cheap. I took my place in line and motioned for Jelle, still weak from the crossing and obviously having difficulty absorbing all the new smells and sounds of the New World.

"I'll purchase our tickets onward," I said to him. "Go find somewhere to rest until I finish."

He nodded gratefully and handed me his pouch of gold coins. I gave him my knapsack with the goatskin packet inside. "This contains everything I own in this world," I said. "That way you know I'll return with your cash."

Jelle nodded again and moved quickly toward the edge of the room with our parcels. He was already starting to look as if he might be ill again.

The line moved slowly as travelers struggled to make their wishes known in many languages. When I was finally able to reach the ticket counter, I summoned every English word and phrase Catherine had drummed into my poor brain to make myself understood.

It was nearly evening before all the business connected with the immigrant department was over. I found Jelle slumped in a corner sound asleep. I stood for a moment gazing down at him. There was a look of childlike innocence about him as he lay there curled up with his cloak pulled tightly about him. I wondered how he would survive the hardships we were sure to encounter ahead. He stirred awake when I tucked his money pouch back into his pocket.

"I've managed to secure passage on the Pennsylvania Railroad to Philadelphia for tomorrow," I said. "We'll take the ferry across the harbor first thing in the morning. From Philadelphia we can travel further west on the immigrant trains."

As night fell, the immigrants began to settle down in their new locality. The interior of the Garden, having been lit by gaslight, looked much more cheerful. Two large iron stoves, between four and five feet high, fed with plentiful supplies of coal, and throwing out considerable heat, occupied each end of two compartments, one being set apart for the males and the other for the females. In a far corner of each room was a kind of refectory, where for 15 or 20 cents you could obtain a half a pint of coffee, a roll, and cheese or butter; but many of the immigrants preferred to purchase their own tea and coffee and prepare it in tin utensils on the stoves. There were two water taps and an iron ladle at each end of the division.

Two uniformed watchmen kept order during the night and attended upon the immigrants. Sleep did not come easily that first night. The bed was nothing more than hard boards and the wind whistled through the open casemates, doors, and windows. This combined with the cacophony of tongues, the squalling of children and the erratic scratchings of a colony of rats made sleep impossible. The snug hammock rocking to and fro on the boat was paradise compared to this. Unable to sleep, Jelle and I joined those standing around the stoves.

As may be imagined, much of the conversation of the sleepless immigrants that night centered around the good or bad fortune they had met with during the day in search of situations and employment. Many came back reporting dolefully and despondently how they had canvassed the city and found all positions filled and no help or hands were wanted. It appeared that the promises of plentiful work and opportunities that had drawn many of the immigrants to make the perilous journey from their homelands, may have been overstated.

A shifty-eyed Dutchman with yellow teeth and hair badly in need of washing sidled up to us. He said his name was Lubbert Groen from Friesland. "These places aren't fit for man or beast," Lubbert whispered with a knowing wink. "I know a place where we can get a decent meal and a draft of good beer." I was immediately suspicious, but any offer of a good meal and something stronger than weak tea, piqued my interest.

We eagerly accepted his offer to escape the inhospitable and overcrowded conditions at Castle Garden. Jelle stuck close to me as we navigated our way through the hordes of immigrants and hucksters pushing and shoving each other through the crowded streets of New York. Lubbert led us to a small pub on Water Street where the air was thick with the smell of smoke and alcohol.

Once our appetites were satisfied, Lubbert leaned toward us. His eyes shifted around the room to make sure no one else was listening. "You seem like honest chaps," he began. "I'm afraid I'm in a bit of a dilemma." He slid a folded piece of paper across the table toward us. "I have just inherited this deed to forty acres of land in America from an old aunt. The land lies along a proposed rail route near Michigan City that will connect it to markets in Chicago. The land will double in price as soon as the road is completed." He paused and glanced over his shoulder to make sure no one else was listening. "The thing is…I've got creditors, you know, and I'm short on cash. I'm desperate to sell the land as quickly as possible."

"Are you sure the railroad will go through the land?" Jelle asked.

Lubbert nodded. "I have a source who practically guarantees it. I'm willing to sell the land for only $400. That's less than half what it's worth!"

Jelle was completely taken in by the story. "I have $400! If it is as you say, I'd be a fool not to take advantage of the opportunity." Watching this scheme unfold, I smiled at the irony of his statement.

Lubbert hesitated and sat back in his chair. "I don't know. You are a young man about to embark on the adventure of a lifetime. You will need all your cash to help you get started in America."

"I insist!" Jelle pulled the cash from his pouch and laid it on the table in front of us. Lubbert's face showed signs of reluctance, but there was no mistaking the greed in his eyes. He reached to pocket the cash, but I placed my hand over the money instead. "Hold on just a minute…" I began, but just as I was about to intervene, there was a disturbance at the door.

"I know he's in here. I saw him come in!" An older gentleman with unkempt hair and his face contorted in anger, made his way toward us. His clothes, once the height of fashion, now showed definite signs of wear.

Lubbert looked desperate to escape. He spoke in a low tone to us, "This poor man is completely mad." Then he stood up and bowed deeply to the distressed gentleman. "Mr. Fitzgerald, I believe," he said in a tone of icy politeness. "What can I do for you?"

"You can pay me back for that worthless deed you sold me," the man demanded.

"I don't know what you're talking about," Lubbert answered.

"Worthless deed?" Jelle asked, as realization dawned. Things were looking bad for Lubbert.

The man advanced toward Lubbert menacingly. "I want my money!" he shouted.

Lubbert strove to maintain an air of unconcern. He waved his hand dismissively. "Don't be ridiculous. I sold you that land in good faith. I'm not responsible if the deed was a fake."

"You're a thief and a liar!" the man exclaimed, clenching his fists in anger. He turned to the other patrons who had shifted in their seats to observe the commotion. "This man defrauded me of my life savings," he declared, pointing at Lubbert, who was beginning to look quite uncomfortable.

Jelle jumped from his seat. "You were trying to cheat me too!"

Realizing the scam was over, Lubbert turned on Jelle, "Go to hell!" he said furiously. He turned back to the man. "And you too," he said to him "You are a stupid, greedy old man who deserved what happened to you!" Then he stormed out of the pub leaving us to pay the tab.

Jelle pocketed the remainder of his cash and turned to me sheepishly. "I guess I have a lot to learn," he said.

"You can start by remembering never to display that much cash in a place like this," I said.

4

We left the Garden the next morning and took a ferry across the Hudson River to board the train west toward Philadelphia. By the time we reached the train depot, it had started to rain, big round droplets that landed with a wet plop on the brim of my hat. Jelle and I were soaked to the skin by the time we got under cover. For at least an hour, or so it seemed, we camped on the draughty, gas-lit platform. It was crowded with a Babel of bewildered men, women, and children, all trying to convey their destinations to a seemingly disinterested porter. The air was heavy and rank with the smell of unbathed bodies and dripping clothing.

Finally, we were led into a long shed that reached downhill toward the river. It was dark, and the wind blew through it from end to end. The building was jammed with passengers and baggage. Porters, infuriated by hurry and overwork, shouted and pushed their way into the upper skirts of the crowd. A white-haired official with a stick under one arm and a list in the other, stood in front of us and called name after name in a commanding tone. As each name was called, a family gathered up its brats and bundles and ran for the hindmost of the three cars standing by for us.

Jelle and I were called to the second car which was devoted to men travelling alone. We were crammed into a long, narrow wooden box, like a flat-roofed Noah's Ark, with a stove at one end and a toilet at the other. There was a passage down the middle with benches on both sides. I maneuvered my way onto one of the benches and motioned for Jelle to settle in beside me.

The train jerked and rolled away from the station, with its load of human cargo. As night fell, a porter came through the car prevailing on passengers to pair up for sleeping. The benches were too short for anything but a young child. Where there was scarcely elbow room for two to sit, there was not enough for one to lie down. However, the backs of the benches could be laid flat and the benches made to face each other in pairs. Jelle and I purchased a board and three small square cushions stuffed with straw and covered with thin cotton. We laid the boards from bench to bench, making a couch wide enough for two, and long enough for a man of middle height. Between the body odor of the other passengers and Jelle's raucous snoring, it was an extremely uncomfortable night.

Nevertheless, the easy familiarity of rail travel was a welcome respite from the chaos and confusion of the ocean passage. As the train sped through the American countryside, the reality of my situation finally struck home, and I was overcome with a sense of sadness and regret. What I had hoped would be a glorious adventure with the woman I loved had instead become a headlong rush to escape her memory. I had naively believed that our love was strong enough to overcome any difficulties we encountered. I could not have been more wrong.

Lainie had pleaded with me to consider a position in her father's business instead of emigrating. But I could not imagine a life for us under her father's strict rule and her brother's disdain. For me, the pull of an independent lifestyle was too strong to be denied. But Lainie could not accept a life without the comforts and social life that she was accustomed to. Neither of us was willing to budge on the issue. It was the only thing we ever argued about.

"Don't you see?" I persisted. "We have no future here. Your father will never agree to our marriage and even if he did, I could never provide the life for you here that you have become accustomed to."

Anger flared in her eyes. "If you weren't so stubborn, you could ask my father for a job in his business. I'm sure I could convince him. He would do anything I ask to make me happy."

"Lainie, we've been over this," I answered, firmly. "In America, I will be able to establish my own homestead. We can be completely independent."

"I can't wait for years while you make your fortune in America," she said, pushing herself away from me.

"It won't be that long. I'll write to you every day. I promise the time will speed by until I am able to send for you and we can be together again. We have a lifetime ahead of us."

"You don't understand," she said, sadly. She stared hard at me for several seconds. When she finally spoke, it caused an eruption in my brain that had been simmering beneath the surface for several months. "I'm pregnant," she said, at last.

#

The high-pitched scream of the train's whistle accompanied by the hiss and sigh of the steam engine announced our arrival in Philadelphia. The station was small and utilitarian, reflecting the railroad's emphasis on long haul traffic. Several passengers left the train here, but they were soon replaced by others carrying a myriad of parcels and packages which they proceeded to beat against us as they attempted to stuff them into baggage compartments and any other available empty space.

At the last moment, a shabbily dressed man came aboard reeking of alcohol. He was aggressively friendly to the other passengers as he moved unsteadily down the aisle. He jostled passengers and mumbled apologies as he proceeded. As the train began to pick up speed, he lost his balance and fell against Jelle, who was seated next to the aisle. "Get off me!" Jelle growled, giving the man a shove. He landed in the seat opposite us. The ruckus attracted the attention of the conductor who was coming through the train checking tickets.

The man made a show of searching for his. "I must have lost it in boarding," he said, apologetically, slurring his words. He made a vain attempt at indignance when the conductor expressed doubt.

"Lost it in the saloon is more like it." The conductor grabbed the man by the shoulders and wrenched him from his seat. He marched him through the car and sent him flying onto the side of the track. It was done in three motions as exact as a drill that had been practiced many times.

The train was still moving slowly, although beginning to pick up its pace. The drunkard got to his feet and dusted himself off. He carried a red bundle, though not so red as his cheeks; and he shook this menacingly with one hand, while the other stole behind him and produced a pistol from his waistband, which he pointed at the train as it rumbled past him. The conductor stood on the steps with one hand on his hip, looking back at the man. For a moment, I feared that violence might erupt, but the drunkard smiled and bowed deeply. Then he turned and staggered back along the track toward town.

"Jezus Christus!" Jelle muttered beside me. "What foreign land have we come to?" Then a look of panic came over his face. He began patting his pockets and rummaging through his bags. "Stop the train! I've been robbed!" he shouted.

The other travelers turned to stare at the young man screaming gibberish in a language they did not understand. The conductor reappeared and tried to calm him. "Calm down, young man," he said. "What seems to be the problem?" Jelle tried unsuccessfully to make himself understood by waving his arms and pointing.

I tried to interpret in what limited English I could muster. "My friend has been robbed," I said to the conductor. "The man you just threw off the train was a thief and a pickpocket."

The conductor shook his head sadly. "We can't stop the train once we're under way. You'll have to wait until we stop at Lancaster to report it. Unfortunately, these things happen all the time. I doubt if he'll be able to recover his losses." The conductor moved on down the aisle collecting tickets and assuring passengers that the situation was under control.

"He took everything!" Jelle exclaimed. "All my money, my father's gold watch, everything I had of value. It happened so fast! He must have robbed me when he stumbled against me."

"You still have your ticket with passage to Chicago and a connection to Wisconsin." I said, trying to reassure him. "You can still make it to your uncle's from there."

Jelle choked back a sob. "You don't understand. My uncle is destitute. The bank is about to foreclose on his land. I was sent here to help him negotiate a settlement. Now he will lose everything, and it's all my fault!" He began to sob quietly, sucking in great gulps of air with each breath.

I turned away from him. I had no words to comfort him. My heart went out to this poor soul with the open and trusting nature. He seemed ill-equipped to handle the evils of the world. He would most likely perish at the hands of some unscrupulous thief if the perils of the journey itself didn't overtake him. But perhaps the hardships of the journey so far had hardened him to be more cautious in the future. I glanced over at him. He had stopped weeping and turned inward.

"It was my own fault," Jelle said, to no one in particular. "I must learn to be more cautious." He rubbed his palms slowly over his face, but the gesture did not erase the worry and concern reflected there. "I just don't know what I'm going to tell my uncle."

Jelle turned away from me and stared off into nothingness. We were silent for the remainder of the trip, each lost in our own thoughts, while the rhythmic chuffa-chuffa of the engine rolled us through the Pennsylvania countryside. We passed through rolling wooded hills, deep stream valleys and fertile soils. Much of the area we passed through was farmland. Small farms dotted the landscape with their neat homesteads and carefully tended fields of grain and tobacco. Cattle and sheep grazed contentedly in the meadows. Occasionally, the train slowed as it moved through a tiny village where children lined the track waving at the train as it passed.

As we neared Lancaster, we noticed small shops run by tradesmen such as blacksmiths, wheelwrights, millers, and storekeepers – indispensable to a rural community – had sprung up along the rails. I felt a tugging at my heart. The pastoral scene reminded me of home. It fed the immigrants' dreams of bettering one's lot through land ownership, and I soon found myself caught in the spell.

A nagging thought wrestled with my conscience and pushed its way to the surface. The goatskin packet was still hidden safely in the bottom of my knapsack with the promissory note tucked inside. Father had said that Jacob Van Pelt had settled in Pennsylvania. I wondered if there were still relatives in the area who would know what to do with the note. Perhaps Jelle's distress was simply an omen, a sign that my future lay here in the rolling hills of Pennsylvania rather than deeper into the unsettled west. I touched the pouch containing the coins that mother had sewn into the lining of my jacket. The germ of an idea began to form in my mind.

The brakes squealed as the train slowed to a stop at the station. I nudged Jelle awake. "I have a proposition to make," I said, handing him the pouch of money still warm from its spot against my heart where it had ridden safely since my journey began. The sunlight glittered off the coins as they spilled out into his hands. "I exchanged my Guilders for American dollars when we landed at Castle

Garden," I said. "There is a little over $1100 here. I want you to have it."

"I can't take this!" he exclaimed.

"I'm not giving it to you," I said. "It's a loan. You can pay me back when you get your uncle's affairs straightened out."

"But this was to be your stake for a place of your own," Jelle protested.

"I'll cash out the remainder of my ticket here in Lancaster. It'll keep me going while I connect with some family in the area."

"You never told me you had family in America."

"You never asked." I gestured to the workers busy loading goods for shipment to the frontier settlements to the north, west and south. "Look at all the activity here. This *city* is obviously a regional distribution center for goods being shipped from Philadelphia," I said. "I should have no trouble finding work here."

Jelle looked at the money in his hand. "I don't know what to say…"

"You would be doing me a favor," I added. "I need to prove to myself that I can make it in America on my own. If things don't work out here, I can still make it to Alto before winter."

He ran the coins through his fingers. "I still don't feel right taking this."

"Think of it as a business deal. I'm sure you learned about money lending from your year at the university. In the absence of organized banks in the west, there will be homesteaders eager to borrow money to stake their claims. If you are wise and keep your senses about you, you could turn this small investment into a profitable business."

Jelle nodded thoughtfully and I could see him running the idea over in his mind. Then a look of consternation passed over his face. "How will I find you to pay you back?"

I thought of the card Catherine had given me when we parted onboard the ship. "I have a contact at the Railroad Savings and Loan Bank in Philadelphia," I answered. "You can deposit the money in an account there in my name once you have things settled with your uncle." I looked out the window as the train pulled into the station. There were crowds of people milling about, but among the

American greetings, my ears detected the language of my homeland. "This is where I'm supposed to be," I said at last. "This is my home."

When we parted in Lancaster, Jelle shook my hand solemnly. "I don't know how to thank you, Harke," he said.

"It's Hank now," I replied. "I've got a new name in a new land. It's a new beginning." The whistle blew signaling the train's departure. Jelle leaned out the window and waved at me until the train rounded a bend and he was out of sight. I felt a small pang of loneliness and regret at leaving the only friend I had in this strange new land, but I had cast my lot and now staked my future on the beauty of the Pennsylvania countryside.

5

I joined a group of Dutch travelers who had also disembarked at the station. The immigrants stood around looking lost and confused. They soon dispersed, joining friends and relatives who were waiting to greet them. One prosperous-looking gentleman strode off purposefully as if he were at home in these strange surroundings. Sensing that he might be a local, I fell in step behind him.

He walked a few blocks into the town, stopping to purchase a newspaper, before turning into a public house. The sign above the door advertised it as Shank's Tavern. I followed him inside and took a seat at a table not far away. The proprietor greeted him as an old acquaintance and the man answered in English. They exchanged a few pleasantries that I did not- understand before I was noticed. As the owner of the establishment ambled over to take my order, I caught the eye of the distinguished gentleman. He smiled and tipped his hat to me before turning his attention to his paper.

"What can I get ya?" the barman asked again. His voice held a note of impatience and I guessed that the question had been repeated more slowly and loudly for my benefit.

Once again, I summoned up the few words of English I could remember, "A cup of tea, please."

Upon hearing me speak, the man at the other table looked up briefly, but then returned his attention to his reading. The barman looked disgusted as he ambled off to fill my order. I noticed that the gentleman was drinking a lager. I remembered Catherine's advice and kicked myself for not trying harder to fit in with the local tastes. The barman returned and brought the man a lunch of rye bread and sausages along with thin slices of yellow cheese, dill pickles and a bowl of hot and spicy, brown mustard. My mouth watered at the sight and smell of the food. The two men spent a few more minutes talking and laughing, before the barman wandered off again. The gentleman continued to sip his drink, but he left the food untouched.

By the time my tea arrived, I was practically salivating. My tea was weak and tepid and did little to stave off my hunger. I took a few of the coins I had received from refunding my ticket and laid them on the table hoping it would cover the cost of my tea. The barman grunted and took one of the coins. I quickly pocketed the remainder. I still needed to find a place to spend the night before starting out early to look for work.

The gentleman set down his paper and looked over at me. He gestured at the food. "Would you care to join me?" he asked, in perfect Dutch.

At first, I was too surprised to answer. "I assume you are Dutch from your dress and accent," the man said. "Do you have family here?"

I remembered the letters in the goatskin pouch. "Yes. They live somewhere in Pennsylvania. Their name is Van Pelt, but I've never met them."

The man's face registered recognition. "I know of some Van Pelts near Philadelphia. They are prominent landowners around Valley Forge." He paused and studied me for a few minutes. "Why are you in Lancaster instead of Philadelphia?"

"I hadn't intended to stop here," I answered. "I was on my way to Wisconsin to join my congregation there."

"Are you a minister?"

"No, but my father has connections there. I was hoping to find work and earn enough to stake my own claim."

The man gestured to the chair across from him. "Come join me. I don't like shouting across the room to talk to you. Besides, you look like you haven't eaten in days." He gestured to the barman. "Bring this man a lager and get rid of this weak piss you call tea."

"My name is Gerhard Boersma," he said, as I sat down.

"Hank De Jong," I answered.

He pushed the food toward me. I tried to restrain myself, but my hunger was overpowering. He smiled as he watched me devour everything on the table. With my hunger satiated, I sat back to enjoy the lager. It was light and refreshing and much better than the tea.

"You never told me why you're here," the man said.

I hesitated, not knowing how much to divulge to this stranger. "I ran out of money," I said, truthfully. "I thought I might find enough work here to help me get on my way."

Gerhard nodded in understanding. "What about your family? The Van Pelts, wasn't it? Why don't you see if they will help?"

"Like I said, I've never met them. I didn't think it would be a good idea to throw myself on their mercy."

"That's probably wise," Gerhard said. He tapped the newspaper he had been reading. It was written in English, but I could make out the words *Philadelphia Record* on the masthead. "I see that the Van Pelt family is engaged in another lawsuit with the government over an unpaid debt from the Revolutionary War. They would undoubtedly assume you were an imposter looking to cash in on the settlement."

I thought again of the promissory note in my bag, but I clamped my mouth shut and said nothing. "Do you think they'll succeed?" I asked, finally.

"I doubt it. This isn't the first time they've tried to collect. The government refuses to acknowledge the claim and the Van Pelts have no paperwork to substantiate it. It's been dismissed in the past as hearsay."

"Why do they keep trying to collect?"

"They claim there is a copy of the note buried in the files of the Continental Congress that verifies the loan. But the records from that time are in such disarray, the government is not willing to take the time or the money to research it, unless the family can produce the original note." My heart took a leap into my throat. Gerhard didn't seem to notice. "His heirs have combed through what little he had left for generations and turned up nothing."

"It sounds pretty hopeless," I said. "Why do they keep trying to collect?"

"The loan keeps drawing interest," Gerhard said. "I imagine it's quite a tidy sum by now."

"There have to be several generations of heirs by now," I said. "It would be impossible to track them all down."

"Jacob Van Pelt died childless, so anything they collect would go to the children and grandchildren of his siblings. Most of them are still residing near Philadelphia."

"I imagine they would be very suspicious of someone who showed up claiming to be a distant relative," I said.

Gerhard nodded and gave me a meaningful look. "I think you're right about that," he said. We sat in silence for a few moments before he spoke again. "You said you were looking for work. By the looks of you, I'd say you're used to hard labor. I own a ranch a few miles from here, and I'm short-handed right now. One of my men is laid up with a broken leg. I could use a hand on my place if you're interested." All thoughts of promissory notes were momentarily banished from my thoughts at the possibility of employment. "I can't pay much," he continued. "Eighteen dollars a month plus room and board."

It sounded like a fortune to me. "I'll take it and be glad for it!"

Gerhard signaled the barman for the bill and rose to leave. "Good. Get a good night's sleep." He handed the barman a few bills. "Riley, here, will put you up in a room upstairs. He'll tell you how to get to my place."

He left without looking back, leaving me to contemplate my good fortune. The barman suddenly became very accommodating. "I'll show you to your room as soon as you're ready," he said. He looked at me with a pointed expression. "There's a washroom just down the hall where you can clean up."

"Thank you," I answered. Then I picked up the newspaper Gerhard had left behind and followed him up the stairs.

I awoke before dawn after a restless night and began the nine-mile walk to the Boersma Ranch. It was located northeast of town in the heart of what the barman had referred to as Dutch country. Seeing the land on foot afforded me the opportunity to observe more closely this land that fortune had dropped me into. The rich soil of the surrounding countryside provided ample space for grazing livestock. I observed occasional ridges standing above the rolling hills and limestone plains. There appeared to be ample drainage for the rivers and creeks that flowed through the region. I stopped to run a handful of soil through my hands. It crumbled easily indicating that it would erode and leave behind rich nutrients to feed the soil.

I had not gone far before a wizened old farmer with a long gray beard stopped his wagon alongside me. His face was tanned and wrinkled from long hours in the sun and his hands on the reins were calloused and hard. "D'ye need a ride?" he asked. "I can take you as far as the road to New Holland."

He spoke in halting English, so I answered him in Dutch. "I'm headed for the Boersma Ranch. Is it near there?"

"*Ja!* Not too much farther to walk from where I'll drop you off." I climbed up onto the seat beside him. He slapped the reins and the horse moved off down the road. "I'm just heading to town for supplies," he said. A train whistled in the distance and the horse pricked up its ears. "The railroads keep expanding through this area, gobbling up everything in their path," he grumbled. "Cities and towns spring up overnight. It won't be long before there won't be enough land left around here for a man to raise his family and make a decent living."

"Is it changing that fast?"

The farmer nodded. "Just last week, a neighbor sold out, loaded up his family and all his belongings, and headed west. I hear there's still plenty of good land available out there."

"What if the railroad continues out west?"

The old man shook his head sadly. "I guess you can't stop progress, but I sure would like to slow it down some."

Curious about my new boss, I asked, "Does the railroad go through the Boersma Ranch?"

"Old man Boersma made certain of that!" the old man scoffed. "The family got a land grant from William Penn back in the day that covered nearly the whole county…more land than any one family could handle alone. When the railroads came to Philadelphia, Gerhard's father was there to greet them. He wined and dined them and put them up on his ranch in high style. Next thing you know, he's got a contract for the railroad to go right through his land all the way from Philadelphia to Lancaster."

"But Gerhard still farms the remainder of the land?"

"Hires out most of the work. Spends most of his time in Philadelphia managing his railroad holdings." He turned in his seat to look at me. "I reckon that's where you come in…working the land while he's off doing other things."

We passed a run-down farmstead with the name Van Pelt etched crudely over the gate. The fence surrounding the property needed repair and the buildings beyond bore the ravages weather and time.

"What happened here?" I asked.

"Oh, that's the old Van Pelt place. They own a big spread up north of here around Valley Forge. Bought this place a few years ago and one of them moved in for a while but couldn't make a go of it. Moved back up north with the rest of the clan and just let the place go."

"Why don't they sell it?"

"They tried." He shook his head sadly. "But the land is no good for farming. Too much limestone rock to contend with. Nothing will grow. Not enough cleared land for grazing either."

I remembered the limestone I had crumbled in my hands on my walk toward the ranch. "What about water?"

"Conestoga Creek runs through the neighboring property. But the owner holds the water rights and won't allow any diversion. Besides, the creek is prone to flooding during the rainy season. Most of the bottom land near the creek gets washed out every year."

"Sounds like you know a lot about it."

"One thing you learn living 'round here…everybody knows everything about everybody else's business." We had reached a fork in the road and he pulled the horse to a stop. He pointed to the left. "That road will take you north to Boersma's place. I'm heading on south to New Holland."

I picked up my things and hopped down off the wagon, "Much obliged for the ride," I said.

He slapped his horse and called back over his shoulder, "Good luck to you."

I stood for a while watching him drive away. Then instead of continuing up the northern fork, I turned back to the Van Pelt place.

For several hours, I waded through the tall grass and overgrowth exploring this namesake place that nature had reclaimed as her own. The windows in the old farmhouse gazed at me forlornly as I approached. The front door hung askew, gaping like a toothless old man. The house had been abandoned for years and was now in an unstable state with its roof partly sunken in. I stepped gingerly onto the sagging porch and pushed aside the door that was secured by a single rusty hinge.

I kicked aside remnants of a life that was long gone—old tin pots, bits of pottery, a raggedy doll. Further inside, the second story had collapsed, creating a ceiling of sunlight and clear blue skies. I picked my way carefully through the debris and exited out the back door where a rusted washtub lay half-buried in the dirt and tall grass. A wooden bucket still hung from its spindle over the well, but when I dropped it down the shaft, I was greeted only by a hollow empty thud as it hit the dry bottom.

I stumbled over the stone foundations of several outbuildings and the remains of a corral fence that had once held the livestock secure. Beyond that lay a large expanse of pastureland for grazing that abutted the tree line marking the banks of Conestoga Creek. With the creek this close to the property line, there had to be a spring feeding into it that could be tapped as a water source.

I turned upstream from the creek and began to follow a line of trees and brush that snaked away to the north up a steep incline. The soil was rockier here and the boulders larger, making the land unfit for cultivation. But something had to be feeding all this undergrowth. At a spot between two large boulders I pushed aside the grass and there it was. Like the promise of a maiden's first kiss, a small spring gurgled up between the rocks and trickled its way down the hill, losing itself amid the grass and brush. I bathed my face and hands in the cool refreshment of the waters and drank deeply. As I rose to leave, I paused to take in my surroundings once more. "One day you will be mine," I said, but only the wind heard my words.

6

I arrived at the Boersma Ranch around mid-morning and I was greeted by a sight that filled me with awe. There were so many buildings! A separate building with a loft overhead and a corral attached housed the horses. I could see a buggy parked inside. Still another building was reserved for the chickens that clucked and picked their way around the yard. I marveled at the idea of separate buildings for livestock. At home, in Gelderland, we lived above the livestock and counted on their warmth during the cold winter nights. Gerhard Boersma must be wealthy beyond my imaginings.

Gerhard met me on the porch with his hands on his hips. Gone was the stylish traveling attire he had worn the day before. He was dressed in western work clothes with a large wide-brimmed hat pulled low over his eyes, but there was no denying his displeasure. "I expected you two hours ago," he said, scowling.

"I had trouble understanding Riley's directions in English," I answered.

He regarded me for a few minutes, deciding whether to believe me. "Well, you've missed breakfast," he said, gruffly. "Drop your things on the porch. We have work to do." He strode away, leaving me to follow in his wake.

Spring planting was complete, so we spent the day clearing the land for next year's planting. It was back-breaking work. I was assigned to dig out the rocks and boulders by hand and load them into a wagon to be hauled away. Then I had to back-fill the holes with new soil and tamp it down evenly. The early autumn sun beat down relentlessly, and I wished several times that I had arrived in time for breakfast. Lunchtime came and went with no sign of stopping. Sweat poured down the back of my shirt, and I longed to stop and rest. But Gerhard kept a watchful eye on me, so I did my best to keep pace with the others.

Although accustomed to hard work back home, that evening my body ached in ways I had never felt before. The evening meal was a welcome respite. I stuffed myself with white bread, pork, bread, butter, and canned fruit until I thought I would burst. Afterward, I fell into my bunk along with the other hands, too exhausted to think of much else.

The next morning, we continued clearing timber, but this time I fortified myself with a hearty breakfast. Some of the hands were assigned to fell the trees in the planting area, while others were assigned the job of loading the logs onto the sled for the horses to pull away. I was assigned to stump removal. The task involved digging around each stump, attaching a heavy rope around the entire stump, and hitching it to the horses who dragged it away for burning. The largest, most stubborn stumps had to be blasted out. This task often interrupted the other work for several hours while the area was cleared, and the dynamite was set.

This work went on for several days. Once the trees and stumps were removed, we cleared the brush and other dense vegetation and thickets to ready the land for planting. Then we moved on to the next field. The work kept me too occupied and exhausted to think about the Van Pelt place, but the seed of an idea had taken root and began to grow in my mind.

One morning, a heavy downpour kept us from the fields. The rain came in huge bursts, running off the roof in sheets that obstructed the view from the windows and doorways of our bunkhouse. A rushing river of dirt and debris washed away anything in its path. The hands all hunkered down inside to await the storm's passing. Some entertained themselves with games of chance. Others napped or entertained each other with stories of their latest exploits in town. I remembered the newspaper Gerhard had left behind at the tavern when we first met. I pulled it out of my bag and spread it out on my bunk. I found the Van Pelt story and tried my best to pick out any familiar words. Although I had picked up enough English words and phrases to communicate my basest needs, I still had not been able to decipher much of the written language.

I was deep in concentration, trying to sound out the words, when I sensed someone standing over me. I looked up and saw a large gruff-looking cowboy standing over me. He had been introduced to me earlier as Ben Crawford. He was taller and heavier than most of the other hands, with squinty eyes and a sinister look about him. "What's the matter, Dutchman?" he asked, with a sneer. "Can't ya read?"

A momentary flashback caused the hair on the back of my neck to rise. For a moment, I was back home with Dirk standing over me, taunting me to strike back against him. I sucked in my breath and spread my hands in a gesture of helplessness. *"ik spreek geen Engels,"* I said, hoping my limited English would send him away.

"Stupid Dutchman," he scoffed. "Why don't you go back to your own country?" He snatched up my newspaper, crumpled it into a wad and threw it into a corner. He drew back his shoulders and threw challenging glances around the room, but no one took the bait. They avoided his glance and continued what they were doing as if he had not spoken. Ben laughed derisively, then he turned and stomped out.

Crawford's words rekindled old feelings of anger and inadequacy that I had tried so hard to repress. I wanted to lash out at him, but instead I felt disheartened and ashamed. Since arriving in America, it had become clear to me that immigrants were tolerated so long as we stuck to our own kind and didn't interfere with those who believed their rights were guaranteed as a result of their American birthright. Even lowlifes like Ben Crawford considered themselves of a higher social standing than immigrants, and they made no effort to hide their disdain.

I retrieved the newspaper and smoothed it out on my bed. The man in the bunk next to mine had not spoken or opened his eyes during the whole altercation. Now, he looked over at me. "Don't mind Ben," he said in Dutch. "He likes to pick on the newcomers. Makes him feel superior."

Olie Caufrid was one of the older hands. He was slight of frame and bent from years of hard manual labor. He had one good eye that didn't miss much that happened around the ranch. The other eye was covered by a thin blue film, the result of some past accident. His teeth were stained yellow from the chewing tobacco he kept tucked between his cheek and his gums. He spoke in the world-weary tones of one who had already experienced a lifetime of pain. He had been in America for several years, coming over during the beginning of the Second Great Migration in the late 1840s, but he still had family in Zeeland. Olie had been kind to me when I first arrived, taking time to translate instructions, and helping me to adjust. He rolled to the side of his bed and rose on his elbow. "What is it you're trying to read?" I pointed to the story about the Van Pelt family. "I've heard of them," he mused. "There's an abandoned homestead not far from here."

"Yes, I saw it on the way here. Do you know anything about them?"

"Hearsay, mostly. They claim that the government owes them money for some long-ago unpaid debt. They've been trying to collect ever since. Just when it looks like they might succeed, some imposter shows up claiming to be a long-lost relative and the whole thing falls apart."

"Do you think there's any merit to their claim?"

Olie shrugged. "Hard to tell. The government doesn't seem to think so. The original Van Pelt died childless without leaving a will or any written record of the debt. It's his siblings and their kin that keep trying to collect on it." He paused and scratched at his beard. "Why are you so interested in them?"

"I was just curious," I answered, with as much innocence as I could muster. "It's a pretty fantastic story."

Olie's good eye pierced my innocent façade. He stared at me for several seconds. There was a sting of suspicion in his voice when he finally answered. "If you ask me, I'd stay clear of them. I understand they don't take too kindly to anyone interfering in their business." He spat out these last words along with the tobacco juice he had been collecting in his cheek. It left a foul stain on the floor beside his cot.

He rolled back on his cot and closed his eyes, but I could tell he was still awake. Olie did not interact much with the other hands, but he kept his good eye on everything that happened on the ranch. I folded up the newspaper and tucked it back into my pack on top of the goatskin packet.

I propped myself up on the bed and stared at the rafters overhead. Ever since my visit to the old Van Pelt place and the discovery of the spring, my thoughts had been consumed with the thought of making the place prosper again. I thought about the promissory note still tucked away in my knapsack. There had to be a way to use it to gain possession of the land. As an illegitimate heir, I had no claim to the inheritance it promised; however, the note must have some value to the legitimate Van Pelt heirs. Perhaps there was a way I could use this to my advantage.

I thought of Catherine's advice to me on the passage to New York: "learn the language and customs of America if you want to succeed." Although she had spent several days teaching me practical words and phrases, my proficiency had not progressed much beyond that.

I turned to Olie who was still feigning sleep. "Is there anyone around here who can teach me English?" I asked.

He answered without opening his eyes or turning toward me. "Gerhard's wife, Hannah, holds classes in the evenings for anyone who's interested. They meet in the parlor in the ranch house, but if you go, you better be on your best behavior. I understand she's a real taskmaster."

"Is that where you learned to speak?"

Olie opened his eyes and snorted an amused laugh. "Not me. School is not for me. I just picked it up from living here so many years. I still can't read or write much. I just make a mark for my name and that seems to get me by."

"Do you think Miss Hannah could teach me to read and write as well as speak?"

"If you're willing to work at it, I imagine so," he answered. He rolled over with his back to me, signaling the conversation was over.

I lay awake for several hours staring at the ceiling and listening to the pounding of the rain on the roof. I had not thought about Catherine since our departure from Philadelphia. I had enjoyed our tutoring sessions more than I cared to admit. I remembered the man who had met her in New York and wondered if this was the brother she was staying with in New York or someone else in her life. The thought of Catherine with another man caused me to recoil as if I had touched a hot stove. Images of her danced across my memory and clouded my mind with guilt. I closed my eyes tightly and tried vainly to conjure up visions of Lainie instead, but all I could muster up was darkness.

$\neq$

Hannah Boersma was a plain woman, but she ruled with an iron hand. She greeted me on the first evening without fanfare. She handed me a slate and directed me to a chintz-covered chair in the parlor. I sat down carefully; afraid I might break it in my clumsiness. There were already several other ranch hands in the room, immigrants like me who spoke English haltingly if at all. They were scrubbed and subdued. I hardly recognized them as some of the same rowdy bunch I worked beside during the day.

Hannah walked to the front of the room and took her place behind a small desk. She tapped a ruler on the desk for attention, although it was completely unnecessary. All eyes were focused on this small woman with her low, sloping shoulders and serious nature. She wore a bell-shaped skirt that was accentuated by a pointed waist. Her hair was parted in the middle and pulled back in a bun at the nape of her neck, giving her a more severe look.

"I assume you are all here to learn English," she repeated slowly and loudly in response to our puzzled faces. Then she sighed and wrote the word in large letters on a slate at the desk. ENGLISH. She pointed to the word and repeated it again even more slowly, then indicated that we should repeat it.

She repeated the exercise with several other words, sometimes pointing at an object in the room and instructing us to repeat the words she spoke and copy the word onto our slates. She berated us if the spelling was not accurate or the letters were unreadable. I found her teaching method far different from the gentle instruction I had received from Catherine on the voyage across the ocean. By the end of the session, I had twelve new English words in my vocabulary, none of which I could use for any useful purpose.

Over the course of the next few weeks, attendance at the class began to dwindle until there were only a handful of us left. This did nothing to deter our instructor. She continued the course of her instruction, adding words to our vocabulary until she eventually began to string together words in simple sentences.

One evening as I was leaving, she called me back into the room, "Hank, may I speak to you a moment before you go?"

She stood at the front of the room with her hands clasped neatly in front of her. Her stern expression left me with the impression that I had displeased her. "Yes, ma'am?" I answered, in the manner she had taught us to respond to her.

"Unlike some of these other idlers, you seem determined to learn," she said, handing me a small book. "Many of the words you have learned are in this primer. I want you to study this on your own and be prepared to read from it at our next meeting."

I thanked her and backed my way out of the room. While the other hands spent their month's pay in town on women and drink, I spent the next few days struggling to decipher the words in the primer and make meaning of the sentences.

At the next session, while the others were dutifully copying words onto their slates, Miss Hannah called me to a chair beside her desk and asked me to read from the primer. Fear gripped my throat at the thought of performing before this small bundle of terror, but I swallowed hard and began, slowly at first, stumbling over the words. Miss Hannah showed remarkable patience with me, correcting the words I got wrong, until I relaxed and began to read more fluently.

In time, life on the ranch settled into a comfortable routine. I spent my days clearing the land for spring planting under the watchful eye of Gerhard Boersma, and my evenings studying the English language under Miss Hannah's strict tutelage. Over time, my body grew hardened to the labor and my mind began to grasp the nuances of the English language. Eventually, I gathered enough courage to ask for her assistance on a project that had been in the back of my mind since I had arrived at the Boersma Ranch.

I waited after class until everyone else had gone. She was busy at her desk and I finally had to clear my throat to get her attention. She looked up, slightly irritated, "Yes, Hank. What is it?"

I produced the wrinkled and yellowed newspaper I had kept all this time. "I'd like to write a letter to these people," I said, pointing to the article on the Van Pelt family.

She looked surprised. "To the Van Pelts? Whatever for?"

"I want to inquire about the abandoned homestead they own near here."

She stared at me with a mixture of incredulity and doubt. "But my husband says that land is worthless!"

"I don't think so. I've walked the property. It needs clearing and the buildings need repair, but I'm not afraid of hard work." I didn't mention the spring I had located.

"Have you spoken to my husband about this?"

"Yes. He has helped me identify what he considers an acceptable offer for the property."

She raised her eyebrows in surprise. "Where would you get that kind of money?"

"I'm a man of few needs," I answered. "Your husband has been generous enough to pay me a good wage and provide me with room and board. When the other hands spent their wages in town, they came to me for loans which I happily provided at a modest interest rate. I've also hired out during the winter to help your neighbors mend fences and chop wood. I have managed to save enough to put a minimum down payment on the property. I was hoping to procure a loan for the remainder."

"A loan? From whom?"

I showed her the card Catherine had given me when we parted. "I have a contact at this bank in Philadelphia that may be able to help."

She turned the card over in her hand and gazed at me thoughtfully for several minutes. "Very well. I'll help you, but we must make this a learning activity. Bring me your thoughts in writing and I will help you compose a proper letter."

I struggled with the wording of the letter for several days. Miss Hannah sent me back several times to rewrite it after her corrections. I decided not to reveal my suspicious heritage in the letter thinking it might be more useful as leverage during the negotiation process. When I finally posted the letter, I could hardly contain my excitement.

For weeks afterward, I watched the post with great expectation, but no response was forthcoming. I had just about given up hope when Miss Hannah again asked me to remain after class. "I think you've been waiting for this," she said, handing me a letter.

I took it with trembling hands. The letter bore the seal of the Van Pelt family. I handed it back to her. "I'm too nervous to try to read it myself." She smiled and took the letter from me and began to read.

Dear Mr. De Jong,

I have received your letter with much interest. The property you have inquired about is, indeed, for sale and we have found your offer quite within the realm of possibility. I will be in Philadelphia on Saturday of next week for some other business and would very much like to meet with you to discuss the purchase of the property in question.

Sincerely,

Ezra Van Pelt, owner

I gave a whoop and impulsively wrapped my arms around Miss Hannah in a bear hug and swung her around. Realizing the impropriety of my action, I quickly released her and apologized.

"No harm, Mr. De Jong," she said, smoothing her hair back in place. "I understand your excitement at this news."

When I broke the news to Olie, his only comment was, "Well, I'll be damned. I didn't think you could do it!"

The other hands congratulated me when they heard the news and broke out their hidden stash of whiskey to help me celebrate. Even Gerhard, who usually did not socialize with his workers, joined in the fun. Later, he took me aside to offer a word of caution.

"I've known Ezra Van Pelt for years," he warned. "He was a shrewd businessman in his day, but he's gotten up in years and turned the management of his affairs over to his son, Gregor." Gerhard paused and scratched his chin. "I'd be careful around him. Gregor is a man of questionable ethics. He wouldn't hesitate to cheat you if he thought he could get away with it."

"Do you think he'll accept the offer of the down payment?"

Gerhard looked concerned. "I don't know. That land had been abandoned for years. I would think he would be glad to be rid of it. Unless…"

"Unless what?"

"Well, you know the railroads are expanding like crazy. Everybody's got the fever. New lines are springing up every day. There is even talk of a spur connecting New Holland to the Pennsylvania Railroad not far from here. Speculators are buying up land at the smallest hint of railroad interest, driving prices way up."

"Have you heard of any railroad interest in the Van Pelt property?"

Gerhard shook his head. "Can't say that I have. But you should be prepared if they try to use it against you during the negotiations."

"If the bank approves my loan request, I hope to make a cash offer."

"That will certainly be in your favor. Just be careful and don't tip your hand too soon."

The excitement and anticipation of my meeting with the Van Pelts kept me awake all night. I rehearsed my offer and imagined how the conversation would go. In the end, due to my superior negotiating skills, I always came away with a deed to the property.

But when the day came to depart, I was filled with sadness and doubt. The Boersmas had been good to me. Gerhard had given me my first job and Miss Hannah had helped me improve my English skills. I said goodbye to her on the front porch. The morning was just beginning to dawn with the promise of a beautiful day to come. The first spring seedlings were just starting to push their heads through the newly thawed ground.

"You've been a good student," she said. "Your English has improved tremendously. I know you will do well."

I wasn't so sure, but I tried to lighten the mood. "Perhaps, when I return, we will be neighbors."

She smiled, but her words were not convincing. "That would be nice."

I left her and went to say goodbye to the men in the bunkhouse. Several came up to me and shook my hand to wish me luck. Ben Crawford was nowhere to be seen. He had made it his mission to mock my efforts to improve my language skills for months. When he discovered that I was hoping to purchase the Van Pelt property, he had laughed derisively and belittled me for having such a foolish idea.

Olie was lounging on his cot, his good eye focused on me as I approached. His health had taken a turn for the worse lately and these days he spent much of his time resting in the bunkhouse. I sat down on the cot next to his. There was so much I wanted to say, but now the words escaped me.

"Don't worry about old Olie," he said, in Dutch. "I've seen many winters come and go and I imagine I'll see a few more before my time is up." I nodded, afraid to look him in the eye lest he should see how difficult this parting was for me. "You go out and make your place in the world big enough for the both of us. I'll be cheering you on each step of the way."

I took his gnarled old hand in mine. It was the first time I had really noticed how frail he was. "You've been a good friend to me," I said. "I will never forget your kindness."

He waved me away. "Go on with you," he said, turning away. "Don't go soft on me." He sounded gruff, but there was no mistaking the emotion behind his words.

Gerhard was waiting in the wagon to take me to the station. We spoke little on the trip to town, just idle talk of the new crop and the work yet to be done on the ranch. We took care to avoid any talk of how we felt about my departure. When we arrived at the station, I picked up my bag with the goatskin packet tucked inside and walked around to shake his hand.

"Take care of yourself," Gerhard said, with a huskiness in his voice I had not heard before. He furrowed his brow in concern. "Remember what I told you about old Van Pelt. He's a tough one. Don't let him get the best of you."

"I'll be careful," I answered. "Thanks again for everything."

He nodded in silent farewell and slapped the reins to the horse. I watched him drive away without looking back. He had provided my first familial connection in America, and I felt the same sense of loss I had felt watching my father leave me behind at the station in Zutphen.

7

I arrived in Philadelphia a day early for my meeting with Ezra Van Pelt. I wanted to meet with Joseph Weller first to try to secure a loan for a cash offer on the property. The city was even noisier and more boisterous than I remembered when I had passed through on the immigrant train over two years ago. The streets were abuzz with activity. Prostitutes and pickpockets conducted their business openly. Most of the city's brothels were in the waterfront area along the South Street corridor and just west of Washington Square, next to the families of working-class families and artisan laborers. It was common for prostitutes to solicit men in public parks and theaters at night and in the business district during the day.

As I was making my way downtown, a young woman of about 18 years stepped up and blocked my way. Her dark hair was pulled into a roll at the base of her neck. Her bosoms peeked enticingly above her bodice in soft round mounds. "From the looks of ye," she said, with a sultry smile, "I'd say yer just in off the range." Her voice carried a thick Irish accent, and I could smell the sweetness of desire emanating from her. She moved closer so that her breasts were almost touching me. "I betcher lonely and wantin' a little companionship." She gazed up at me with half-closed eyes.

Although I had never passed up the chance of kissing a pretty girl with nice breasts, visions of Lainie still burned in my heart. I took a step back from her. "I am engaged to be married," I lied. "I'm on my way to meet her now."

The girl's expression changed suddenly, and her smile turned to a sour menacing snarl. "So ye think yer too good for the likes of me, is that it?" She turned on her heel and flounced away from me, her plump bottom swaying with each step. Then she turned to face me and lifted her skirts just enough to give me more of a glimpse of her ankles than was necessary, and to entice my imagination on what heavenly delights lay higher up. "Here's a peek at what you'll be missing then" she said, as her laughter echoed down the street.

I took the card that Catherine had given me on the ship from my pocket and studied the address, trying to find some clue about the location identified there. I finally gave up and stopped an elderly gentleman wearing a tailcoat and a top hat and asked directions to the Railroad and Loan. He looked at me suspiciously, taking in my heavy woolen pants, deep-pocketed vest and bandana. For practical reasons, I had adopted the style of dress common in the American West, which is obviously why the prostitute had assumed I was just in off the range.

"Two blocks down on the right," the man said, tersely pointing behind him. "You can't miss it." Then he hurried away as if to rid himself of the unpleasant encounter with me.

The Railroad Savings and Loan was an impressive structure built of stone with large glass windows on either side of a heavy oak door. Inside, the place was a beehive of activity. To the left was a row of caged windows where atrons lined up patiently waiting to deposit or withdraw funds. The air buzzed with the hushed sound of their voices. Occasionally, a teller could be heard to shout, "Next!" above the hum of voices.

Immediately behind the tellers was a large black vault. To the right were a series of desks partially hidden behind low walls where bank officials conducted other bank business in semi-privacy.

I had just spied a door with the words **Joseph Weller, President** stenciled above it, when the door opened and a tall, slender woman with auburn hair appeared in the doorway. I didn't recognize her at first, but when she turned in my direction, there was no mistaking the quiet intelligence behind the soft gray eyes. She didn't notice me at first, but I couldn't help but exclaim at the sight of her, "Catherine! Catherine Weller."

She stopped and looked at me with a puzzled expression before her face brightened in recognition. "Harke? Is that really you?" She came toward me holding out her hands in greeting. "I hardly recognized you," she said. "What are you doing here?"

I took the hands she held out to me. They were as soft as I remembered, and I was reluctant to release them. "It's Hank now.

I'm here on business. I'm trying to buy some property and I was hoping to secure a loan to help with the purchase."

She raised her eyebrows in surprise. "I thought you were headed out west."

"Much has changed since we parted," I said. "But fate has intervened to bring me here today." I briefly told her of Jelle's robbery, and my decision to stake his journey while aborting mine. I explained how I had met Gerhard Boersma who had given me my first job in America, and how I had saved and scrimped to amass enough to make a down payment on my own land in Lancaster County.

"My goodness!" she exclaimed when I stopped to catch my breath. "You've had quite the adventure."

A distinguished-looking gentleman with a commanding presence came to stand behind her. He wore his slightly graying hair swept to the sides to show off his handlebar moustache and mutton-chop sideburns. It was evident from his manner and style of dress that he was accustomed to the deference of others.

Catherine turned and planted a gentle kiss on his cheek. "Father, this is Harke, I mean, Hank De Jong. You remember, we met on the voyage over and I helped him with a few English phases."

Joseph Weller held out his hand to me. "Oh, yes. Catherine spoke highly of you. She told me you were quite determined to make a go of it in America."

Triumph at this unexpected stroke of good luck, roared through me. I had not expected to get a direct introduction to the man who held my future in his hands, and it took every ounce of control I possessed to keep my voice calm. "Yes," I said, shaking his hand. "That's why I've come to see you."

Weller looked at me doubtfully, but Catherine interjected. "Hank left Holland with the goal of attaining independent land ownership. During our tutoring sessions, I was impressed with his drive and determination. He is interested in buying some property not far from here." She paused and weighed her words carefully. It was not in her nature to speak in haste. "I really think you would be wise to hear him out."

Before he could answer, Catherine turned to face me. "I am anxious to hear about all that has transpired since we last met," she said, transfixing me with her thoughtful gaze. "Father and I will be dining at the Savoy just down the street this evening. If you are available, why don't you join us?"

I was somewhat taken aback by the brashness of her invitation, but her father laughed. "Don't be shocked by Catherine," he said. "She is quite the modern woman. Do join us if you can."

I thought about the small amount of cash I carried with me. I had planned to hand over the major part of my savings to Ezra Van Pelt as a good faith down payment. Dinner at a fine restaurant had not been part of my plans, but a glance at Catherine's expectant face changed my mind. I bowed stiffly. "I would be happy to accept your invitation to dine this evening."

I stood by awkwardly as Catherine took her leave. She had changed. When I first met her, she was aloof, careful in her motions and sparing with her words. She seemed resigned to her position as a business observer rather than participant. Now she seemed more alive. The confident way she had advocated for the meeting with her father and invited me to dine signaled a woman who was made for action, not passive acceptance.

Joseph Weller gestured toward his office. "Well, young man, if Catherine says I must meet with you, then I must."

"She can be quite convincing," I said, following him into the office. "On the way to America she told me that she hoped to one day run her own company!"

"She's a headstrong and stubborn young woman," Weller said, pointing me toward a chair. "I just hope she isn't too impetuous and that she listens to some sound advice before plunging into something she'll regret later." He took a seat behind the large wooden desk that dominated the room. "But to be honest," he added, "I'm not so sure the ruthless world of big business is a good fit for a woman's more delicate sensibilities."

I smiled when I imaged Catherine's response to her father's opinion of the female temperament. "Catherine doesn't strike me as the type who would shy away from a difficult situation," I said. "She's extremely determined. It wouldn't surprise me if she made it happen."

"Catherine has her own ideas about business," he said, smiling. "I try to advise her as best I can."

I took a seat in the stiff-backed chair he pointed to. "I'm sure she would be wise to listen to your expert counsel on these matters."

I glanced at the large framed paintings of victorious Union soldiers that adorned the dark wood paneling. "Catherine mentioned that you were quite active in supporting the Union cause during the Civil War," I said.

Weller turned his gaze to the paintings. "I was commissioned as a special agent for the state of Pennsylvania to sell treasury bonds overseas," he said. "But these days I'm more interested in the expansion of the railroads into the northwest territory."

"As I was leaving the Netherlands, I heard talk of your proposal to attract Dutch settlers to the area."

A spark of interest gleamed in Weller's eye at the mention of northwest settlement. "Is that why you've come to see me?" he asked.

"Actually, I'm interested in purchasing the old Van Pelt place near New Holland," I answered. I laid out my proposal as Miss Hannah and I had outlined it in my letter to Ezra Van Pelt. I explained my plan for making the land profitable for farming and ranching by harnessing a small spring to bring water to the land. He raised his eyebrows slightly and leaned back in his chair when I mentioned the Van Pelts, but he said nothing until I finished.

"Why are you so interested in this particular property?" he asked. "I understand the place has been abandoned for years. It will take a lot of work for one man to make it profitable. There are other properties I could steer you to that might be better suited to the enterprise you have in mind."

I hesitated, unsure of how much to reveal. "I feel almost a familial connection to this property," I said. "It reminds me of the Netherlands and the family I left behind." The sentiment was partially true, but more than that, I believed I might be able to leverage the note buried in the goatskin pouch to my advantage in the purchase.

Weller leaned forward in his chair. "The Van Pelts are valued customers of this bank and one of our primary stockholders," he said. "Their business connections are vast and involved. Therefore, I feel it is my duty to tell you that there is another party interested in that property."

My heart sank. Another offer. I had not considered this possibility. I was not prepared for a bidding war over the land. Like a drowning man struggling for air, I desperately tried to make sense of his words. "But you just said the property wasn't suited for farming and grazing," I protested.

Weller cleared his throat and appeared to be searching for words. "I don't believe the party in question is interested in farming the land. You might say he's more of a developer."

"I don't understand."

"He wants to develop the land for other uses," Weller explained. "He's made a generous offer that I'm quite certain the owner will accept. I doubt if you could match it even with a cash offer."

My dejection at hearing this news left me speechless. My mind struggled to comprehend this situation. I had put all my hopes on the acquisition of this land. I had walked the property several times since my initial visit, planning all the improvements I would make. In my mind, I had rebuilt the house and corral, cleared the land, and harnessed the spring to water the crops I would plant. To see all my hopes and dreams disintegrate in the space of a few minutes, was incomprehensible. "Perhaps when the Van Pelts hear my plans for improving the land…" I began.

"Perhaps," Weller interrupted, "but as my clients and in the best interests of the bank, I would have to counsel them against it. They would be foolish to pass on the current offer." Weller rose and extended his hand. "I'm sorry that I can't help you with this. But if you are interested in another piece of property, please do not hesitate to call on us. Catherine seems to think highly of you, or she would never have asked me to speak with you."

We shook hands and he ushered me out of his office. The door closed behind me with a sense of finality, and I stood for several minutes in numb disbelief at what had just happened. But I was not prepared to give up so easily. I thought of the promissory note I carried with me. Perhaps there was another way.

I was still in somewhat of a daze as I wandered back out into the street. My meeting with the Van Pelts was scheduled for the next morning. Although there was already a strong offer on the table, the meeting had not been canceled. I assumed this meant that the family was still willing to hear my offer. I had hoped to purchase the land on my own without having to leverage the promissory note as part of the bargain. Now, it seemed that the note was all I had left. I just wasn't sure how much it was worth to them.

I walked aimlessly for a few blocks while I tried to come to terms with my new situation and plot out a plan for negotiating with the Van Pelts. Without intending to, I found myself in front of the Savoy Hotel. With a sense of panic, I remembered that I had agreed to meet Catherine and her father for dinner here tonight. I weighed the awkwardness of dining with Catherine's father after his denial of my loan request, against the thought of seeing Catherine again. I remembered the direct way she had spoken to him at the bank. Perhaps her father would be more amenable to my proposition in a relaxed atmosphere with Catherine by his side.

I caught a glimpse of myself in the hotel window. I looked out of place against the backdrop of stylish people inside. I was taller than most, big boned and rugged. I was fresh off the range and my clothes were threadbare and hung shapelessly on my lanky frame. If I were to be taken seriously in my negotiations with Joseph Weller Noand the Van Pelts, I would first need to look the part.

Washed and scrubbed and freshly decked out in a new suit of clothes, I returned to the Savoy early that evening to meet Catherine and her father. Catherine arrived shortly thereafter and the sight of her left me momentarily transfixed. She was dressed in a domed bell-shaped skirt with a fitted bodice that emphasized her small waist. The pale blue color accentuated her cool gray eyes. Her hair was coiled atop her head, highlighted by the candlelit room in a mass of sunshine and flame. I rose to greet her and helped her into a seat across from me. I caught my breath as I leaned over her. Her hair smelled of sweet jasmine and she dropped her paisley shawl to reveal smooth white shoulders. "Will your father be joining us this evening?" I asked when she was seated.

"Father asked me to convey his regrets," she said. "I'm afraid Mother has taken a turn for the worse, and he decided it would be best if he stayed in to be with her."

"I'm sorry to hear that," I said, taking my seat and trying my best to sound disappointed. "I hope she is soon better."

Catherine shrugged sadly. "Unfortunately, the doctors do not hold out much hope."

I suppressed an urge to reach across the table and touch her. "I'm so sorry to hear this. I had no idea she was so ill."

"Mother has been in failing health for some time. It's been really hard on my father to see her suffering so."

"And for you as well, I assume."

Catherine's eyes glistened with tears. "I won't deny that it has been painful to see her in decline. She was always such a vibrant woman. Mother was quite involved in her family's dry goods business until her health began to fail."

"That must be where you get your drive and ambition," I said.

"I'm sure that's part of it," she said. "But you must not underestimate my own abilities."

"I didn't mean to imply…," I stammered.

Catherine's smile lit her face from within, creating a warmth that drew me closer to her. She shifted slightly in her chair and dismissed the remark with a wave of her hand. "There is no need to apologize. It is a common misconception that women are incapable of managing their own affairs," she said. "But let's talk about you. It's been a long time since we parted in New York. Your English has improved since then."

"I'm still learning," I answered, grateful for the change in topic. "My vocabulary is still limited, and I sometimes have trouble expressing my thoughts clearly."

"You must continue to practice if you expect to prosper here."

I nodded. "I've been taking classes at the ranch to learn to read and write in English."

"Tell me about the ranch and what brought you to Philadelphia. I want to hear all about it," she said.

I launched into an eager description of meeting Gerhard Boersma and working on the ranch. In my excitement, I alternated between Dutch and English when the words failed me. I spoke of exploring the abandoned Van Pelt homestead and my hopes for making it prosperous again.

"How did the meeting with my father go?" she asked when I stopped for breath. "Did he agree to help with the financing on the land?"

"The meeting didn't go as well as I had hoped," I answered, shaking my head. "He told me there was already another offer on the property." I paused to control an unexpected swell of emotion. "I had pinned all my hopes on the purchase of this land." My voice caught in my throat and I swallowed hard to conceal my disappointment.

Catherine watched me struggle for composure for a few minutes. Then, she reached across the table and touched my hand with her long, tapered fingers. The warmth of her touch caused a thin hot wire inside my chest to vibrate like the strings of a finely tuned violin. "I can see that you are upset. I think it might be easier to express your feelings if we speak in Dutch," she said. "Why don't you tell me what happened."

Her eyebrows knitted together in thought as I related my conversation with her father. "A developer?" she asked. "Given the location, I doubt that he is interested in farming the land. That can only mean two things: he is interested in mining, or he is interested in the railroad rights."

"Either way, I don't hold out much hope of winning a bidding war against a speculator," I said.

"What made you decide to purchase this particular piece of land?" she asked.

"I just felt a strong connection to it. The place has been vacant and neglected for some time. I have enough saved to make a good faith deposit on the land. I thought I might appeal to the owner's sense of pride. I know I could make the place prosperous again."

She knitted her brows together thoughtfully. I could tell she did not have much faith in the idea. "The Van Pelts are wealthy land speculators. It will be difficult to strike a bargain with them. Is there anything else you can leverage to help pay for the land?"

I thought again of the promissory note. "There might be something, but I'm not sure how much it's actually worth." I produced the weathered article from the *Philadelphia Record* about the Van Pelt family and spread it out on the table between us.

She quickly scanned the article and then glanced up at me in confusion. "I don't understand."

"I think I may possess the promissory note for this loan." Her eyes widened in amazement while I relayed the story my father had told when I left for America.

"That's quite a story!" she exclaimed. "I have heard stories of that awful winter at Valley Forge. Washington's army and the British were both camped nearby. They relied on food from the same small farmers in the area to feed their troops. The difference was that the British offered gold in payment, but the Americans could only offer paper promises. Some patriots took the scrip with the promise that it could be redeemed for gold after the war. Van Pelt must have been one of them."

I nodded. "And I have the note to prove it."

"How can you be sure the note is authentic?" she asked.

"I have the letters that Jacob Van Pelt wrote to my great-grandmother all those years ago. It's clear that he had no knowledge of his illegitimate child."

"And you know for certain that your grandfather was the son of Mr. Van Pelt?"

"Only the story passed as it was passed down over the generations," I said, shaking my head. "But the letters prove that Van Pelt left my great-grandmother the promissory note. And my father handed it down to me. So, I believe that I could claim a rightful inheritance, regardless of my grandfather's birthright."

"Why don't you go directly to the government with the note?" she asked.

"From what I understand, the family has tried for over 70 years to collect on the debt. Even though there is no doubt about their lineage, the government has refused to honor the debt without proof of the loan. Since my lineage is not proven, I would have to prove that the letters were authentic and that the note was not a forgery. That could take years."

"What makes you think the Van Pelt's will believe your story?"

"I don't know. But from what I understand, the only thing holding them back from collecting on the debt is the lack of a promissory note documenting the existence of the loan. Producing this note could force the government to go back into the records to authenticate it. I thought it might be worth a try."

Catherine's gray eyes clouded with worry. "That could be dangerous. If your claim is legitimate, it would supersede all others. Their claim to the inheritance would be worthless as long as you are alive and are in possession of the note." She folded the newspaper and pushed it across the table to me. "There's no telling what someone might do if they knew you had the note."

I tucked the paper away and surveyed the room suspiciously, suddenly aware of the impact of her words. The other diners appeared oblivious to our conversation, but my glance fell on two men seating across the room from us. The man facing me was tall and slim with a long nose and thick dark eyebrows that almost grew together in a menacing scowl over his eyes. His companion had his back to us so I could not see his face. He was modestly dressed in comparison to his more flamboyant companion. Bits and pieces of their conversation floated our way.

The two men were engaged in an animated discussion about railroad rights. The tall man raised his voice and gestured broadly. "I'm telling you, the most direct route between Reading and New Holland is right through this land. You can't go wrong on this deal. Most of the land through that part of the state is already settled. You will not find farmers, who have invested their lives in the land, willing to give up their rights to the railroad." The other man nodded thoughtfully, and the conversation continued at a lower volume so that I could not make out what they were saying.

Catherine followed my glance. Her view of the two men was obscured by the other diners, but she had also heard their conversation. "Railroad mania," she whispered, leaning toward me. She inclined her head slightly in the direction of the two men. "I saw it happening all through Europe. Speculators pour money into railway shares setting up new companies and proposing new routes. The smaller railroads often must purchase the land on which to lay their tracks from private individuals. This leads many investors on modest incomes to invest their life savings on the purchase of land they believe is in the right of way for a new rail route. Unfortunately, many of these deals turn out to be fraudulent and the roads are never built."

"You seem to know a lot about this."

She smiled, shyly, "You forget. My father's work focused on raising foreign capital for railroad expansion through the West. I learned a lot from him. Someday I plan to put all this knowledge to good use in my own company."

Her eyes glistened with excitement and I remembered Weller's concerns about his daughter's enthusiastic ambitions. "It sounds like a dirty business."

"It certainly can be if you don't know what you're doing. Railroads have been heavily promoted as a foolproof venture and a way to gain a quick return. One should always exercise extreme caution before investing."

"Wise words for any investor," I said, pointedly.

Catherine raised her glass, "I take your point," she said with a smile.

A burst of laughter from the two men diverted our attention and I saw them shake hands and raise their glasses in a toast. "They must have come to an agreement," I said.

The two gentlemen rose from their table and took their leave without looking in our direction. When they had passed, Catherine leaned toward me again. "Actually, now is the time to invest in the railroads. Smaller companies are buying up land all over the country to build spurs that will connect to the larger rail lines and service the smaller communities."

"I hear that the railroads are expanding westward at a rapid pace," I mused. "Towns and settlements are springing up along the routes at an astounding rate. It won't be long until the West is completely settled."

"Have you given up on the idea of homesteading?" she asked.

I considered the question for several minutes, and I felt the intensity of Catherine's gray eyes as she waited for my response. I had become so consumed with owning the Van Pelt land that my original plans for settling in the west had faded into the background. "I wouldn't say that I have given up," I answered. "I guess I'm still struggling to find my place in America. When I embarked on this journey, I had only one aim: to connect with other Dutch settlers in Wisconsin and build a homestead there."

"But now?"

I stared back at her. "Now, I'm not so sure."

"You once told me that homesteading was not a choice for you, it was your destiny."

"I still believe that," I answered. "I'm just not so sure that my future lies out west."

Our dinner arrived and Catherine and I turned our conversation to lighter topics. Catherine regaled me with stories of the New York Carriage Parade she had witnessed during her time in the city. Catherine's soft voice rose and fell like the swell of the ocean on the night we met. The light danced off her eyes as if tiny stars flickered behind her lashes. Streaks of gold glinted through her thick auburn hair and I imagined what it would be like to pull it loose and let it fall about her shoulders.

She amused me with her imitation of the New York society ladies in their carriages. "One could often see the aristocracy, the new smart set, the pretenders, the celebrities and the notorious in the same procession," she laughed.

A vision of Lainie mimicking the ladies of London society flashed across my memory and then disappeared. "It must have been quite a sight," I said, ignoring the pang of guilt left behind by the fleeting memory.

I had become so enamored by my companion that I barely noticed the lateness of the hour. I found myself not wanting the evening to end. I helped Catherine into a coach outside the restaurant and paid the driver from the cash I had saved for the down payment on the Van Pelt property. I would have to do without breakfast, but I had no regrets.

She turned to me. Her face was only inches from mine. "Please be careful," she said, softly. Her voice carried the warmth of a summer breeze although tiny snowflakes were beginning to cling to her hair and eyelashes. "America can be a ruthless temptress for those who are not schooled in her ways. There are many who will stop at nothing to improve their own lot in life."

"I will take your advice to heart," I murmured, unwilling to let her go. We gazed at each other silently, unsure of the moment. The air between us went hot and humid, full of scent. I forced myself to keep my breath regular. There was neither room nor time for the unaccountable and ridiculous vagaries of attraction in this moment, especially with a woman who was so clearly aware of her personal charm. Then she leaned out of the carriage and kissed me lightly on the cheek. I felt the warmth of her breath on my face. She pressed a note in my hand. "This is my address here in Philadelphia," she said. "I am anxious to hear how your meeting goes with the Van Pelts." Then she was gone, leaving me feeling confused and elated.

8

Ezra Van Pelt was waiting for me when I arrived at the appointed location the next day. He was a small frail man with graying hair and stooped shoulders who looked as if the slightest wind might carry him away, but he was not alone. A younger man was seated next to him. His tall angular body was folded stiffly into a chair that looked much too small for him. His lips were turned up at the ends in a sinister smile, adding to the aura of evil around him. The shock of recognition caused me to momentarily halt in my tracks. It was the same man I had seen at the restaurant the previous evening!

I approached them with a mixture of apprehension and dread. The younger regarded me suspiciously under his heavy brows. The older man rose with some effort and introduced the younger man as his son, Gregor Van Pelt. "I am meeting with you as a courtesy," Ezra began, in a voice that crackled with age. He looked apologetic and somewhat chagrined. "But I must tell you that Gregor and I have discussed the matter and the property you inquired after is no longer available for sale."

I had prepared myself for this response. "I understand that there has been another offer for the land, but I believe you will still want to hear my offer."

Ezra motioned to the chair across from him and sat down. "Very well then. I'm willing to listen, but I am doubtful that it will be worthwhile. I have already agreed to sell the land to another buyer."

I placed the money I had saved on the table in front of him. "I know that the average price of land in Pennsylvania is $25 per acre. I am prepared to offer you a cash deposit of $1500 today for the 160 acres you own along the Conestoga Creek, along with a generous share of the profits until the land is paid off."

I recognized the slight glimmer of greed behind his yellow eyes at the sight of the gold coins before him. For a moment, I thought he might change his mind. "I appreciate your offer," Ezra said, kindly, "but the land is located on a rail route. I have been offered more than twice that amount from the other buyer."

I had prepared myself for this argument. "I'm sure you are aware that smaller railroad companies are going under every day. The Pennsylvania Railroad already has a spur to New Holland," I said. "It is highly unlikely that another company will risk putting in a road so close to it. Besides, the land is covered with trees and rocks and the buildings are in disrepair. It could take years to clear the way for the railroad and your buyer would most likely have to default, leaving you with nothing."

"That's really not our problem," Gregor interjected. "The buyer knows the risks involved. If he defaults on the deal, we will simply foreclose on the land and sell it to someone else."

I ignored him and spoke to the older man, hoping to appeal to his family pride. "I can make the land prosperous again. It will no longer be a blight on the Van Pelt family name." Ezra winced at the thought of besmirching his family name.

Gregor answered again. "The Van Pelt family is well-respected in this area. We are barely known around New Holland. Besides, the land will no longer bear our name."

I decided to play my ace. "What if I told you that I was a direct descendent of Jacob Van Pelt?" I asked him.

A smirk played across Gregor's lips. "I'd say you were a liar."

"What if I can prove it?"

The old man laughed. "That's preposterous! Jacob Van Pelt died childless. Everyone knows that."

Gregor leaned across the table and sneered at me. "I guess that makes you an imposter."

I could feel the anger welling up inside me. I clenched my fists and willed myself to remain calm, but the insult had jarred me, causing me to be reckless, so I plunged ahead. "I have letters proving that Jacob Van Pelt visited the Netherlands during his privateering days. He met my great-grandmother and they fell deeply in love. Unfortunately, her parents would not allow them to marry. Van Pelt left the Netherlands without knowing that the woman he left behind was with child. That child was my grandfather."

Ezra knitted his eyebrows into a straight line across his forehead and snorted derisively. "That's ridiculous! There was no child."

"Van Pelt never forgot about the girl he had once loved so deeply. He wrote to her often in the hopes that they might one day be reconciled." I continued. "As he was dying, he sent her the only thing he had left of any value." I laid the goatskin packet on the table. "This packet contains the promissory note from George Washington, dated December of 1777 promising to repay Jacob Van Pelt in the amount of $450,000 for cash and supplies provided to the Continental Army."

Gregor's eyes narrowed and his voice became a sinister hiss. "There is no record that such a note ever existed. You don't know what you're talking about."

I removed the note from the packet and laid it on the table. Gregor reached for it, but I quickly covered it with my hands. "Not so fast. I am prepared to hand over the note in exchange for the deed to the property in question."

Gregor regarded me suspiciously. "How do we know the note is legitimate?"

I tapped the goatskin packet. "I can also produce the letters Jacob Van Pelt wrote to my grandmother granting her possession of the note. So even without proof of any direct descendance from the Van Pelts, the note was hers to pass on. It has passed from father to son in her family throughout the generations until it was eventually passed down to me." I paused before continuing, to let them take in the importance of this information. "The promissory note is signed by Washington himself. It won't take much to authenticate the signature."

Ezra had been silent during this exchange, but now he rose to his feet, screaming with the energy of a young man. He came at me with fists flying. "Lies! It's all lies! There is no note. No bastard child. This is all a forgery to get me to sell you the land at less than half what it's worth. Well, it's not going to work. You're an imposter trying to swindle an old man out of his land." His screaming had attracted the attention of those nearby who now turned to stare at us.

Gregor was also on his feet. He pointed at me and screamed at the gawking crowd, "This man is a crook and a cheat!" His shouts attracted the attention of several other men, who rose to their feet and started toward me. Their menacing glares left no doubt about their intentions. In an instant, my fickle memory took me back to the schoolyard where Dirk and his friends had taunted me for being weak and unworthy. I felt the familiar prickly sensation at the back of my neck that signaled a readiness to fight back. Instinctively, I squared my stance and raised my fists, but my saner instincts warned me that I had little to gain in a fight with Van Pelt and much to lose. I backed away from them. "You will regret this," I said, gathering up the scattered papers and stuffing them back into the goatskin packet.

Gregor's words hit me like a slap in the face. "You are nothing but a fraud and a fake, masquerading as something you're not! Even if the note is authentic, you can't prove you came by it honestly. For all we know, the letters you hold are all fakes, written by an accomplice. How do we know you are who you say you are?"

I steadied my voice and tried to sound reasonable. "You may be right. The promissory note may be of more value to you than it is to me. That is why I came to you first. It can be yours in exchange for a deed to the land in question."

"How dare you!" the old man shouted as I gathered up the cash and the goatskin pouch and tucked them back into my shirt. "The Van Pelts are a respectable family. I will not have our name sullied by someone like you." He tried to move toward me again but instead, he collapsed weakly into his chair from the exertion. "Imposter," he said again, but his voice was little more than a gasp.

The word still rang in my ears as I backed away from them and hurried from the tavern. I was angry with myself more than the Van Pelts. In my desperation to purchase the land, I had allowed myself to be goaded into showing my hand too soon. Now I had nothing left to bargain with.

Outside, a light rain was falling, and a ghostly mist shrouded the streets. I walked without purpose, head down, with my hands shoved deep into my pockets, berating myself for my foolishness. I don't know how long I walked before I became aware that I was being followed. Heavy footsteps behind me matched my own. I stopped to see who was behind me, but there was only silence and the shadows dancing eerily in the rain. I remembered how I had recklessly emptied all my gold coins on the table to show the Van Pelts the seriousness of my offer. Anyone nearby could have seen the money and followed me, hoping to take advantage of my carelessness. I continued walking and the footsteps resumed. I ducked into an alley and crouched in a sheltered doorway, hoping to catch sight of whoever was following me. The footsteps paused momentarily on the street and then moved on. I caught sight of a large, dark frame silhouetted against the light, but I couldn't make out any of the features.

I took a longer, alternate route back to my hotel room, stopping periodically to check behind me. My room was on the second floor, so it would have been difficult for anyone to go up without being noticed. Nevertheless, I opened the door carefully and glanced around the room before entering. Everything was in order just as I had left it. I latched the door behind me and breathed in the stale air still tainted with the scent of the last inhabitant. I raised the window slightly to let in some fresh air and the thin curtains billowed in protest. The rain had stopped. Several people were on the street in addition to the usual array of prostitutes and pickpockets, couples strolling arm-in-arm, and businessmen rushing home after work. It was impossible to tell if one of them was the dark shadow that had followed me.

I crossed the room and the floorboards squeaked under my feet. I knelt and discovered a loose board. I pried it up and carefully tucked my gold in the space it revealed. Then I added the goatskin packet to the stash and tapped the board back into place. The first shreds of moonlight shining through the jagged curtains cast an eerie glow on the room. I checked the street below, but the only sight was an old peddler woman with a basket of apples and a pair of lovers exchanging last minute kisses in the shadows.

The memory of stolen kisses lingered sweetly on my lips. Lainie and I had also delighted in sneaking away from the others whenever we could. We gave little thought to the consequences of our love and we were blind to all the warning signs. Lainie's father made no secret of the fact that he disapproved of our relationship. When Dirk intervened to convince his father that betrothing Lainie to the Governor's nephew would secure his future and give him the inside track for increasing his investments in railroad bonds overseas, he forbade us to see each other. Our situation appeared hopeless. But we still found ways to be together.

The Dutchman

For the price of a few sweets, Lainie and I engaged the services of the widow Franke whose eyes had dimmed with age, but whose heart still remembered the passions of youth. She requested that Lainie come and read to her from the scriptures after church services since she was too feeble to attend the service herself. I would meet her there and then we would sneak off to our special place. But like most young lovers, giddy with our love, we grew careless.

The old woman was distraught and Lainie was in tears by the time I arrived at the widow's home that morning. Before I could ask the cause of their distress, Dirk appeared in the doorway.

"Harke, I'm so sorry. He followed me!" Lainie cried.

Dirk advanced toward me menacingly. He pinned me against the wall with his face only a few inches from mine. I could smell his hot breath and feel the anger pulsing through his veins "I told you to stay away from her!" he hissed. "She's too good for the likes of you. You have nothing to offer her. She's going to marry Leen Van de Donk."

Van de Donk was a short, dumpy man with thinning hair and a face full of warts, who was fifteen years Lainie's senior. He leered at Lainie each time she passed and made lewd remarks about their marriage night. The elder Van de Donk was the official representative of the central government in Gelderland. He not only represented the province in its dealings with business, he also played an important part in the appointment of municipal mayors, a position Dirk coveted.

Lainie began to sob more loudly. She moved toward us and laid a pleading hand on Dirk's arm. He shoved her away roughly, causing her to fall against a table. She cried out in pain and I fought against Dirk's grip to go to her, but he held me fast.

"She's marrying Leen Van de Donk and that's the end of it!" he hissed. "The engagement will be announced next month at the King's Day Festival. This marriage will seal the futures of our family. I will not allow you to ruin it!"

Before I could respond, he punched me in the stomach and I doubled over, gasping for air. He raised his knee and caught me sharply in the face. Blood gushed from my nose and the gash beneath my eye. Dirk laughed. While I was still gathering my wits about me, he grabbed Lainie by the arm and dragged her away. "Don't come around her again!" he shouted. "The next time, I won't be so gentle."

I sat on the edge of the bed and dropped my head into my hands. Anger throbbed through the veins in my temple and I touched the scar that ran from my cheek up to the corner of my eye. It would forever remind me of Lainie's tearful pleas and Dirk's threats. I had dreamed of a life with Lainie by my side, but that dream had ended with Lainie's death. I had left Gelderland with plans to homestead in the west, but the contents of the goatskin packet had led me to the Dutch country of Pennsylvania instead. With my hopes of establishing myself as part of the Van Pelt legacy now in ashes, I had not given much thought to an alternative plan.

The sting of rejection burned in my mind. I had failed to attain the bank loan I needed and my negotiations with the Van Pelts had ended in disaster. A cold wind whistled through the partially open window and wrapped its icy fingers around my brain. Catherine's words returned to haunt me. America could indeed be a cruel temptress — luring you as a land of boundless opportunity and then laughing in your face when you reached for it.

#

I awoke the next morning with a pounding headache. The sun was already pouring through the window and the noise from the street indicated that the city was beginning to stir. The bottle of whiskey I had purchased to celebrate the successful conclusion of the Van Pelt deal lay empty on the floor beside me. I stumbled to the basin and poured cold water over my head, but it did nothing to alleviate the pain. My stomach growled and reminded me that I had not eaten since yesterday morning. The stiffly formal clothes I had purchased for the meeting with Van Pelt lay in a heap, so I dressed in my ranch clothes and left without giving a thought to the stash I had hidden under the floorboards.

I had just settled in with my food when I heard my name called from across the room. "Harke! Is that you?" I looked up to see Jelle striding toward me. "I've been looking for you. I've just come from the bank and they told me you were in town."

He sat down across from me. He had matured since I saw him last. Gone was the round, cherubic face with the innocent eyes. In its place was a well-dressed, confident young man who seemed quite at home in his surroundings. He signaled a waiter for coffee.

"Jelle? I hardly recognized you. What are you doing here?"

"I came to take care of some business," he said, smiling mysteriously. He leaned back in his chair, sizing me up. "It was a stroke of luck to find you here. What have you been up to since we parted? You look like you've just come in off the range."

"As a matter of fact, I have," I answered. I told him of finding work on the Boersma ranch and saving enough to make a down payment on my own land. I left out the part about my family connection to the Van Pelts and instead lamented the fact that the deal had not come to fruition. "But, Jelle…" I said. "From the looks of you, your luck has obviously improved since I left you at the station in Lancaster."

He laughed. "Our luck, you mean."

I was puzzled. "I don't understand."

Jelle spread his arms expansively. "America is indeed the land of opportunity and I have managed to take advantage of its bounty."

"I never doubted that you would succeed in America," I said. "So, I take it you were able to save your uncle's homestead?"

"Better than that!" he exclaimed. "My uncle's land happened to be situated near a major rail line. Because of the ease of shipping crops and livestock to the markets in Chicago, the value of the land was worth its weight in gold! I was able to sell the land for enough to set my uncle up in his own business in town."

"I'm happy for your good fortune," I said. "But I still don't see how your good luck affects me."

"It's a wonderful thing, the railroad," he said, grinning broadly. "I can make the trip to Philadelphia in two days and to Chicago in one." He took a sip of his coffee, made a grimace, and pushed the cup away. "I still can't get used to the taste of this stuff. I can't imagine why Americans are so taken with it."

"It's not so bad once you get used to it," I said.

"It was a stroke of luck to find you here," Jelle continued. "You remember our agreement when we parted on the train?" I must have looked confused, so he continued to enlighten me. "When my own money was stolen, you lent me money to reach my family. I promised to pay back with interest."

"Yes. I do remember that. I'm happy that things worked out for you."

"After I sold the homestead to the railroad, I invested the money in railroad bonds." His eyes gleamed with excitement and he leaned toward me eagerly. "I have just come from the bank where I deposited your initial investment, plus the interest I promised you."

It took several minutes for what Jelle was saying to register in my mind. I had to admit that I had not really expected Jelle to make good on the loan. I had felt compassion for a scared young man alone in a strange land and acted on impulse to help him on his way. Jelle watched in amusement while I tried to understand the implications of this new information.

"So, what are your plans now?" he asked. "Will you go back to Lancaster?"

I shook my head sadly. "I don't think so There is nothing for me there. Most of the land available for homesteading is already taken, and what is left is too expensive. The Van Pelt place was my best hope."

Jelle's eyes flashed with excitement. "Then come to Wisconsin with me!" he said. "There is still good land available there. But the railroads are moving west at breakneck speed, so the opportunity won't last long."

"I don't know…" The dream of owning land in the Pennsylvania Dutch country was still fresh in my mind. I had staked all my hopes for the future on setting down roots here. The thought of giving up and starting over again was painful.

"What's keeping you here?" Jelle asked, slyly. "Is it a woman?"

I thought briefly of Catherine. The soft brush of her lips against my cheek still lingered in my memory. She was not only beautiful; she was smart and independent. But the only thing I could offer her now was a dream. It had not been enough for Lainie and I had no illusions that it would be enough for Catherine. Her life here was filled with the trappings of wealth and prosperity. Once again, I felt that my desires were reaching beyond my grasp and could only lead to more pain and heartache. "No," I answered. "There is nothing keeping me here."

"Then it's settled," Jelle said, rising. "I'm leaving for Wisconsin first thing tomorrow." He pulled a gold pocket watch from his vest pocket. "I have some other business to attend to today, so I will see you at the station in the morning." He scribbled some numbers on a scrap of paper and handed it to me. "Here is the account number at the bank where your money is deposited. I think you'll find it's all there just as I promised."

I watched him stride away, marveling at the changes that had occurred since we had parted ways on our journey west. I turned the note over in my hand. In addition to the account number Jelle had included the balance. It was almost $2,000!

#

When I returned to my room later that morning, I noticed that the door had been tampered with. There were splinters on the floor indicating that someone had pried it open. I opened the door carefully and looked around. The room had been ransacked. The curtains were closed, throwing the room into semi-darkness. It took several minutes for my eyes to adjust to the dim light.

The intruder was sitting in the chair by the window with a pistol lying haphazardly in his lap. Even in the dim light, I could tell who it was. "The door was open, so I came on in," Gregor said. I willed myself not to glance at the floorboards where my valuables lay hidden.

"Did you find what you were looking for?" I asked, indicating the mess in my room.

"I didn't think you would be stupid enough to leave it behind, but I couldn't take the chance," he answered, carelessly.

"Is that why you had one of your goons follow me home?"

He laughed but the sound was hollow and mirthless. The light caught the evil glint in his dark hooded eyes. "I work alone," he said. "Much less chance of mistakes that way."

"Have you decided to take me up on my offer for the land?" I asked. "A cash down payment plus the promissory note in exchange for the land."

Gregor laughed derisively. "And what about the letters? What's to prevent you from using the letters to try and claim your right to the inheritance later?"

"You have my word. The letters are my insurance. With the note in your possession, the government would have to take you seriously. Once I relinquish the letters, my life is of no further use to you."

"Your word!" he sneered. "That may mean something where you come from, Dutchman, but here a man's word is only as good as the next offer."

"What is it you want?" I asked, taking a seat on the edge of the bed where I had a full view of my stash beneath the floorboards.

He walked toward me and placed the muzzle of the gun under my chin. I could smell his sour breath. He pointed the pistol at me and pulled the trigger. It clicked harmlessly, but nevertheless, I flinched at the sound. He laughed. "I want everything…the letters and especially the promissory note…anything you have that ties you to our revered ancestor." He paused and pressed the nuzzle of the gun against my throat. "And I always get what I want."

I gestured around the room. "You've already searched everywhere. The note and the letters are safe where you can't get them. If you kill me, you will never find them."

The anger flashed in his eyes. He clicked the gun again and I willed myself not to react. He bared his yellow teeth in an evil sneer. "You said yourself that the note is of no use to you," he said. "Why not save us both the trouble and hand it over now?"

"I came to you hoping to make an honest business deal," I said. "But now I realize that you are motivated more by greed than honesty. Handing over the note would never be enough for you. While I am alive, I am a threat to you. But killing me removes all hope of ever attaining the note."

"There are other ways of getting what I want," Gregor said, leaning toward me menacingly. "In the meantime, I want you to live in fear, not knowing when or where you'll see me again. I want you to flinch at every sound. I want you to wonder if the next time, the gun will be loaded."

Gregor tucked the gun into his belt and started toward the door. His threat triggered memories that collided in my brain making it nearly impossible to separate the past from the present. Visions of Dirk pushing my face into the dirt, taunting me, and threatening my family with ruin streamed through my mind. I felt the anger rise in my throat and I propelled myself off the bed toward Gregor's retreating figure. But he slammed the door before I could get to him, and I heard his laugh echoing down the hall as he left.

I slumped against the door and let the flood of familiar emotions wash over me. Gregor had made my decision much easier. He was determined to have the promissory note and would do whatever it took to get it. If I remained in Philadelphia, he would never let me have a moment's peace.

I lifted the floorboards and found that the goatskin packet was untouched along with my gold stash. The gold would help me to establish a new life in the West, but the letters and the promissory note were a liability I could not afford. Gregor had made it abundantly clear that he would stop at nothing to get his hands on the documents. It was obvious that I couldn't risk carrying them on my person where he might overtake me. I needed to leave them in a secure place, and I could only think of one person to trust.

The rented coach deposited me in front of the address Catherine had given me. "Are you sure this is the place?" I asked, looking up at the impressive façade.

The driver gestured toward the mansion at the end of the winding drive that snaked its way behind the iron fence. "This is it." I climbed out of the coach and the driver clicked his horse and drove away.

I stood for several minutes taking in the grandeur of the place. The Boersma house on the ranch was dwarfed in comparison. A two-story masonry building with a three-story tower stood behind the iron fencing, commanding the attention of all who passed. Three large porches wrapped the exterior of the house and four stone chimneys reached high above the steeply slanted mansard roof. I made my way up the drive toward the house which was surrounded by a large garden filled with a variety of trees, plants, shrubs, ferns, and flowers, creating the illusion of a wild forest.

I stepped beneath the arched portico and timidly approached the large, ornate front door. I dropped the knocker and the sound echoed through the halls beyond. Eventually, I heard footsteps approaching from behind the door. A stern-looking woman in a starched apron greeted me with a look of disapproval. I was dressed in the clothes I had worn on the train, suitable for the ranch, but clearly not appropriate for calling on someone of such a high social standing.

"The service entrance is in the rear," she said, preparing to shut the door.

I held out the note Catherine had given me. "I'm Hank De Jong," I stammered. "I'm here to see Catherine Weller."

The woman took the note and looked at it skeptically. "Wait here," she said, and shut the door, leaving me standing outside. I began to think that this visit was a huge mistake. I had taken a few steps in retreat, when the door opened again, and the woman reappeared. "Follow me," she said curtly, turning on her heels.

I followed her into a sitting room with painted and stenciled walls and an elaborate ceiling design. The room was bursting with accessories, furnishings, and fabrics, all designed to showcase the wealth and social standing of the inhabitants. Polished parquet floors formed a border for the large patterned carpet. Two button-backed chairs with carved mahogany arms flanked the heavily draped window. The woman gestured towards them. "Please have a seat. Miss Weller will be with you shortly."

I tried to make myself comfortable in this stiff, formal room with its marble fireplace and gilded mirrors, but all I could think of was how out of place I felt surrounded by all this opulence.

"Hank!" Catherine said, coming toward me. "What a surprise!" I rose to meet her. She was even more beautiful in the afternoon light. She wore a high-necked gown of green satin with embroidered trim and the many layers of fabric swished gently as she approached. "I wasn't expecting you. What brings you here on such short notice?"

"I've come to ask you a favor," I said, when we were seated by the window.

"Of course. I'm happy to assist in any way I can."

I produced the goatskin packet. "I was hoping that you would keep this safe for me until I can return for it."

Catherine's eyes clouded with concern. "Are these the papers you spoke about? The ones connecting you to the Van Pelt family?"

I nodded. "I have no further use for them at this time."

Catherine laid the packet gently in her lap. "I take it the meeting with Van Pelt didn't go as you had hoped," she said.

"I'm afraid not," I answered. "Van Pelt refused my offer. The elder Van Pelt has obviously turned his business operations over to his son, Gregor. My impression of the younger Van Pelt was that he could be quite ruthless. He made it clear that he was unwilling to negotiate for the land I wanted." I paused to consider how much to reveal to her.

She regarded me silently for a few moments. "So, what are your plans now?" she asked.

"I've decided to pursue my future out West," I answered. "I ran into my old friend, Jelle Schippers yesterday. He says there is still land in Wisconsin available for homesteading." I paused to gauge her reaction. "I'm leaving with him first thing in the morning to check it out."

"I'm truly sorry to hear this," Catherine said. "When will you return?"

"I'm not sure."

"Can't you go back to the ranch?"

"No," I said, shaking my head. "I have no future there. But Jelle says the railroads are expanding rapidly though Wisconsin and will soon open up the markets in the west."

"It's true that prosperity seems to follow where the railroad goes." She sighed and there was no mistaking the sadness in her voice. "I envy the adventure you're about to undertake. If it weren't for mother's illness…" She let the words trail off.

I followed her gaze to the neatly folded hands in her lap, long tapered fingers cradled together, palms facing upward in a gesture of supplication. I wanted with all my heart to take her hands and press them to my lips. She raised her eyes to mine and for a moment, I was lost in the clear depth of her eyes. "Will you write?" she asked. "I'd love to know how you're getting on."

"My future is uncertain at this point," I answered. "I'm not sure where I'll end up or what I'll do, but I promise to write whenever I can."

Unlike Lainie, Catherine made no attempt to dissuade me from my decision, although a part of me wished that she would. When she saw me to the door, there was a sadness in her gray eyes as if a curtain had descended between us. I felt that she was as hesitant to part as I was. I kissed her hand in parting and left her standing there. I was overcome by a familiar feeling of sadness and loss, but I resisted every instinct to turn back and look at her as I made my way back down the winding lane to the road.

PART II

*Self-redemption is the first step
to exoneration from guilt.*
—Dennis E. Adonis

9

Jelle was waiting for me when I arrived at the station early the next morning. When he saw me, his face lit up with the same boyish glee I remembered. "It's odd," he said, "but I feel as I did when we first embarked on this journey together."

"I've made some mistakes along the way," I said, nodding in agreement. "I just hope I can redeem myself this time."

"I'm confident that things will be different," Jelle said, as we joined the crush of passengers boarding the train. "We are no longer venturing into the unknown. I have connections in Alto and I know the land is fertile and excellent for farming. With the railroads expanding through the area, it is now easier than ever to ship goods to markets in the east. I think you'll find that Wisconsin offers greater opportunities for independent land ownership than Pennsylvania." He kept up a constant chatter until the train left the city behind and the Pennsylvania countryside began to recede into the distance. The early morning sun stretched its long shimmery fingers through the trees as if it were pleading for me to stay. This land still held a special allure for me. I thought I had found a home here and a place where I could prosper and start anew, but that was not to be.

As we crossed Pennsylvania into northern Ohio, Jelle slept with his head rolled back and his mouth wide open. Occasionally he would breathe in sharply and release a loud snort. Jelle stirred briefly as I squeezed past him to go stretch my legs, but he didn't wake up.

Darkness fell as I paced the aisles of the train. Jelle and I had upgraded to third class, but we still didn't have the privacy of first-class sleeping quarters. It didn't really matter. I was too keyed up to sleep anyway. I wandered into the lounge where a group of railroad barons were gathered. I sat a few tables apart from them, but I could still hear most of what they were saying.

"I'm telling you," one of the men said. "the demand for contract labor is what is holding up construction on the Northwestern Pacific Line. It will never be finished at this rate." I recognized this as the line Joseph Weller was promoting. I leaned forward to hear more of their conversation.

"I thought you were using Chinese labor for that," another man said.

"We use the Chinese to work on the treacherous part of the line through the mountains. They are the only ones willing to work in such dangerous conditions."

"Why don't you use them on the rest of the line through the flatlands?"

"The unions have gotten involved and forced the railroads to hire more white workers," the first man answered. "But most of the white workers refuse to work the mountain routes, so we have no choice but to hire the coolies for that."

"I've seen their camps along the rails," one man muttered with a grunt of disapproval. "They stand there bareheaded and indifferent, with their hands in their pockets. Hundreds of them along the line, waiting patiently for the next order to move on. I wish we could rid ourselves of the whole lot!"

The dislike of the Chinese was pervasive among railroaders. The Chinese workers occupied a strange space where they were both detested and essential. They were treated as virtual slaves, racially inferior, and exotically alien. The conversation unnerved me, and I retreated to my seat.

The train slowed as we neared Cleveland, and Jelle stirred himself awake. He stretched out his legs and yawned, "We should reach Chicago by tomorrow afternoon," he said, sleepily. "We'll change trains there."

As the train ground to a halt at the station, the sun was just beginning to push its way through the gray haze that blanketed the city of Cleveland. The city's location allowed it to receive a large flow of raw materials and to ship out finished products, and the sky was clouded with the smoke from their factories. In the distance I could see the steam coming from the smokestacks of the Standard Oil Company. The depot was already buzzing with noise and activity. Dock workers busily loaded pallets of mass-produced products onto rail cars for shipment to markets in the east and west.

We soon left Ohio behind and began to skirt the southern border of Michigan where the land was covered with sand and sawdust. It was littered with stumps and branches from loggers who gave little thought to the land they were leaving behind. I nudged Jelle awake as we neared Michigan City. "This is the area where Lubbert was trying to sell you his land deed," I said to him. "The loggers have left no barriers to erosion on cutover land and the dried debris creates an enormous fire hazard. You are lucky to have avoided his scheme."

"I have you to thank for that," Jelle answered. "I was too eager to believe the stories of quick riches in America."

"Don't be too hard on yourself," I said. "It's easy to fall prey to schemes like that. Unfortunately, I'm sure Lubbert found someone else who was willing to part with their hard-earned cash.'

The train rounded the southern edge of Lake Michigan and the great city of Chicago soon came into view. As the train neared the station, I was overcome by the powerful stench of manure. "What on earth is that smell?" I asked, covering my mouth and nose with my arm.

"It's the stockyards," Jelle answered. "Ranchers bring their cattle here from all over the country to be slaughtered and shipped to markets in the east." We passed pens where cattle and hogs bawled and squealed while they languished in the muck and mud. Children spilled from the doorways of overcrowded slums nearby. They seemed oblivious to the filth and odor.

I wiped my eyes with the sleeve of my coat. "The smell is overpowering. It's no wonder that Chicago is reported to be the filthiest city in America." I mumbled. "How can anyone bear to live here?"

"There are fine homes along the lake on the city's north side where the smell is barely detectable," Jelle answered. "But down here, it is mostly immigrants who work in the city's stockyards, factories, and railroads. They work for much less than it costs to hire white workers."

I shook my head sadly. "Most immigrants came to America seeking a better future. They thought America was the land of economic opportunity. Instead, they find that there are never enough jobs, and when they do find work, they are taken advantage of and paid less than other workers."

We picked our way carefully over the mud and puddles toward our connecting train for Wisconsin. "We should reach Waupun by tomorrow afternoon." Jelle said, "My uncle will meet us there and we'll travel the remaining few miles to Alto by wagon."

Jelle became more animated as the train rumbled through more familiar territory. I listened with half an ear while he extolled the virtues of life in Wisconsin and the potential for success that lay in the path of the railroad's expansion. "This area is called The Rock River Valley," Jelle said, pointing out the window at the lush countryside. "The south branch of the river rises north out of Fox Lake and flows east right through Waupun." Jelle's enthusiasm for his adopted land was beginning to take hold of me. I had to admit that the valley held some of the most beautiful and fertile land I had ever seen.

Otto Schippers met us at the station in Waupun. He was a small, round man with narrow, close-set eyes and a large open smile. He pumped my hand enthusiastically in greeting. "Jelle has told me all about you," he said, his voice thick with a Dutch accent. "You saved my Jelle from certain disaster on the journey to America and we owe you a huge debt of gratitude." He shouldered my bag with difficulty and loaded it into the wagon to take us the last few miles to Alto. "You must stay with us until you find suitable lodging," he insisted. "My wife has supper waiting and is anxious to meet the man who saved us from ruin."

I raised my eyebrows to Jelle who shrugged sheepishly. "I may have embellished the story somewhat in the telling."

Otto kept up an excited chatter during the wagon trip to Alto. He told us of the hardships he had endured as one of the first homesteaders in the region and the difficulties of shipping crops to market at the ports along Lake Michigan before the railroads. When we arrived in Alto, he proudly pointed out his shop on the main street. Otto and his family lived above the shop and I could see two small heads peering at us from behind the curtains as we passed. He left Jelle to show me around while he tended to the horse and wagon.

Alto was a prosperous community of about 800 Dutch settlers. According to Jelle, many of them had arrived in 1844 from

Winterswijk in the Netherlands. They had erected a log meetinghouse, which served as the spiritual and community center. Several small businesses, including Otto's haberdashery, lined the town's main artery. "We are only 68 miles west of Milwaukee," Jelle said, proudly. "The area is already showing promise of maturing into a vibrant and prosperous community. You could do well by settling here."

While the area was certainly impressive, it held none of the allure that had initially captivated me in the Pennsylvania countryside. However, I resolved to give it a chance. "You may be right," I answered. "But first, I must find room and board, and some means of employment."

"I may be able to help with that," Jelle said.

Later that day, he introduced me to a Dutch tradesman who, like many other immigrants, had achieved success by becoming a farmer and landowner. He offered me room and board to help with the work of clearing trees, shearing sheep, harvesting grain, cutting, and husking corn, and chopping firewood in preparation for winter.

Although I had become somewhat accustomed to the living standards of American farmers during my time with the Boersmas, I still marveled at the level of comfort enjoyed by farmers here as opposed to those in my homeland. Even here in the relatively unsettled western lands, farmers enjoyed a comfortable living standard. People lived in two-story houses, had excellent furniture, and drove in buggies and coaches. They proudly turned out for Sunday services in their finest clothes, creating quite a display of fashion. I thought of father's strict adherence to piety and somber, conservative dress. There was no doubt, he would have disapproved of such a display of fashion and considered it a serious fault, but Lainie would have loved it.

Lainie thrust her bottom lip outward in a pretty pout. Despite Dirk's threats, we had still managed to steal a few minutes to be together. "What am I to do?" she lamented. "The dress arrived yesterday from Amsterdam and it's hideous! If I'm to be forced into this marriage, I should at least be able to choose my own gown."

Lainie's engagement to the Governor's nephew had been announced on King's Day over our protests. I watched helplessly as she was promised to a man she detested. He leered at her, making no attempt to conceal his lust. Dirk and his father smiled in approval as he led her away to receive the congratulations of the crowd.

I recoiled at the thought of this horrible man raising the child Lainie carried – my child. Lainie was still early in her pregnancy and the tiny seed that grew inside her had not yet begun to show, but her breasts were already alluringly full. I stroked her hair. "You don't have to go through with this, you know. You could leave with me tonight and we could start a new life in America."

She looked up at me with tearful eyes. "It would kill my father if I left. You know he's not in good health. Sometimes I think this marriage is the only thing keeping him alive."

"But what about us...what about our child?"

Lainie stroked her belly and looked up at me with sad eyes. "I will hold you in my arms each time I caress our child. Nothing can take that from me. Our child will be a constant reminder of our love."

"But what if your husband suspects the truth."

Lainie's eyes clouded with anger. "He's a stupid man who cares for nothing but himself. I doubt that he will even acknowledge the child." Lainie could tell that I wasn't convinced. "Don't you see?" she implored, taking my hands in hers. She gazed up at me with pleading eyes and my heart flipped in my chest. "It's the only way. Our child will have the best things in life. All the best schools. He'll want for nothing. I'll see to that."

As much as I hated to admit it, Dirk was right. I could never provide the life Lainie was accustomed to if I stayed in the Netherlands, and she was not prepared to endure the hardships of life in the American West. But that did nothing to ease the cold grip of pain around my heart.

I shivered and slapped my arms against my chest to generate warmth. The first cool days of October were already signaling the coming of more long cold days ahead. My first winter in Wisconsin had made me hunger for the balmy ocean breezes that moderated the temperatures in my homeland. Winter arrived in Wisconsin with a vengeance and refused to leave. The daytime highs rarely reached above freezing, and at night, the temperature dropped so low that water froze on the stove. The snow was deep and constant. My boots and clothes instantly became soaked with snow and ice if I dared to venture outside. My clothes perpetually hung by the stove to dry whenever I came inside.

"I don't believe I can endure another Wisconsin winter," I said to Jelle as we sat in his uncle's kitchen devouring hearty bowls of pea soup. The fall harvest was complete, and the entire community was beginning the process of locking down in preparation for the onset of colder weather.

"I thought you liked it here," he said, making no attempt to conceal his surprise and disappointment.

"I do," I answered quickly, "but good land here is expensive and already occupied, and permanent status as a farm laborer or tenant is not what I had in mind."

"Where will you go?" he asked, shoveling a spoonful of sausage and vegetables into his mouth.

I longed to return to the rich Dutch country around Philadelphia, but land there was also out of my reach. Besides, it would be too easy for Gregor to find me there. I pushed my bowl away and rubbed my stomach in satisfaction. It would be difficult to leave behind the traditional Dutch meals provided by Jelle's aunt. "I hope to reconnoiter with another Dutch colony in Pella, Iowa," I said. "I've heard there's still good land available there."

"Iowa…" he said, pushing himself away from the table. "The St. Paul and Sioux City Railroad is moving west at breakneck speed, but I hear there is still government land available for homesteading in the northwestern part of the state along the railroad."

"I've seen the proposed route of that line," I answered. "It crosses some of the most sparsely populated areas of the entire country. Nothing for miles around but dry, barren land not fit for man nor beast."

Jelle was undeterred. "I've heard claims that locomotives passing through the arid plains will actually stimulate the development of rain clouds."

"You can lay track to the Garden of Eden," I laughed, "but what good is it if the only inhabitants are Adam and Eve?"

Jelle sighed in resignation. "I can see that your mind is made up and there's no changing it," he said. "But staking your own claim can be expensive. Why not stay here another year until you can set aside enough to get you started on your own?"

I shook my head. "Pella is a hub for the Des Valley Railroad from Keokuk to Des Moines. I should have no trouble finding work on the railroad until I can afford to stake my own claim."

"Railroad work certainly pays well," Jelle mused, "but it can be extremely dangerous. Railroad executives care little for safety. Workers must go between the cars for coupling and uncoupling and ride the cars to work the brakes, not to mention the number of derailments and collisions."

"I don't plan to make it my life's work," I said. "I just want to earn enough to stake my own claim."

"Money won't help you if you are seriously injured or die on the job," Jelle said, pulling a railroad timetable from his pocket. "But if you are determined to go, your best option is to return to Chicago and connect from there since there is no direct line to Pella from here." He folded the timetable and put it back in his pocket. "When will you leave?"

I swallowed and looked away from him. Jelle had become like a brother to me. My decision to leave had not come easily. "Your family has made me feel welcome here," I said, "They have treated me like one of the family and I can't thank you enough for everything you've done for me, but if I am to achieve my goal independent land ownership, I must go where good affordable land is still available. The longer I wait, the more difficult it will be to say goodbye." I choked back an unexpected flood of emotion. "I plan to leave within the next couple of days."

10

Nowhere was the thin veneer of wealth more evident to me than in Chicago in 1871. Haphazardly constructed wooden slums existed alongside the stone mansions of the newly rich. The exorbitant fortunes amassed by bankers, railroad tycoons, and other titans of industry were but a glamorous layer of gold that masked the stark inequality and social ills as the working classes and poor were forced to work more and more for less and less.

Even though I knew what to expect this time, the noise and the horrendous stench of the stockyards still made my eyes water. I wiped my eyes with the sleeve of my coat. I headed out into the muddy streets, past two mammoth elevators that stood on the banks of the river. Shipping containers lined the harbor between the elevators and the railway building. The track was constructed on trestlework made of piles filled with stone and protected on the lake side by a breakwater. Just beyond the track, a large park, nearly one mile in length, was almost entirely covered with water and green slime.

The train to Pella did not leave until the next day, so I decided to look for accommodations nearby. I passed a rowdy saloon specializing in beer and liquor sales by the drink, with food and lodging as secondary concerns, and decided to quench my thirst while I checked on the availability of a room for the night.

The saloon was a circus of activity and noise. The proximity to the rail station was a constant reminder of the myriad of rail lines fanning out from the city in all directions. The ground shuddered constantly from the rumble and hiss of trains arriving and departing from the station. The place was filled with workers enjoying a freedom and independence through drinking and gambling that was a world apart from their closely supervised factory and railroad jobs.

Their voices created a cacophony of sound that reverberated off the walls and echoed through the building. After booking a room, I found a table near the edge of the throng and ordered a beer.

A group of rowdies was seated at the bar where a drinking game was in progress. A tall, thin man with a narrow, pinched face and an aquiline nose stood at the far end of the bar watching the activity. His hat was pulled low over his eyes, but there was no mistaking his identity. When he noticed my stare, he tipped his hat to meWe s and then turned away.

I had not seen or heard from Gregor Van Pelt since I left Philadelphia. I assumed that he had given up on his threat to get the promissory note, and yet somehow, here he was! The sight of him triggered familiar feelings of anger and resentment and I felt the blood rush to my head. I rose from the table and started toward him, but my attention was momentarily diverted when a drunk bumped against me and asked for money; his words were slurred, and his eyes were already bloodshot. I shoved him away and he staggered off to accost someone else. When I looked again, Gregor had vanished.

I rushed outside, hoping to catch a glimpse of him, but the conflagration of narrow streets flanked by wooden buildings and sidewalks made it easy for him to disappear. I stopped to catch my breath and was once again reminded of my proximity to the stockyards. I continued to wander the streets aimlessly hoping to gain a respite from the smell. I crossed the river and found myself near the center of town where the air was cleaner and tinged with the sound of carriages. Enticed by the aroma of fine food, I suddenly realized I was starving. I slipped into a nearby restaurant and was having dinner alone when I saw her.

Catherine was even more stunning than I remembered. She was dressed stylishly in a gown that accentuated her narrow silhouette and ended in a train with more fullness at the back. She entered in the company of a tall gentleman who carried himself with an air of confidence and self-importance that I found presumptuous. He kept his face turned away from me so I couldn't get a clear look at him. He tipped the host, and they threaded their way through the guests on the far side of the restaurant to a prime table for two just out of the main traffic flow.

The gentleman took a seat with his back to me behind an ornate screen. While I could not make out much of their conversation, I could tell that the gentleman was trying his best to impress her by ordering the finest wine and expensive dishes that he asked to be specially prepared by the chef.

Catherine was seated so that I could see the tilt of her head and the gentle curve of her jaw as she smiled at her companion. I found myself lingering over my meal so I could steal glances in her direction. When they finally rose to leave, they passed by my table and Catherine stopped short. "Hank! Is that really you?" she exclaimed, placing her hand on my shoulder. I rose and her hand slid down my arm leaving a tingling sensation that sent shock waves through my body.

She introduced me to her companion, and I suppressed a gasp. There was no mistaking the dark hooded eyes and long slender nose. "Gregor, I believe you know Hank De Jong," she said.

I felt the hair on the back of my neck rise. Catherine tossed me a meaningful glance, but before she could say more, I extended my hand. "Yes. We've met," I said.

Gregor's eyes narrowed to two evil slits. He inclined his head slightly in acknowledgement but did not take my hand. "Yes. Mr. De Jong approached me about a business deal about a year ago. Sadly, we weren't able to reach an agreement."

"Mr. Van Pelt is representing a Dutch investment firm interested in building a spur that will connect Father's Northwest Pacific line to a line running north through Iowa," Catherine continued. "He was just filling me in on the details."

Van Pelt cleared his throat. "We really must be going, my dear," he said, taking her elbow. Catherine carefully removed herself from his grip. "Why don't you get me a cab," she said. "I'll meet you outside." Van Pelt's face reddened at the rebuke, but he said nothing. Instead, he bowed and left to do as he was bidden.

A few more awkward moments passed before Catherine said, quietly, "May I sit down?"

Embarrassed at my lapse of manners, I quickly pulled out a chair and helped her to seat herself before taking the chair opposite her.

"I know what you must be thinking," she said at last. "But you're wrong."

"It's none of my business who you have dinner with," I said, with a shrug. "But I must admit that I was surprised to see the two of you together."

"It was strictly business, I assure you," she said. I watched as a myriad of emotions crossed her face. "The Van Pelts have been my father's clients for years. Gregor represents a Dutch investment company that is selling bonds for the Des Moines Valley Railroad. Father suggested that I meet with him to hear his proposal."

"Is that why you're in Chicago?"

She lowered her eyes. "Mother passed away this winter," she said softly, struggling to keep her voice steady. "Her death has been hard on Father. He has decided to move to Chicago to escape the memories and be closer to his railroad business." A tiny smile graced her lips. "He is convinced that he can make Duluth the new Chicago. We are staying with friends on the north side of town until the home in Philadelphia can be sold and suitable living arrangements can be made in Chicago. The move will allow Father better access for leading groups of businessmen on junkets to the west where he hopes to persuade them to invest in his Northwest Pacific Railroad across Canada to the Pacific."

"Is that why he's interested in Gregor's proposal?"

She paused as if considering how to continue. "He's not the one who's interested. Mother left me a small inheritance. I was thinking of investing it in Gregor's railroad spur."

I hesitated, unsure of how to proceed. "Are you sure Gregor is trustworthy?"

Catherine stiffened her back and arched her eyebrows. "He comes with Father's recommendation. The company he represents is well known in the Netherlands. They have already completed a line from Keokuk on the Mississippi River all the way to Des Moines. Besides, I have spent years following my father's business. I know it almost as well as he does. I've looked over Gregor's prospectus and it looks quite promising."

There was an edge to her voice, but I ignored it and proceeded without caution. "I just don't want you to rush into something you may later regret."

"I assure you that I have taken the necessary precautions."

"Still…"

"Please..." she interrupted. "Don't lecture me. I'm quite capable of taking care of myself."

I felt the blood rise beneath my collar and sting my ears. I struggled to reply, but no words would come. The silence hung between us for several seconds while her soft gray eyes held me spellbound. I found myself unable to look away. "Let's not argue," she said, at last. "What brings you to Chicago? I thought you were headed to Wisconsin."

"One winter in Wisconsin was enough for me. I'm on my way to Iowa to join up with another Dutch settlement there."

"Still pursuing the dream, I see," she said, and I felt myself bristle at her tone. The words of Lainie's father resurfaced in my brain. *"You are nothing but a dreamer! You'll never make it, and you will soon be back here begging for my help."*

"You forget," I told her, somewhat testily, "America was founded on an immigrant's dream. I am only following in the footsteps of those who came before me."

"I didn't mean to sound critical," she said, contritely. She furrowed her brow thoughtfully. "I told you once that I believed you would succeed," she said, softly. "I stand by that assessment."

"I hope you're right," I answered.

"I still have the packet you left with me in Philadelphia," she said. "Would you like to have it back?"

"No, I'd like to continue to leave it in your care if that's acceptable to you," I answered. "But please don't let Gregor know you have it. There's no telling what he would do to get his hands on it."

"You mustn't worry about me," she said, with a smile that caused my heart to leap in my chest. "I can take care of myself." She rose to leave. "I assure you that your inheritance is secure with me. I will keep it safe until you return for it." An awkward silence hung between us. We stood facing each other. The air between us was charged with electricity. I felt myself move toward her.

"Excuse me, Miss Weller," the waiter said, apologetically. "The gentleman outside asked me to tell you your cab is waiting."

With the moment lost, she turned away to speak to the waiter. "Tell him I will be right there." Then she turned back to me. "Good luck," she said, softly. "I won't say goodbye. While I am the guardian of your inheritance, I can assume that you will one day return for it."

"You can be assured of that," I said.

She turned to go, and I watched her glide toward the door with apparent disregard for the admiring stares that followed her. I thought again, how lovely she was. Seeing Catherine again had stirred my senses. Time was slipping through my fingers. I had been in America nearly three years and I was still no closer to acquiring my own land. I was suddenly consumed with a sense of urgency to stake my claim out west.

I took my time on the walk back to my hotel. The evening was warm and dry and the wind off the lake filled the air with the smokey scent of evening cooking fires. I was lost in thought as I neared my hotel and did not notice the two men slouching near the building. Suddenly, they were upon me. Too late, I remembered that I still had my money pouch in my coat pocket. It contained all the money I had saved to stake my claim out west. Ordinarily, I would have secured it in the hotel, but I had not gone to my room after leaving the saloon. The men dragged me into the darkness of the alleyway. One of them pinned my arms while the other one beat me almost senseless. I was badly outmatched, and I have no doubt they would have finished me off then and there if not for the gunshot that echoed through the night.

"Leave him be!" a voice shouted, startling the men.

One of them grabbed the money pouch from my pocket and then they ran into the night, leaving me crumpled and bleeding. One eye was already starting to swell shut and my mouth was filling with blood.

Gregor Van Pelt was standing at the mouth of the alley. I caught the glint of a large steel revolver in his hand. "You don't waste any time, do you?" he said to me.

I tried to get to my feet but slumped back against the wall. My head throbbed. I spat out the blood and wiped my face with my sleeve. "What are you talking about?" I mumbled through swollen lips.

"I'm talking about the lovely Miss Weller. It was hard to miss the obvious attraction between the two of you."

I spat the blood from my mouth and wiped my face with the sleeve of my jacket. "Is that what this was about?" I asked.

He laughed derisively and tucked the pistol into his waistband. "This was just a little bonus. I told you, I work alone. I don't know who those thugs were, but in the future, you might want to be more aware of your surroundings when you walk alone at night in this part of town."

I made another attempt at rising to my feet. I was able to achieve success by bracing myself against the wall for support. "Is this another of your lessons on life in America?"

He shrugged. "I could have let them kill you."

"Why didn't you?"

"You have something I want. I thought we might make a trade."

"You no longer have anything I want."

"That may be true…for the time being…but things can change quickly. I'm sure our paths will cross again. The next time we meet you may think differently." He curled his lips into a sinister sneer. "I'm sure Catherine told you we are about to go into business together. She's a lovely young woman. I look forward to our continued association." A mirthless chuckle rumbled up from his throat as he touched his hat in farewell. Anger surged through my veins and I struggled to regain my strength to go after him, but my knees buckled beneath me and I slid back to the ground.

Gregor's parting words left me more convinced than ever that there was more to his meeting with Catherine than she suspected. I knew that he was not to be trusted. I had tried to caution her, but she was headstrong and determined. My mind reeled between rational thought and the emotional desire to keep Catherine from making a serious mistake. I wanted to try to warn her again, but since her father had recommended Gregor to her, there was little chance she would listen to me. She had made it clear that my opinions and especially my interference were not welcome. In the end, I decided to put off the decision until morning.

The hotel manager said nothing about my appearance when I stopped at the desk to pick up my key. I assume he was accustomed to such things given the proximity of the hotel to the stockyards. I undressed and cleansed my wounds as best I could. My body rebelled against the beating each time I tried to move. I touched the soreness in my ribs and nearly cried out in pain. I caught a glimpse of myself in the chipped mirror that hung over the basin. One eye was partially swollen shut and there was dried blood on the cut under my eye. The thugs in the alley had relieved me of most of my savings and my hopes of staking a claim out west had vanished along with it.

11

I had just drifted off to sleep when I was awakened by the shrill sounds of panic in the streets below. I sat up in my bed. I was bathed in sweat. The air was filled with smoke and the noise from the street rang with the high-pitched screams of women and children. I rushed to the window and beheld the masses of fleeing humanity against a backdrop of flames. Burning fragments of wooden parapets, sheets of roofing metal, signs and scuttle-doors were blown by the fiery wind, and with blazing fury swept down upon those fleeing in the streets with a terrific roar. Loose horses and cows, as well as people of all conditions on foot and in wagons were hurrying half-blinded through the streets together.

I dressed quickly and hurried into the streets. The heat of the fire greeted me like a blast furnace. The air was filled with the frantic cries of husbands, wives, parents, and children forced apart and lost to each other in the sudden desolation and horror of the fire. Bits of tarred paper and canvas along with myriads of smaller sparks swept down upon me, blinding me, and filling my lungs with smoke. I pulled my coat around my face and joined the throng of those escaping toward the river.

By the time firefighters were able to make their way through the crowds, the fire had grown and spread to neighboring buildings and was progressing toward the central business district. The river was lined with lumber yards, warehouses, and coal yards, along with barges and numerous bridges across the river. I crossed the South Branch of the river through an area that had previously been thoroughly burned and that I hoped might act as a natural firebreak to provide an escape route.

As the fire grew, the southwest wind intensified and became superheated, causing structures to catch fire from the heat and from burning debris blown by the wind. I joined the crowd moving north, trying to stay ahead of the flames. Around midnight, flaming debris blew across the river and landed on roofs and the South Side Gas Works. With the fire across the river and moving rapidly toward the heart of the city, panic set in. When the courthouse caught fire, the building was evacuated, and the prisoners jailed in the basement were released. A few minutes later, the cupola of the courthouse collapsed, sending the great bell crashing down into the inferno.

I continued my nightmare journey toward the northeast where the fire had not yet crossed the river. The air swirled around us, spinning flaming debris high into the air. I watched helplessly as a large piece of flaming debris sailed languidly high into the air where it was caught by the wind and blown across the main branch of the river where it landed on a railroad car carrying kerosene. The fire was soon raging across the city's north side. Catherine had said that she and her father were staying in a home on the city's north side. I headed toward the fine homes along the lake's north shore in the hopes of finding her.

A short time after the fire jumped the river the second time, a burning piece of timber lodged on the roof of the city's waterworks. Within minutes, the interior of the building was engulfed in flames and the building was destroyed. With it, the city's water mains went dry and the city was left helpless. As the fire continued unchecked from building to building, block to block, I joined the ranks of volunteers who entered and searched houses for survivors, sometimes dragging bewildered, fainting or suffocating people from their homes by force with their clothes on fire. Finally, late into the morning of October 10, it started to rain, but the fire had already started to burn itself out.

Over the next three days, I assisted in search and rescue efforts around the city in the vague hope that I might hear news of Catherine and her father. In the aftermath of the fire, several makeshift relief warehouses were hastily set up around the city. The mayor established a Relief Center at the First Congregational Church, out of harm's way on Washington Street in the West Division. I still had not been able to discover any news about Catherine and her father, so I decided that this would be the best place to start.

The church had been turned into a temporary city hall and was enlisting volunteer special deputies to preserve order and curb the looting as well as providing food and water to the burned-out and homeless. Another area of the church had been set aside as a temporary hospital to treat those injured and burned in the fire. This is where I found Catherine. She was covered in soot and grime, but her face was bathed in light, reflecting the same grit and determination that had drawn me to her when we first met. But beneath it all, she displayed a deep sense of caring and compassion. She seemed unfazed by the scent of burned flesh and clothing as she moved from place to place directing the doctors and nurses to those in direst need. The sounds of agony and loss filled the air. Some people cried out in pain. Others stared blankly into space as if they could not comprehend the circumstances that had led them to this point. Catherine stopped beside a woman who was weeping inconsolably and gathered her into her arms. She rocked the woman back and forth and stroked her charred face until the woman calmed herself.

Catherine looked up when she saw me coming toward her. "Hank! Are you all right?"

I kneeled beside her. "I'm fine. Are you hurt?"

Catherine shook her head. "I'm one of the lucky ones," she said. The woman in her arms began to moan softly and someone came and gently led her away. Catherine's shoulders sagged sadly. "That woman and her husband managed to escape their burning home," she said, "but her husband rushed back inside to rescue the baby." Catherine's voice caught in her throat. "He never came out." I reached out and took her in my arms and she sagged against me. "That poor woman," Catherine said. "I cannot imagine the pain she must be feeling. I believe the greatest loss one can ever feel must be the loss of a child," she said.

I held her close and stroked her hair. "Yes. The experience completely demolishes you, and you spend the rest of your life nursing a pain that will never go away."

Catherine pulled herself away from me and for a moment I was lost in the deep sorrow in her eyes. "You sound as if you speak from experience," she said, softly.

"Remember the woman on the ship whose child was buried at sea?" I answered, quickly. "She was never the same after that."

"I remember," she said, and the sadness in her voice nearly broke my heart. "I don't think I understood her pain at the time. I was on the outside looking in. But after tonight I don't think I'll ever be the same."

I read the sadness and exhaustion in her face. "How long have you been here?" I asked.

"We were forced to flee last night along with our friends," she said. "but father wanted to check on the situation at the bank. I refused to allow him to go alone. Luckily, the bank was also spared, but we were caught in the flood of refugees fleeing for their lives."

"What about your father? Is he all right?"

"Yes. "He has been called to a meeting upstairs with other city leaders. They are working on a plan for maintaining order in the city and handling the rescue efforts. I chose to stay here and help wherever I could."

"What will you do now? Do you have a place to stay?" I asked.

Catherine nodded. "Our friends returned to their home this morning when it was evident that the fire had spared it. Father and I can stay there for a while." She gestured around at the cots filled with dazed and suffering survivors. "In the meantime, I will do whatever I can to help out here." She turned back to me. "What about you?" There was a pleading in her gray eyes that tugged at my heart.

"I'll help with the recovery efforts until I can continue my journey west," I said. I didn't mention the thugs who had stolen my money the night the fire broke out or the fact that I was now penniless and homeless.

"Are you sure you have to go?" she said.

Every fiber of my being begged me to say I would stay with her, but the city would eventually rebuild itself and the social and economic classes that had separated us before would still be there. If Catherine and I were to ever have a future together, I would first need to establish myself as an independent landowner. "I can't stay," I answered, mustering all the strength I could find. "This city must devote all its resources to helping those displaced by the fire. It would be wrong of me to take work that might help someone feed their family and rebuild their lives here." I paused and swallowed the lump that had risen in my throat. "As soon as the trains are running again, I'm headed for a Dutch settlement near Pella, Iowa."

I could sense her disappointment as Catherine pulled away from me. "I understand," she said, somewhat stiffly. "Our lives seem to be traveling along separate paths. Perhaps when we recover from this devastation, I can once again pursue my own dreams."

I helped her to her feet. "Can I take you to your friend's house?" I asked.

"No," she answered. "I'll wait for father."

We stood together for several minutes surveying the mass of human suffering and loss. Something had broken between us. It was as if our destinies were pushing us apart. Then she turned and kissed me on the lips. She tasted of smoke and fire. "Good luck," she said. "Perhaps fate will bring us together again when the time is right."

12

I left behind the smoldering ruins of Chicago with a sense of sadness and regret—not so much for the devastation of the once great city, but rather, for the way Catherine and I had parted. It was obvious that there was the beginning of something between us, but that we were neither one in a position to pursue it. Nevertheless, I found it impossible to put those feelings aside. Instead, I vowed to do everything in my power to earn a place in her affections.

Carefully tilled farmland soon gave way to virgin grassland as the train sped across Illinois into Iowa. I longed to slow down and appreciate the possibilities of the land I was passing through. Perhaps this had been my problem all along. Perhaps I had been moving so fast in pursuit of my dreams that I had sabotaged my own success. Perhaps I needed to quit chasing the dream and work on living it. It was with this new sense of resolve that I left the train in Pella.

My first impression of the Pella settlement was that it was nothing more than an overgrown village. The main road into town was only a dusty path. Residences and businesses had been hastily constructed; hotels stockyards, and lumber yards appeared to have sprung up with little or no planning. Until the line was completed to Des Moines, Pella had been the terminus for The Des Moines Valley Railroad out of Keokuk. As such, the town had its own depot and even a roundhouse in which to rotate the engines to travel back to Keokuk and the shipping channels on the Mississippi River.

Short of cash and out of options, my first order of business was to find work and lodging. I approached a man in the railyard who appeared to be in charge, "I understand the Des Moines Valley Railroad is planning a northern spur connecting the line to the

Northwest Pacific Line," I said, recalling Gregor's proposal to Catherine. "I was hoping to find work laying track."

His response set off alarm bells in my brain. "I don't know nothin' about that," the man answered, shaking his head. "You must be mistaken. The only rail work on that line is heading west to Des Moines and that's just about finished." He looked me up and down. "If it's work you're looking for, I could use a good hand in the yard."

The yard was the beating heart of the railroad, and the work involved constant movement. Trains moved; workers ran and jumped onto moving cars; shopmen worked with whirring belts and drills and saws that bored and cut. Trains moved in and out of the yards; workers made and repaired cars and locomotives in the shops. My work involved coupling railcars and operating railroad track switches to facilitate the movement of railroad cars within the yard. I came to think of railroads not as just trains moving up and down mountains and across the continent, but as shorter bursts of motion as trains switched cars, adding them and dropping off, or as the small movements involved in coupling cars together with iron pins.

I was assigned to work with an American named Charlie Truesdale, coupling and uncoupling the railcars heading to different markets. Charlie had been a blacksmith before coming to work on the railroad. He was a large man with huge coal-stained hands. His face was permanently etched with lines from the grime and coal dust collected there over the years. He had a weakness for the cheap whiskey sold in the saloons clustered near the tracks, and often staggered into work with the remnants of the previous nights' debauchery still clinging to him.

After many years of pounding iron over a hot forge, Charlie was better equipped than I to handle central Iowa's humid climate. Summers were especially hot and sticky, and the heat radiating off the railcars created truly uncomfortable and sweaty conditions. By early June, the weather was already unbearably hot. The only shade to be found was under the railcars, but they provided little relief from the sweltering heat.

I had been sweating profusely and was suddenly overtaken by a bout of dizziness. I stumbled over to a spot where I had left a jug of water and gulped thirstily. No sooner had I emptied the jug than I was overcome with nausea and vomited it all onto the dirt at my feet, along with the entire contents of my stomach. Charlie found me collapsed on the ground next to the empty jug.

"Christ, man!" he swore. "Whatja do? Drink the whole thing at once?" I mumbled an incoherent reply. "Stupid Dutchman," he grumbled. Taking a soiled handkerchief from his pocket. He took another jug that he had reserved for himself and poured some water onto the rag. "Here," he said, handing it to me. "Suck on this." I took it greedily and did as he instructed. It tasted of dirt and sweat, but the trickle of moisture down my throat was heavenly relief. Charlie poured more water into a tin cup and set it down. "Don't drink this or you'll heave it all up again," he ordered. "Use it to keep the rag wet and keep sucking on it." I tried to stand, but my legs collapsed under me like a newborn calf. Charlie watched my efforts and shook his head with disgust. "You'd best just lay here until you get your strength back." He walked away from me muttering something that sounded like "Dumb Dutchman," and returned to his work.

Charlie was part of that vast shifting army which built the great railway lines of the country. They were an ill-disciplined and increasingly rebellious and resentful bunch. As soon as their shift was completed, most headed straight for the many gambling halls and whorehouses near the tracks to relieve themselves of their wages. Many of them returned the next day bleary eyed and hung over from the night's revelries. On such occasions, errors in judgement were all too common, often leading to serious injury and sometimes death.

Charlie returned from one of these outings looking much worse for wear. "You look like hell," I said, when I saw him that morning. "I'm not sure what good you'll be to me today."

He drew himself up in a show of bravado. "I'm still more man than you'll ever be," he bragged, but I could smell the whiskey on his breath.

"We'll see about that," I said.

We were attaching two cars that had been detached from one another for maintenance. Charlie stepped between the drawbars to guide the coupling link and pin by which the car is drawn. At the same instant, the engineer received the signal to go and slacked back, catching Charlie between the bars. He did not utter a sound, but I remember the look of terrible agony, of utter despair, in his white face as he clutched the iron that was pressing out his life, straining at it in an endeavor to hold it back. In a second the engineer slacked ahead, and the poor fellow leaped from the track like one springing from the path of threatening danger, to fall lifeless beside the rail. The accident caused an initial buzz of excitement, but once the body was carried off, work resumed as usual, leaving me shaken and angry.

Charlie's death underscored the increasing division between labor and management that festered just beneath the surface of the industry. As railroad workers, we were just part of the machinery of the railroad—actively mediating between machines and nature, and constantly moving. Workers ran and jumped on moving cars; shopmen worked with shirring belts and drills and saws. Charlie's death was merely an unfortunate incident. One more life had been extinguished in the unfeeling, unfriendly struggle. That was all.

After Charlie's death, I found myself unable to concentrate or work without seeing my friend's face or hearing his gruff voice everywhere I turned. The vision of his body in agony haunted me—no sound, the white face, the body straining at the bar crushing it between the cars, the way the dead body appeared to leap rather than crumple. The incident renewed all my feelings of guilt. I should have called out to him in warning. I should have stopped him from stepping between the bars. Perhaps I could have saved him.

I directed my anger at the situation toward anyone or anything that crossed me. Yard fights often followed in the wake of my wrath with little or no provocation. I overindulged in anything that would dull my senses and block out the memory. I began frequenting the same haunts and seeking the same diversions that other railway workers enjoyed. I stopped reporting for work at the yard and wallowed in oblivion, drowning my sorrow, and indulging my baser appetites.

Following one of these binges, I awoke with the sun burning my eyelids and a throbbing headache. I stretched out my arms to block the sun and knocked an empty whiskey bottle off the table by the bed. It clattered to the floor, waking the woman sleeping by my side. She rolled to face me and rubbed the sleep from her eyes. She reached out to stroke me gently.

"Good morning, luv," she crooned.

She was older than most of the other whores. I didn't know her name, but she was clever and funny and as lustful as a tomcat. She had ways in bed that I had never heard of, and she made me play games I had not even imagined. She had a sensual face and warm brown eyes and big soft breasts. Most of all, she helped me to forget.

I lay back on the pillows and closed my eyes. "What day is it?" I asked.

"What difference does it make?" she answered. "Do you have a wife waiting at home for you?"

I pushed her hand away. "No wife. No one waiting."

"Why aren't you married yet?" the woman asked. "A man like you should already be taken. You're not like the rest of those railroad hooligans who come in here."

I turned away from her. The lacy curtains at the window were torn and ragged. They floated and billowed in the wind as if they were participating in a macabre dance. The mention of marriage reminded me of Lainie. A sad memory floated up out of my consciousness.

They buried Lainie in her wedding dress on the day she was to be married. I was not allowed to attend the funeral, but I watched the proceedings from afar. The ceremony was held in the largest and oldest church in the city, St. Walburgis, which dated from the eleventh century. It was a Gothic building containing the monuments of the former counts of Zutphen, a fourteenth-century candelabrum, and a monument to the Van Heeckeren family. Lainie hated the place. She said it was dank and cold and smelled of death.

"There was a girl once," I said, at last.

The woman laid her head on my chest and threw one plump thigh over my knees "What happened?"

"Things didn't work out," I said, evasively.

"But you still love her," the woman said.

I rolled out of bed and pulled on my trousers. "I don't think one ever forgets their first love," I answered.

"You must have been very young," she said.

I nodded. "Too young," I said. "And very naïve about the ways of the world. We thought that our love was strong enough to overcome all the obstacles."

"But it wasn't."

I reached for my shirt and pulled my arms through the sleeves. "No. It wasn't."

The woman persisted. "But that was a long time ago. Hasn't there been anyone since then?"

I paused in the buttoning of my shirt while thoughts of Catherine teased my memory. I saw her smile and felt the warmth of her kiss. I remembered the sad longing in her eyes when we parted after the fire. Like Lainie, she was also out of my reach. I had no home, and no life to offer her. "No one," I said, curtly.

I finished dressing and tossed some bills on the bed. "Will I see you again tonight?" the woman asked.

"I don't think so." I answered. "I need some time to myself."

She pulled the sheet around her and propped herself up on the pillows. "Well, whatever it is that has you all tied up in knots, I hope you'll soon be able to resolve it. You have a future ahead of you if you can put it behind you."

"You've been very kind," I said, leaning to kiss her on the cheek." But it's time for me to face the world again."

The sunlight was even more blinding when I stepped out onto the street. I breathed in deeply, allowing my lungs to clear away the cobwebs of debauchery that had formed there. A long, shrill whistle announced the arrival of the 10:00 train from Keokuk.

When I arrived at the yard, the foreman met me with his hands on his hips. "I see you finally decided to show up," he said. "Well, you needn't have bothered." He turned on his heel and called back over his shoulder. "You can pick up your check in the office."

I took the news with some degree of relief. Although the money was good, life with the railroad was not to my liking. The expansion of the West demanded labor. But the railroads, and Americans in general, believed that the purpose of labor was to apply the final touches that turned nature into a garden. The workers were the serpents in this garden and were, therefore, dispensable. Young workers often moved from job to job until they reached an age where they became a liability to the railroad. An aging worker was a vulnerable worker. He was forced to stifle his resentment and bow his neck to the slavery his employer demanded. This was not the life I envisioned for myself.

I picked up my last paycheck and left the yard. At the depot, a group of Dutch travelers had just arrived from Keokuk. They chattered excitedly while they awaited the removal and transfer of their luggage. The sound of my native tongue drew me toward them. "Where are you folks headed?" I asked. They turned to stare at me curiously. I had spoken to them in Dutch, but I still wore the trappings of an American railroad worker. "I'm originally from Gelderland," I said, by way of explanation, and received several nods of approval in response.

A stocky gentleman dressed in traditional Dutch clothing and clogs stepped forward toward me. "We're headed to Sioux County in northwestern Iowa," he said. "We hear that good land is still available to be claimed there along the checkerboard plats granted to the railroads."

The remnants of the dream I had deferred during my time in Pella resurfaced in my brain. It had been almost six months since I had left Wisconsin with plans to homestead in Iowa, but I was no closer to realizing that dream than I had been when I left my homeland. The economic conditions in Pella mirrored the circumstances in the Netherlands that had propelled me to leave. I had made several inquiries about land ownership in the area, but the best land was already taken, and the rest was either too expensive or untillable. There was no future for me here.

"I'm headed there as well," I said, impulsively.

The gentleman looked at me skeptically. "You don't look like a farmer," he said.

"My family were farmers in Gelderland where I grew up," I said. "I've been working my way west since I emigrated over three years ago."

The gentlemen nodded appreciatively. "Our train leaves in two hours and you're welcome to join us. But we have no provisions to spare. You'll have to fend for yourself."

"I've been working on the railroad here, so you don't have to worry," I answered. "I can pay my own way. I won't be a burden to you."

I joined the Dutch travelers and boarded the train amidst a chatter of excitement. Their enthusiasm for their new life was contagious. They were driven by the immigrant's dream of independence in a land where they would be free to worship and live as they chose. They were embarking on a mission of their own choosing and they had thrown all their energies into making it a success.

Although I, too, had begun this journey with high hopes, I had been distracted by the lure of quick riches and easy promises. I had temporarily lost my way by trying to capitalize on my heritage with the promissory note. When that had ended in disaster, I had followed Jelle to Wisconsin, hoping to find the promised land there, but the harshness of the climate had driven me away. And finally, I had joined the ranks of those enticed by the money and romance of the railroad. Nothing had worked in my favor. It was time to set my own course for the future and accept the hardships and sacrifices that went along with it.

13

I parted company with the others at Sioux City and hired a horse-drawn wagon to take me north as far as Le Mars, Iowa. At that point, my ride ended, and I walked for miles, deep into the heart of the rich grasslands of northwest Iowa where the virgin prairie was yet unbroken by a steel plow. There was not a home in sight. I was totally alone. As far as the eye could see, the land rolled gently. In the distance, hills pierced the line separating land and sky. In the lower parts, near where the streams emptied into a river, the grass was tall and sprinkled with wildflowers.

I admired the view from the crest of a hill where the grass was shorter. As I gazed on this beauty spot, it seemed to dance before my eyes. The quality of the soil was so rich that it would need no fertilization for the first 20 years. I gathered up a handful of soil and threw it into the air. It hung there suspended in space before the wind carried it away. "This will be my home," I said to the wind. "This is my destiny."

A few miles farther on I came upon a new Dutch settlement in the making. The settlement was called Orange City in honor of the Dutch Royal House of Orange. Like all Hollanders, these settlers cherished their homeland, where many of their families still lived. Orange City was little more than a few hastily constructed buildings lining a dirt street.

The town's founder, Abraham Lenderink, had come over with his wife, Emma, during the first emigration wave from Zutphen in Gelderland, the same depot town I had emigrated from in 1868. They were people of great courage and kindness. Abraham was a large man with wide-set, intelligent eyes and a body already bent from years of hard labor. His quiet thoughtfulness reminded me of my father. His speech was slow and deliberate, and one tended to stop what they were doing and pay close attention when he spoke.

As the unofficial leader of the colony, Abraham's advice on settling on the Iowa prairie was much sought after. Although I still had every intention of making it on my own, I recognized that survival on the harsh prairie was best served by being part of a family unit. So, when Abraham offered me food and a straw mattress in the barn above the livestock in exchange for my help in preparing his land for next year's planting, I accepted.

After one of Emma's hearty meals one evening, I followed Abraham out onto the porch where he was busy sharpening an axe. His youngest son, Stephen, sat at his feet throwing sticks for one of the old dogs to fetch. Every so often Abraham would check the sharpness of the blade he was working on by running the edge of it along his bare arm to see if it would shave off the hair. I watched him silently for a few minutes.

"Was it difficult when you first came west to settle?" I asked.

Abraham grunted in reply but didn't look up from his task. "The first years of homesteading are filled with sacrifice and suffering," he said. "Emma and I arrived in America with little more than the clothes on our backs. We lived in a sod shanty for the first five years until we could afford the wood to build a proper home. By that time, we had three more mouths to feed."

I looked out at the well-maintained farmstead with its barn and corrals, surrounded by acres of farmland. It was hard to imagine that this land had once been barren, untamed prairie. "How did you manage all this by yourself?"

"Emma helped. We started with just ten acres. Broke the sod by hand and planted enough corn and potatoes to get us through the winter."

"That first winter must have been hard."

Abraham nodded and continued sharpening the axe. "Even though we were careful, food and firewood were scarce." He paused as if trying to find the right words to continue. When he spoke again, his voice was so soft I could barely make out the words. "Emma lost our first baby during that winter."

An old memory flashed through my mind and I felt a lump rise in my throat. "That must have been hard on you," I said.

Abraham made a sound deep in his throat. "Harder on Emma. She still hasn't completely gotten over it." He finished sharpening the axe and set it aside.

I stared out over the expanse of Abraham's homestead, taking in the land rich with the promise of next fall's harvest and the cattle grazing in the pasture. "When I see what you have built here, I am even more determined to do whatever it takes to build something like this for myself."

Abraham looked at me skeptically. "Your courage and ambition have helped you make it this far alone," he said. "But it takes more than that to endure the hardships and difficulties that lay ahead."

"What do you mean?"

Abraham tapped his chest. "It takes heart. You must understand that the prairie has its own heart. She is like a woman. She is moody and will sometimes turn on you for no apparent reason." Abraham looked out over his land. "She can never be tamed, but if you treat her with love and respect, she will produce and care for your needs."

I often thought about Abraham's words during the long winter nights while I huddled in my bed with only the lowing of the cows beneath me to keep me company. I had tried to bend Lainie's will to match my own with disastrous results. Catherine was also a strong-willed woman. I wondered if she had followed through on her plan to invest in Gregor's railroad scheme. My initial attempt to caution her against Gregor Van Pelt had only caused her to stiffen her resolve. Shortly after I arrived in Pella, I had written to warn her again when I learned that there were no plans to extend the Des Moines line. But there had been no response.

More and more, I found my thoughts turning toward the future and my life in America, but my thoughts turned not to Lainie, but to Catherine. I would often awaken in the middle of the night with her face, not Lainie's, on my mind. Her soft gray eyes peered into my heart and the electricity of her touch caused me to thrash about until I was fully awake. But as time passed, the images blurred until it became difficult to tell which woman haunted my dreams at night.

"How much do you love me?" Lainie asked. We had managed to sneak away from the others and retreat to our special place by the river. It was late spring. The air was heavy with the scent of wildflowers and the damp grass covered the earth like a soft blanket.

"More than life itself," I answered. It was a game we often played. Each time she asked the question, I responded with the utmost sacrifice I was willing to make for her.

She pointed to the river flowing languidly at our feet. "More than the river that feeds your fields?"

"More than that."

"More than the land that you love so much?"

"Even more than that."

"More than the God you worship in secret?"

I pretended to hesitate. "I'd have to think about that one."

She laughed and punched me playfully on the arm. "I thought so! When you can answer that last question truthfully without hesitation, I will follow you to America."

"Then I will forsake my religion here and now. When can you be ready to leave?"

"Blasphemy!" she exclaimed. "We wouldn't get far before God would strike you dead on the spot. Then what would I do? I couldn't possibly live and raise our child without you."

I drew her to me. I ran my fingers through her hair loosening it and causing it to fall around her shoulders. I breathed in the scent of her. I held her face in my hands and kissed her tenderly, the warmth of our embrace sending shock waves through my body. How could I possibly allow her to marry someone else? There must be a way to stop this engagement.

"Come away with me now. Right this minute," I implored. "We'll go to England. I'll find work in the shipyards until I can earn enough for our passage to America."

She pushed me away from her and gazed into my eyes. "Of course," she said. "I will follow you anywhere."

I awoke with a start. The face that looked so lovingly into mine was not Lainie's, but Catherine's! I sat up in my bed. Although the air in the room was frigid and frost covered the woolen blankets I was using for warmth, I was drenched in sweat. I threw off the blankets and sat upright. The animals stirred below me, the steam from their breath wafted up towards me like tiny tendrils of smoke. The wind howled through the cracks in the walls in a mournful wail. The shock of the icy air filling my lungs brought me to my senses and I began to shiver. I slapped my arms against my body to generate warmth and pulled the blankets higher around my shoulders.

I berated myself for my foolishness. There was no hope for a relationship with Catherine any more than there had been with Lainie. The societal distance between us was greater than the miles that separated us, and there seemed little hope that I could close that gap any time soon. Although Abraham had been generous, I had yet to establish my own claim.

My melancholy began to lift when the spring sunshine finally arrived to warm the land and the ground began to thaw. The air smelled of new growth and new beginnings and I was once again filled with hope for the future. Abraham helped me to file a homestead claim four miles east of town on 80 acres of the verdant open prairie in the V-shaped corridor between the Floyd River and its West Branch. I moved out of the barn and built a homestead shanty that was little more than a dugout covered with a sod roof.

After a long day spent breaking up the virgin sod, and planting crops on my claim, I collapsed on my cot at night surrounded by the earthy smell of sweat and soil. I thought of Catherine in her fine house with the long winding lane and the ornate drawing room. I remembered the scent of her hair and the softness of her touch. I longed to see her again, to feel the warm touch of her skin on mine. I her wrote a long letter extolling the beauty of the landscape and the potential for great wealth for those willing to work hard and endure the difficulties. I checked the post regularly for her reply, but there was no word from her.

The sweltering summer heat had just given way to the first cool nights of fall when I observed a crew of surveyors working their way down the Floyd River valley, preparing the way for of the St. Paul and Sioux City Railroad which was to commence next year. I rushed to Abraham with the news.

Before I could speak, he greeted me with news of his own. "I've just learned that the state has received a land grant for the construction of a railroad from Sioux City to the southern border of Minnesota at a point between the Big Sioux and the West Fork of the Des Moines river."

"That line will pass within a mile of my property!" I exclaimed. "It will open us up to the markets in the east."

Abraham nodded. "It's already luring new settlers to the area. Hundreds of Dutch Americans from Marion County have already transplanted to this area to stake their claims along the railroad," Abraham said.

"It won't be long until all the land available for homesteading will be taken up by the new settlers." I mused. "The only option left will be to purchase land from the odd numbered sections owned by the railroad at double the price."

"If that's the case, the bank in Sioux City will be busy writing mortgages," Abraham said. "The only problem is that there are so many restrictions now that prevent the National Banks from directly investing in mortgages and the long-term market. Many of the settlers may not qualify."

"It's too bad we don't have someone here who could support expansion in the community," I said. "If the settlers are unable to acquire the mortgages they need, they will most likely move further west."

Abraham scratched his chin. "The only answer is a small independent bank that isn't tied to the federal treasury."

Jelle had predicted that the rapid expansion of the railroads in the west would spur new settlement in the area. He had a nose for business and had done quite well by providing mortgages to the settlers in Wisconsin. His last correspondence to me had indicated that he was looking for ways to expand his business.

"I know someone who runs an independent mortgage business in Wisconsin," I said, thoughtfully. "Perhaps we can convince him to come west."

Abraham glanced at me with interest. "It might be worth a try," he said, hopefully.

I stopped by the post office that afternoon to send a cable to Jelle alerting him of the opportunity here in Iowa. The postal clerk looked up and smiled when he saw me. "This just came in," he said, handing me a letter. "I believe you've been waiting for it."

I immediately recognized the familiar feminine slant of the writing and tucked the letter away to read in privacy.

The clerk smiled knowingly. "Hope it's good news," he said.

I hurried outside and tore open the letter and read with dismay what Catherine had written.

My Dearest Hank,

Please forgive me for not responding sooner, but things have been in a bit of a turmoil here. The city has been rapidly working to rebuild after the fire and I have been busy with my volunteer work. Father's business has recovered, and railroad speculation is running rampant as the transcontinental lines are completed connecting Chicago to the west coast. He spends much of his time away on junkets with investors.

You were correct in warning me that Gregor Van Pelt was not to be trusted. He is a ruthless swindler of the worst kind. I should have listened to your warnings, but I was headstrong and stubborn. Father also urged me to be cautious, but the figures Gregor presented and the promise of his prospectus for building a railroad spur that would extend to my father's Northwest Pacific line sounded too good to pass up. Unfortunately, Gregor disappeared after the fire, but not before he had managed to secure my entire inheritance for his railroad scheme.

Once the smoke cleared, we discovered that there was never actually any plan to build the road he proposed. and the construction company only existed on paper. Van Pelt managed to defraud all his investors and abscond with the money. I hear that he has gone to west to work his scheme on other unsuspecting and gullible investors. Father has hired a detective to search for Gregor and bring him back to face justice.

The days pass slowly, and I am often alone. I think of you often and hope that your adventures in Iowa prove more successful than my own weak attempt at independence. You have always had a vision of what you wanted to achieve in life, and I know you have the passion and courage to succeed. In the meantime, I continue to hold the packet you left in my care and anxiously await your return to retrieve it.

Yours,

Catherine

I folded the letter and tucked it away. Catherine's words had filled me with despair and longing. I had hoped that my warning about Gregor's railroad scheme had reached her in time to dissuade her from investing her inheritance with him. But Catherine had been desperate to prove that a woman could survive in the world of business, and she had rushed into a decision with her heart instead of her head. Now she seemed defeated and lost. I knew exactly how she felt, and my heart ached for her. I had also encountered obstacles that had led me to detour from the path I had set for myself. I knew that Catherine was strong. She could overcome this. She had to understand that it was only a temporary setback.

I returned to the telegraph office and wrote out my message to Jelle describing the rapid settlement of the area and the coming of the railroad. I briefly outlined my proposal to him and asked if he could meet me in Chicago the following week to discuss the matter further. I waited while the clerk tapped out the message, then I gave him one more message to send to Catherine.

14

The Chicago fire had taken lives and ruined fortunes, but it had also provided the city with an opportunity to rebuild itself from a new vision. The city's rebuilding efforts had drawn architects and city planners from all over the country eager to experiment with new techniques in an atmosphere of continual construction. New brick and stone buildings were already beginning to arise in place of the acres of wooden structures that had made up the old Chicago.

I met Jelle at the station and led him to a small café away from the stockyards. Jelle's appearance had changed significantly since I saw him last. Gone was the pudgy waistline and round child-like face. In its place was a slim figured young man with a full head of wavy hair and long mutton chop sideburns. His jacket and matching waistcoat and trousers were beautifully tailored, no doubt the handiwork of his uncle, the haberdasher. He carried a top hat and a small valise. He looked every bit the prosperous businessman. His face lit up with a familiar boyish grin when he caught sight of me.

"Hank! It's so good to see you." He pumped my hand enthusiastically.

"You've changed!" I exclaimed. "Business must indeed be going well."

Jelle laughed. "I can't complain. Farmers in Wisconsin are eager to expand their holdings and I am more than happy to oblige with a mortgage."

"I gather your uncle's business is prospering as well," I said, admiring the cut of his suit.

"Quite well," Jelle laughed. "And things must be going well for you as well. I am eager to hear about this business proposition in Iowa you wanted to discuss with me. Your cable said you were meeting someone else in Chicago. Am I to assume there is competition for my business?"

"Not at all. I'm meeting Catherine Weller. You remember, the woman who was tutoring me in English on the ship."

Jelle smiled knowingly. "Ah, yes. The tutor. Are you here for a refresher course then?"

"We have continued to correspond since we parted. She most recently wrote to me that her family had suffered a severe financial setback due to a bad business investment with Gregor Van Pelt."

"Wasn't that the family you tried to negotiate with for the property in Pennsylvania?"

"The very same. I thought I would check in to see how she's doing."

Jelle seemed to sense that my interest in Catherine was more than friendly concern for her welfare, and he did not press me further. "Well, I am anxious to hear of the business proposal in Iowa that you wrote of."

I eagerly launched into a description of the rapid settlement in the area around Orange City and outlined the need to establish a banking institution that would supply mortgages to pioneers wishing to purchase the railroad land for settlement. He nodded several times and asked a few questions to clarify his understanding. "It sounds promising," he said, "but I will need to see the area for myself."

"We can leave right away."

"I have some business to conclude here in Chicago first, but another day should take care of it."

"That sounds perfect. I'll make the arrangements."

"I'll need to cable my bank in Wisconsin to let them know I'll be gone for a few weeks," Jelle said, scratching his chin thoughtfully.

I gave him a meaningful look. "You may also want to purchase some decent travel clothes. We will need to travel part way by wagon and the going is quite rough."

Jelle laughed. "Yes, my uncle keeps me dressed in the height of fashion these days. He says I must look the part if I'm to be taken seriously in this business."

I glanced at his fine leather shoes and spats. "And get yourself a sturdy pair of boots while you're at it."

"You could do with an updated wardrobe yourself," he said. "You're not going to impress a lady dressed like you just came in off the range."

I glanced at the shirt and pants Emma had sewn for me. I had borrowed a jacket from Abraham that was much too big and hung loosely off my shoulders. My felt hat had also seen better days. "What do you suggest?" I asked.

"I've picked up a few ideas from my uncle," Jelle said. "Just leave everything to me."

#

I hesitated outside the Ambassador Hotel where Catherine had suggested we meet. I tugged nervously at the tight collar on my new shirt. My new shoes pinched my feet, but I welcomed the pain. While I had rehearsed many times what I wanted to say to Catherine when I saw her again, I found myself almost paralyzed with anxiety. It had now been almost four years since we had first met. I often thought of that moonlight meeting on the ship deck as the real beginning of my journey. From the moment I first heard her voice, my thoughts began to focus on the future rather than the past—on what lay ahead rather than what I was leaving behind. Since then, my thoughts of the future had always included Catherine. But every time I thought of the sprawling mansion in Philadelphia and my sod hut on the prairie, I awoke in a cold sweat over the hopelessness of it all. Now, as I prepared to meet her again, my stomach was churning and turning somersaults. I touched her letter where it rested near my heart.

I took a deep breath and approached the hotel desk. The clerk was a severe-looking young man with hawkish eyes and a long, pointed nose. He was sorting mail into boxes behind the desk and I had to clear my throat to get his attention. He glanced at me with a disparaging look, irritated at being disturbed. I gave him my name and asked for Catherine. Almost immediately, his entire countenance changed, and he became much more accommodating. "Oh, yes!" he said. "Miss Weller is expecting you. She asked me to send you right up." He gave me the room number and without another word turned back to his task.

Anxiety flooded through my veins. My heart pounded faster with each step. I tried to remember the speech I had rehearsed, but the words had escaped my memory. Catherine opened the door at the first knock. Her face was flushed, and her hair hung in loose waves around her shoulders. We stood facing each for other without speaking and it seemed like time stood still. It was as if all the dreams and fantasies that had tormented me during the long, cold Iowa winters were urging me forward. I wanted to reach out and take her in my arms. I wanted to cover her face with kisses. Still I could make no move. Then she reached out and pulled me into the room.

The air was thick with the scent of desire. Her face was flushed, and her eyes were shining. "It seems like forever since I saw you last," she said. "I've missed you."

Instead of answering, I reached for her. I placed my hand at the small of her neck and tilted her face toward mine. She came into my arms eagerly and we pressed our bodies together with a hunger that surprised us both. I kissed her, lightly at first, not sure of her response, then more urgently. I felt the tip of her tongue tease my lips and I opened my mouth to receive it. She tilted her hips toward me, sending me an undeniable message with her whole body. I plunged my hands deep into the softness of her hair and pulled her closer against me.

She placed a hand on my chest. "Wait," she said. "I've waited so long. I want to do this right." She took my hand and led the way into the bedroom.

Our lovemaking was slow and deliberate, unlike the urgent rutting that characterized my passionate moments with Lainie. We took our time discovering and pleasing each other until we could wait no longer. Afterward, Catherine rolled into my arms, curling herself onto my chest. We lay together quietly, stroking each other tenderly. She gently traced the scar on my cheek with her soft fingers. "You never told me how you got this," she said.

I turned away from her and stared up at the ceiling. A tiny spider made its way along the carved molding at the edge of the room. "It's nothing," I said. "Just a reminder from a past life."

"We all have something in our past lives, that caused us pain," she said. "Some of us wear our scars where everyone can see them, and others keep them hidden deep inside."

I turned back toward her. "What is it that has caused you pain?" I asked.

"Causes," she corrected. "I don't think I've put it behind me yet. I thought that by investing in Gregor's scheme, I would be able to show my father that I could be a capable businesswoman. Instead, it only served to reinforce his opinion that women have no place in business."

"You can't let one mistake keep you from pursuing your dream," I said. "You must use the experience to help you move forward."

She smiled. "Is that what you have done...why you are so motivated to stake your own claim in America?"

"I suppose so," I answered, pulling her close. "But I feel that I have finally found my place. With news of the railroad expansion, new settlers are flooding into northwest Iowa. I'm taking my friend, Jelle, to see it in the hopes that he will open a small bank to write mortgages for them. If things go well, I will soon be able to build a two-story frame house with a barn and corral."

"I can't wait to see it," Catherine said.

I pulled her close and kissed her. "I don't want you to see it," I said. "I want you to share it with me." I rolled onto my back. "It's just that time and distance keep pushing us apart."

She slipped out of bed and padded across the room, not the least bit ashamed of the moonlight glowing off her naked body. She pulled the goatskin packet from a drawer in the dresser against the far wall and brought it to me. "I've kept this safe for you." She lowered her eyes. "I hope you don't mind, I read some of the letters. They're beautiful. It is obvious that Van Pelt was deeply in love with your grandmother. He was clearly not the cad that Gregor is."

I looked at the letters she had spread out before me. "I can't bring myself to read them," I said. "It just seems so personal. I feel like an intruder."

"You shouldn't," Catherine said. "These letters indicate that love can endure even when distance and circumstances intervene."

"What good is an enduring love, if it didn't bring them together?" I asked.

"The fact that your grandmother kept these things all these years shows that Van Pelt still held a place in her heart. Perhaps that was enough for her."

I, too, had been holding on to memories of the past. I picked up one of the letters and caressed it with my fingers, willing the words on the page to help me understand not only the past, but also the future that might have been. "Holding on to memories is not always a good thing," I said. "They can come in a rush of emotions and force you to relive a bad experience."

"But memories of happy experiences can reshape how we see ourselves and help us through the difficult times," she said. "Maybe your grandmother kept these things for that reason." She picked up the promissory note. "Van Pelt clearly wanted to leave your grandmother something by which to remember him. He left her the only thing he had of any value."

I took the promissory note from her hands. It represented years of sacrifice in pursuit of a higher ideal. Its contents could bring great wealth or great despair to whomever held it. "Perhaps we should destroy this," I said. "Now that Gregor knows I have it, he has no hope of collecting on the debt without it. If he knows you are holding it for me, there is no telling what he would do to get it."

"Don't be absurd!" she exclaimed, snatching the note away. "We can't destroy it. It's the only thing proving that the Van Pelt claim has merit."

"The note has no real value to me," I said. "My hereditary claim would be too difficult to prove, and it is too dangerous for you to keep it in your possession. You could be putting your life in danger."

"Don't worry about me," she said. "Nathan, the clerk downstairs, looks after me when Father is away. He is very loyal. No one gets by him." Catherine put the packet back in the drawer. "I made sure these were never out of my sight when I left Philadelphia. But if it will put your mind at ease, I will put them in the vault at the bank first thing in the morning."

I kissed her once again and she rolled on top of me. She held me in her hands and gently put me inside her. She was in charge and I liked it. Her breasts brushed against my face and drove me mad; I bucked, and she pushed harder. I lifted and heaved. For the moment, the whole room rocked and there was no one else in the world but the two of us.

When I awoke the next morning, the sun was already peeking over the horizon. Catherine lay curled in the crook of my arm with her hair spread out like flaming ripples on the pillow. Another memory floated through my brain…a memory of golden gossamer strands drifting in the water.

Catherine stirred in her sleep and I kissed her awake. She opened her eyes and smiled sleepily. "You're awake early," she said.

I brushed a strand of auburn hair out of her eyes and kissed her tenderly. "Jelle and I are leaving for Iowa this morning," I said.

She sat up in bed and pulled the bedclothes around her. "So soon!" she exclaimed. "I was hoping we would have more time together."

I reached out to touch her, but she recoiled. I had dreaded this moment since I had first held her in my arms and felt the warmth of her body next to mine. But there was no escaping the fact that our lives traveled on different paths. I lived in a sod hut on the prairie and she was accustomed to a grand house filled with beautiful things. I was not sure that Catherine understood or was ready for the kind of sacrifice a life on the prairie offered. "You know how I feel about you," I said. "But my future lies out west."

"Then take me with you!"

"I can't," I said, reaching for my clothes.

"So, you're just going to leave?" Her eyes flared in disbelief. "What about us?" Tears formed at the corner of her eyes and my heart broke into tiny pieces.

"You don't understand," I said, shaking my head. "Life on the prairie is full of hardship. We still lack all the things that make for a civilized life. Besides, your father may not approve of our relationship."

Her gray eyes flashed with anger. "Don't underestimate me," she said. "I'm not afraid of hard work and I can handle my father's criticism."

"I believe you," I said, "but you must understand how your father will feel about our relationship. You are his only daughter and he dotes on you. He may not take kindly to your being whisked away to a life of hard work and deprivation on the prairie."

"Let me worry about my father. He would never stand in the way of my happiness."

"You can't be sure of that and I can't risk coming between the two of you."

Catherine was headstrong and stubborn, just as Lainie had been. She was a woman who knew what she wanted in life and was not afraid to go after it. However, I had no reason to believe that her father would ever consent to allow his only daughter to forsake her birthright and follow me into the wilderness. Even if her feelings for me had grown as mine had for her, I could not take the chance of angering him. I knew too well the consequences of such a confrontation.

Catherine's anger hit me squarely and I reeled from the impact of it. "Why do you keep throwing obstacles in the way? What are you afraid of?"

In the face of her accusations, all the feelings of guilt and shame that I had worked so hard to bury rose to the surface. I had poured my heart and soul into my relationship with Lainie, and it had ended in heartbreak. I desperately wanted a relationship with Catherine, but I refused to put myself between her and her family. "You must trust me," I said. "In time, I will be able to support you in a manner that will please your father and I will be able to ask for your hand properly. In the meantime, I must ask you to be patient."

She struggled to hold back the tears, "I can't guarantee to wait much longer, Hank. You must promise me that the time will be soon."

"I promise," I said, kissing her.

#

By the time I reluctantly left her to meet Jelle, a small crowd had gathered just down the street from the hotel. Nathan left his post and joined me on the sidewalk. "What's going on?" I asked.

"It's another one of those railroad promoters promising wealth and riches to those willing to take a chance on investing.," he answered. "There's a new one nearly every day, since the railroads announced plans to extend their westward lines."

"What's this one up to?"

"I hear he's selling bonds to support the construction of a new line following the old mail road from Mankato south to Sioux City."

I frowned. The grant for the line being surveyed near my homestead had been conferred by the state of Iowa on the Sioux City and St. Paul Railroad Company and would pass about 30 miles west of the old mail road. If this new line were constructed, it would be in direct competition with the approved road. "Do you think it's legitimate?" I asked.

Nathan shrugged and scratched his head thoughtfully. "He claims to represent the St. Paul Land Company. The new line would allow towns further west to ship directly to the Chicago markets instead of hauling everything overland. I have a copy of his prospectus you're interested."

Just then, the promoter wrapped up his spiel and there was a general surge forward as people scrambled to take advantage of the opportunity he promised. As the crowd dispersed, the promoter straightened his lanky frame and glanced in my direction. For a moment, I was frozen in place. As recognition dawned, the man turned and strode off up the street.

By the time I was able to move, Gregor was already several yards ahead of me. I saw him turn down a side street and I followed as quickly as I could, but he disappeared before I could reach him. I walked a few steps further, but there was no sign of him. I had just given up the pursuit when he said, "Are you looking for me?"

I whirled around to face him. He was leaning languidly against the building, smiling at me with a triumphant sneer, his hooded eyes barely concealing the evilness there. He motioned back toward the hotel. "You must have had quite a night of it," he said. "I take it Miss Weller is in fine spirits this morning."

It was a comment rather than a question. I felt the familiar tingling in my spine as the anger rose to my neck. I lunged at him, but he blocked my blow and struck back, sending me reeling.

"Leave her out of this!" I shouted. I stumbled to my feet and squared off to face him again. "Why are you even here? I thought you had gone west after the fire."

"I did," he answered, "but now that the city is rebuilding, there are more opportunities here."

"Opportunities to peddle your fraudulent railroad schemes that cheat honest people out of their life savings, you mean."

"Fraud is such an ugly word," he sighed. "I simply take advantage of the system's lack of control."

"You sold bonds to Catherine for construction of a worthless railroad that existed only on paper!"

He shrugged. "It's just the way the business works. It is the responsibility of the investor to check the legitimacy of the company, not mine. I'm sure Catherine will land on her feet. After all, she has her father's money to fall back on." He took a few steps toward me. "She really is lovely, isn't she?"

My body coiled to strike him again. "I'm warning you. Leave her alone."

"Or what?" he asked, raising his eyebrows. His response only stoked my anger and I struggled for control. "You needn't worry," he said with a snide grin. "My interest in Catherine is strictly business. You have something I want, and I thought she might be able to convince you to part with it."

I took a step toward him. "I told you to leave her out of this!"

"Why don't you save us both the trouble and hand over the note right now?"

"I told you, I don't have it."

"If you don't have it, then you must have given it to someone for safe keeping," he said, glancing up the street toward the hotel.

"Catherine knows nothing about this!"

"Perhaps you're right," he said with a smirk. "But it's only a matter of time until I get what I want. I always do." He pushed past me and headed off down the street. "I'm sure we'll meet again," he said, tossing the words over his shoulder. "I hear there's money to be made in northwest Iowa."

15

Before leaving Chicago, I warned Nathan to keep a careful watch on Catherine and not let Gregor come near her, but it did little to relieve my feelings of dread. My earlier excitement about accompanying Jelle to Iowa was replaced with the guilty feeling that I was leaving Catherine in grave danger.

"Why so downcast?" Jelle asked. "I thought you were excited about this venture."

"I am," I answered. "It's just that I left Catherine with a situation that could place her in harm's way."

"In what way?" he asked.

"I'm afraid she may become a pawn in a threat Gregor has against me."

Jelle shifted in his seat and regarded me seriously. "If we are going to consider going into business together, I think you should explain."

"I suppose you're right," I said. "There should be no secrets between us." As we traveled north from Chicago to Wisconsin, I told him the story of the goatskin packet and Gregor's threat to do whatever it took to get it.

"If it means nothing to you, why not just hand it over?" Jelle asked.

"As long as I'm alive, I'm still a threat to him," I answered. "If I were to come forward to claim my rightful heritage, it would jeopardize his claim."

"So, what do you plan to do?"

"I'm not sure. I thought that by moving west, I could just disappear, and he wouldn't be able to find me. Now I'm not so sure."

"What makes you say that?"

"I ran into him as I was leaving the hotel. He was selling bogus shares for a rail line running parallel to the St. Paul and Sioux City Railroad that I told you about. I think he may be on his way to Iowa to work his scheme there."

Jelle pulled his coat aside to reveal a small silver pistol. "Then we had best be on our guard," he said.

I gaped at the gun in surprise. "I certainly hope it doesn't come to that!"

"In my business," Jelle said, "one cannot be too careful."

We stopped briefly in Wisconsin to allow Jelle to arrange for the management of his business while he was away. Then we crossed the state into Minnesota to the newly established station in St. James. Along the way, we passed several abandoned townsites that had fallen prey to railroad speculators promising wealth and prosperity to those who would bring their businesses to the bleak and empty prairies. Jelle observed the dismal landscape with skepticism. "I'm not sure I share your enthusiasm for this area," he said.

"Don't let the desolation discourage you," I told him. "The land in northwest Iowa is virgin prairie and will produce bountiful crops for years to come."

"We'll see," he said. "If it is as you say, I'd be a fool not to take advantage of the situation there. I've seen the prosperity that follows the expansion of the railroad. Getting in at the beginning before other investors sense the opportunity, could prove to be quite lucrative." He glanced at me with a sly grin. "But I think there may be another reason for your urgency in this matter, and I suspect it might have something to do with Catherine Weller."

I felt the blood rush to my face, but I sheepishly agreed. I told him of my feelings for Catherine and my hopes for a future with her. "She's a wonderful woman," I said. "But I can't ask her to give up the comforts she enjoys in the city until I can offer her something more than a sod hut on the prairie."

"The expansion of the railroad will undoubtedly bring prosperity to the region just as it has in Wisconsin," Jelle answered. "Cities and towns will soon spring up all along the line. The comforts of city life will soon follow."

"A steady stream of pioneers is already flooding into the area," I said. "I'm just not sure how much longer Catherine will wait for me."

Jelle grinned and poked me in the ribs good naturedly. "If she is as smitten with you as you are with her, the creature comforts will make no difference to her."

I took his ribbing in stride but found little comfort in his words. I had underestimated the need for creature comforts with Lainie and I did not want to make that mistake again.

From St. James, we traveled by horseback, following the railroad construction line westward to Worthington and on south to Orange City. The country along the line of the land grants was a wholly uninhabited prairie with no road or trail or shelter for man or beast. However, as we approached Orange City, we saw that progress on the railroad was proceeding at a dizzying pace. Townsites had been platted and stations opened along the line. Hotels and stores would soon follow.

We passed settlers with teams coming in from the east who were following the trail westward. "Look!" I said to Jelle. "These pioneers are not failures drifting from an old fragmented community, but rather opportunity seekers who have chosen to move west to fulfill their ambitions and continue the tradition of family farming."

Jelle frowned. "But they appear to be pushing further westward. I don't see many of them settling here."

"They're looking for free land to homestead," I said. "But if we can provide these settlers with the capital, they need to purchase the land, they will stay and set up their homesteads here near the railroad instead."

"I see what you mean," Jelle answered, thoughtfully. "It takes money to relocate and start a new life in the west."

"Yes," I agreed, "but as you can see, what started as a trickle has become a steady flow of migration. They believe it is their destiny to settle the west."

Jelle smiled. "Then perhaps it is our destiny to help them."

Abraham met us in Orange City where we were assailed by the incessant thud and screech of hammers and saws. The town was buzzing with activity. Huge stacks of lumber lined the street where builders were busy at work. "What's going on?" I asked. When I left for Chicago a little over a week ago, the main street was little more than the telegraph office, mercantile store and saloon anchored by the building that served as the community center, church, and school. Now, new buildings were taking shape all along the town's main artery. "Where did all this lumber come from?"

"The railroad brought it up from Sioux City to Le Mars. Then we hauled it here in wagons," Abraham answered.

I gestured toward a large two-story building going up next to the mercantile. "What are they building?"

Abraham followed my gaze. "That's the new hotel. With the railroad extending through here next year from Le Mars north to St. James, we'll have a direct connection to the markets in St. Paul."

"News travels fast," Jelle said. "I saw this kind of boom happen in Wisconsin when the railroads expanded through there."

"Three new families arrived this week and more are on the way," Abraham said, proudly. "They are already asking about the possibility of mortgages to purchase land along the railroad."

"I'm impressed with what I've seen so far, and the possibility for growth looks quite promising." Jelle said, thoughtfully. "I can at least set up a temporary office to help the settlers get started with the cash they will need to buy land and supplies. If things go well, we can consider a more permanent situation."

"That sounds great!" Abraham exclaimed. "I'll let them know."

"If you'll direct me to the telegraph office, I'll wire my office in Wisconsin for enough capital to get started," Jelle replied.

Jelle wired his manager in Wisconsin that he was extending his stay in Iowa to test the market for expansion. He wasted no time setting up a temporary branch office for his business in the back room of the mercantile. Abraham and I agreed to serve on his board of directors. After completing all the necessary paperwork, the Independent Bank of Orange City was soon open for business.

News of a local lender offering low interest mortgages spread rapidly and Jelle was quickly inundated with settlers seeking homestead loans. He required half the cost of the land as a down payment with the remainder paid off in regular installments over six years. If the loan defaulted, the land was forfeited and later sold at auction. It was a simple operation, but one that proved quite lucrative. Jelle was so busy writing mortgages during the first few weeks that he set up a cot in his office for sleeping, and seldom left his office except to eat.

By early summer, the first crop on my new homestead filled me with hope and anticipation that my hard work would finally reap rewards. Everywhere I looked, I saw fields of corn, wheat, and other grains, promising a plentiful fall harvest. I wrote to Catherine that I believed my dreams of success as an independent landowner were finally within reach and that we could soon be together again.

Then it happened.

On a clear August day in 1873, the sky darkened and filled with a cloud of grasshoppers coming from unknown regions of the Northwest, full grown and hungry. They alighted in myriads on every field of grain, and within an hour the ground was bare. After completing the devastation of the growing crops, they filled the ground with eggs and then departed; no one knew where they had gone. It is impossible to describe the sense of consternation and defeat I felt as every hope of a crop of any kind for that season disappeared. Many of the early pioneers became discouraged and packed up their belongings and returned to the east.

It seemed that once again, my hopes for a bright future were in doubt. I wired Catherine with word of the grasshopper scourge. I tried not to sound discouraged and reassured her that although every hope of a crop for this season had disappeared, I was determined to try again. But, in the meantime, I would have to ask for her continued patience.

Several weeks passed and I still had received no reply. I worried that this latest setback had been too much for Catherine to bear. Once again, I felt the life I had hoped for slipping away from me. Not only were my hopes for a bountiful crop in ruins, but the life I had hoped for with Catherine now seemed completely out of reach. Faced with grave apprehensions about the coming year, I threw all my efforts into plowing the fields in preparation for next spring's sowing, hoping it would not only destroy my doubts, but also the grasshopper eggs that lay buried there.

I continued to check the post whenever I was in town hoping for a response from Catherine. It was early October before I finally heard from her. When I picked up the envelope at the post office, I noticed that it was quite heavy, unlike the brief notes that Catherine usually sent. I waited to read her letter until I was alone, fearing that it contained bad news. When I finally geared up my courage, I tore open the envelope and read with dismay what she had written. The banking firm of Joseph Weller and Company had been forced to close its doors on September 18, 1873.

Catherine lamented that her father's firm had overextended itself by investing too heavily in the Northwestern Pacific Railroad project. Stock market crashes in Vienna, Austria that summer had prompted European investors to divest their holdings of American securities, particularly railroad bonds, she explained. Without cash to finance operations and refinance debts that came due, many railroad firms, like her fathers, had failed.

According to Catherine, the only thing saving them from complete destitution was her father's interest in a small silver mine in Utah. Charles had taken control of the family business and was confident that, in time, he would be able to satisfy the company's creditors. However, the stress of the situation coupled with her ill health had been too much for Charles's wife, and she had died just a few weeks ago. Under the circumstances, Catherine informed me that she had decided to move to New York to be with her brother during this difficult time, while her father remained in Chicago to handle the business there. She left me an address where she could be reached but made no mention of rekindling our relationship.

Overcome with despair, I replayed Catherine's words in my mind. The railroad industry involved a huge amount of money—and risk. Railroads were the nation's largest non-agricultural employer, and banks and other industries were heavily invested. So, when Joseph Weller and Company closed its doors, it would most likely touch off a series of events that could encompass the entire nation.

I arrived at Jelle's office to find him looking tense and worried. The latest cables lay strewn haphazardly on his desk.

"Have you heard?" I asked, breathlessly.

He nodded sadly and pointed to the newspaper on his desk. The headline blared the news in all capital letters. "The collapse of Weller's firm has set off a major economic panic that will be disastrous for the nation's economy."

"Will we be all right?" I asked.

"I think so," Jelle answered. "I've been going over the figures all day. I'm afraid that inflation and rampant speculative investment in railroads have put a massive strain on bank reserves. Credit has dried up, foreclosures are more common, and banks across the country are failing."

"What will happen when farmers start withdrawing funds this fall to cover the costs of harvesting and transporting their crops?" I asked.

"I think we'll be okay," he said. "Our balance sheet is built on stable funding sources—long-term loans or retail deposits that are either unable or unlikely to flee in the event of a panic." A dark expression came over Jelle's normally congenial countenance and his voice took on an edge that I had not heard from him before. "But money will get tight. And when money gets tight, borrowing costs rise."

"Are you sure we can weather this storm?"

Jelle leaned forward with his elbow on his desk, "There may be more foreclosures when settlers are unable to meet their loan obligations," he said. "But the land held by the bank is not going to be a liability. In fact, I have already been contacted by a cartel in Sioux City that is buying up foreclosed land as fast as it comes up for auction."

"But the grasshoppers have devalued the property!" I exclaimed. "The cartel is buying at sharply reduced prices and making a profit off the hardships of the pioneers."

Jelle wiped his brow with a sweat stained handkerchief and rubbed his temples as if that would relieve some of the tension. He looked as if he had not eaten or slept in several days. He spoke with the weariness of one who had exhausted all hope of a better solution. "You must understand that sometimes business decisions are made by capitalizing on the difficulties of others. Deals like this almost always result in winners and losers. So far, I have been able to keep us afloat by tapping some of the resources from my business in Wisconsin, but I'm not sure how long I can continue to do this." He drummed his fingers absently on the papers strewn across his desk and stared out the window at the empty street. When he looked back at me, his voice was filled with sadness and pleading. "Look," he said. "If you want to keep your homesteaders from losing everything, it is absolutely critical that you solve this grasshopper problem as quickly as possible."

I left Jelle's office feeling more discouraged than ever. The railroad expansion we had counted on to bring prosperity to the region was now in doubt and farmers were suffering due to falling prices for export crops such as wheat and cotton. To make matters worse, the grasshopper plague was still unresolved. More and more settlers were packing up their belongings and leaving or selling the infected land at steeply discounted prices. And yet, there appeared to be no alternative for those who remained but to plow the land and hope that the winter frost would destroy the grasshopper eggs.

There was little chance that the problem would solve itself, and I was rapidly running out of hope. I had left my homeland hoping to make my way in America, but it seemed that America was determined to thwart my plans. I clung to the belief that I could build a life on the prairie for Catherine and me if I could just weather this latest setback. But with Catherine now half a continent away from me, it seemed that the odds of renewing our relationship were as slim as those of overcoming the grasshoppers. Now, with the country in panic, my crops destroyed, and Catherine more out of my reach than ever, I struggled to maintain my will to survive. I could not imagine that my life could get any worse.

But I had not anticipated the blizzard of 1874.

January 7 dawned bright and clear, with hardly a cloud in the sky. Around noon, the air changed, and an eerie stillness blanketed the prairie. Not a breath moved, not a sound was heard; the stillness was both audible and impressive. Soon rapidly rolling clouds appeared in the northeast, and in the southwest a dark line of clouds appeared moving rapidly without any internal movement. As the two fronts met, a terrific wind blew from the northwest. The rain began soon afterward and changed to sleet later in the afternoon. Then the sleet became ice, making it almost impossible for man or beast to travel. Businesses in town closed and only the most daring ventured out.

As the temperature dropped, families gathered up what fuel they could and prepared for a long cold night, not dreaming that the storm would last for several days. Sometime during the night of the first day, the sleet turned to snow. As the night wore on, the snow laden wind increased in ferocity. The air became immediately filled with snow, so heavy and whirling and blinding that visibility was down to three feet. Snow began to sift through the smallest cracks in houses and stables. The snow was so wet that within a few minutes a person's clothes were wet through as if by rain. I gathered what fuel and supplies I could and hunkered down in my hut listening to the high-pitched squeal of the wind while the snow drifted through the cracks in the walls.

Most of the new arrivals had never endured a winter on the plains and were unprepared for the cold and snow. Many of them had constructed dugouts in hillsides, or they had thrown together claim shanties, meant to be temporary housing until a soddie or frame house could be built. Fuel was scarce on the treeless prairie. Having just arrived from the east, many settlers had only a day's supply of buffalo chips and a meager supply of food. By evening, some houses had snowdrifts inside. Many of those who ventured outside did so attached to a rope. An unfortunate few who did not take this precaution were lost in the storm.

While the settlers' shelter and food supply were inadequate, provisions for the livestock were even poorer or nonexistent. Some people led their horse or milk cow into their houses. Much of the livestock that was left outdoors perished. Cows suffocated in the deep drifts and trains were stuck for days.

The next morning, the sun was not visible. My hut was bathed in blackness. I tried to light my lamp, but the wind whistled through the cracks and blew it out, leaving me with only the glowing coals from the stove to see by. The entire world was a mass of swirling snow and howling winds. Not even my winter in Wisconsin could compare to the blizzard's frigid winds. I rationed my fuel just enough to keep a small fire burning in my wood stove where I melted snow to make weak coffee, but it did not provide much warmth against the bone-chilling cold. That night, I lay awake listening to the chorus of voices in my head, accompanied by the whistle and moan of the wind. *"I will see her dead before I let her marry you!" Dirk screamed. "I want you to live in fear," Gregor snarled. "I want you to flinch at every sound. I want you to wonder if the next time, the gun will be loaded."*

On the morning of the third day, I awoke to find the fire in my hut had gone out and the snow I had been melting on the stove had turned to ice. This final blow sent me into an incomprehensible rage. I threw the pot across the room where it thudded against the walls of my hut and rolled across the floor. I lashed out angrily at a God who had forsaken me. "Why have You abandoned me?" I screamed. "What have I done to deserve all this misery?" But the only answer came from the howling of the wind.

The blizzard unleashed its fury without letup for three long days. It blinded the eyes, cut the skin like a shower of needles, confused the mind, and smothered the breath. Fearing the worst, I poured all my hopes and regrets into a long letter to Catherine. I told her about leaving my home in the Netherlands to escape the memories of a future that would never be. I had been filled with anger and blame. Although my father had hoped I would find salvation by joining with others of our faith in America, I could not embrace his strict religious views. My faith had been tested with Lainie's death and found to be lacking. I had fled my home in Gelderland to escape the persecution and guilt I felt over her death, but a part of me also blamed God. He had deserted me when I needed him most. I told her how she had given me a lifeline in America that had kept me afloat while I learned to navigate this new land. If I survived this ordeal, I told Catherine, I still held out hope that we would one day share a future together. I sealed the letter and placed it in plain sight under the oil lamp. If I did not survive, I hoped that whoever found me would see that she received it.

Finally, by the evening of the third day, the winds began to decrease. The next morning a hazy sun forced its way through the overcast skies. People began to slowly venture out, searching for family members, checking on neighbors and looking for lost livestock. Many dugouts were completely covered over with snow and the occupants had to dig themselves out or were dug out by neighbors. More than 70 people died.

Abraham organized the community to help those in need. We shared provisions, organized search parties, and rounded up lost livestock. Jelle temporarily suspended all collections, and he advanced payments so the settlers could replenish their supplies. Everyone pitched in to help their neighbors. We had survived the worst that nature had to offer and yet we had not been defeated. I witnessed first-hand the mental reservoir of strength that people call on in times of need to carry them through without giving up. As I worked beside my neighbors that winter to rebuild our lives after the storm, I felt a glimmer of hope returning to my spirit. I gave little thought to my own misfortunes, or to the letter that remained secure in its place under the oil lamp in my hut.

16

By the spring of 1874, the fields that had been devastated by the grasshoppers in the previous summer had been cultivated and re-seeded and were once again promising a generous return. But the grasshopper eggs lay just below the surface of the soil awaiting the warmth of spring. Then the newly hatched grasshoppers would burst forth to devour the young seedlings before they could reach maturity.

Every day another wagonload of dejected homesteaders headed back east with their belongings, leaving behind the remains of their broken dreams. Jelle had been forced to resume foreclosure procedures against several of the settlers to keep his business afloat. "I hate to do it," he said, sadly. "But what choice do I have? I have extended the loans as long as I can, but if I wait any longer, the bank will go under. Then everyone will lose."

In the distance the mournful sound of a train whistle signaled the departure of more families from the area. If the railroad were to remain solvent, it would need to check the stampede of disheartened settlers and restore confidence in the area. But with whole counties along the line devastated by the grasshopper plague, there was little hope that this land would yield a profit anytime soon. The situation would become a great deal worse if something were not done at once. There had to be a way to defeat the grasshoppers.

The train whistled again, and I could hear the distant sound of the iron wheels on the track as it picked up speed. I kicked a bent piece of tin out of the road. It was bent down slightly at the front to form a scoop and a larger section was bent up higher at the back. I picked it up and studied it for several minutes while the germ of an idea formed in my mind. What was needed was a method of scooping up the eggs without damaging the growing crops. I had an idea, but I would need help to make it happen.

On the way into town, I passed another dejected family fleeing the grasshopper plague, their wagon loaded with all their earthly possessions. A bony cow with her hips protruding at sharp angles plodded along behind. The man appeared stoop-shouldered and beaten and the woman looked frail and weak. In the back of the wagon, tucked in between odds and ends of furniture, two small children rode in silence, their dark eyes projecting an atmosphere of despair and hopelessness.

I arrived at Jelle's office to find him sitting morosely with his head in his hands. Piles of papers and ledgers were strewn over his desk. The air in his office smelled of dust and gloom. Since his business in Wisconsin was still solvent, Jelle had been able to call on New York's money center banks to supply the cash he needed from their reserves. He had managed to weather the financial crisis and meet the demand for withdrawals during the panic. However, if the grasshoppers were not alleviated in time to save this summer's crop, he did not hold out much hope of a full recovery. He would have no choice but to shutter his business here and return to Wisconsin.

Abraham was standing by the window when I came in. He shook his head sadly as the family in the wagon passed by. "Something has to be done!" he exclaimed. "Many of our people have already left the area because of the grasshoppers. I'm afraid more will follow if something isn't done."

Abraham's youngest son, Stephen, was on the floor playing with a half-grown whelp. He was a precocious child of about the age of five, with a mop of unruly hair and large brown eyes that peered out from a perpetually dirty face. He followed his father around like a puppy, peeking curiously at me from behind his father's large protective body and asking a million questions.

My own child would have been about Stephen's age had he lived. My heart twisted when I thought of the child…my child. I always thought of the child as a son. I imagined him with a strong back and his mother's fair hair and good looks. But that dream died with Lainie and it existed now only to cause me pain.

I reached down to pet the dog, and he nipped playfully at my hand. "Where did this guy come from?"

"The Jacobsons left him behind when they moved back east." Stephan answered, scratching the pup behind his ears. "Papa said I could keep him."

The Jacobsons were only one of many of the homesteaders who had packed up what belongings they could fit in their wagon and moved back east where they hoped to recover from the losses incurred by the grasshoppers.

Abraham shook his head. "Whole counties in southwestern Minnesota and northwestern Iowa are in this condition. People are demoralized. It could become a great deal worse if something isn't done to stop it."

I nodded in sympathy and turned to Jelle. "That's why I've come to speak with you. I have an idea that might turn things around and earn us a substantial profit as well."

A glimmer of hope flashed across Abraham's face. "What do you have in mind?" Jelle put down his pencil and folded his arms. They waited expectantly for me to continue.

I laid the bent piece of tin on Jelle's desk. "The grasshopper eggs are buried just a few inches below the surface," I said. "Think of this as a piece of sheet iron. We'll bend the iron plates down a few inches at the front edge, and at the rear edge we'll turn up a strip of about six or eight inches wide to form a kind of sled like this." I demonstrated using the bent piece of tin. "When the eggs start to hatch and the crops are growing, we'll cover these plates with tar. We'll attach a horse to the sled and drag it over the growing crops. The eggs will collect in the tar without damaging the crops."

"But how can we ensure that the eggs won't hatch anyway?" Abraham asked.

"At the end of each trip across the field, the pans will be cleaned with a shovel and the residue burned to ensure that the eggs are destroyed," I answered. "Then the plates will be rebrushed with tar and a return trip made over the adjacent ground until the entire area is cleared."

Jelle had watched the demonstration with great interest. Now, he sat back in his chair and scratched his chin. "Do you really think it will work?"

"What choice do we have? If we do nothing, we know the grasshoppers will continue to devastate our crops and lay their eggs every year. I believe that in the beginning, one man will be required to manage each horse and sled, but as they become used to the work, the horses can be connected by lines so that a man at each end and one to spare could guide a line of eight or nine horses. In this way, we would eventually be able to clean about 16 acres at every trip across the field without damaging the crop."

Jelle shook his head. "It sounds promising, but how will we finance such a proposal?" he asked, skeptically.

"I want to form a syndicate with some of the other men in the area to purchase land from the railroad," I answered. "We'll approach the railroad for a loan to purchase the infected land. It is in their best interests to help us. I believe we can purchase two townships located in the heart of the grasshopper district at a greatly reduced price."

Abraham raised his eyebrows. "But that land is infested with grasshopper eggs! It's worthless unless we can get rid of them."

"Settlers are still heading out west to Dakota and anywhere beyond the grasshoppers," I answered. "I propose that we intercept the migrating settlers and hire them to help us clear the land of grasshoppers."

"What makes you think they will want to stay and help us?"

"They'll be paid to break new ground this fall and plant the fields next spring. The chance of employment will encourage new settlers and keep those here who would abandon their homesteads," I explained. "Once the land is cleared of grasshoppers, we'll sell it back to the settlers. They will stay and set up homesteads near the railroad. In the end, we will all prosper, especially those of us who can get in on the ground floor."

Abraham scratched his chin thoughtfully. "It might work," he said.

The thought of potential earnings from the project caused Jelle's eyes to light up. "I like the sound of it, but how can you be sure your plan will work?"

"I only need enough capital to clear 20 acres to begin with," I answered. "Once we demonstrate that the process will work, we can sell the idea to the railroads and begin to purchase and clear more land."

"And if we are successful on a small scale, then the neighboring farmers may be able to save their own crops by similar efforts," Abraham added.

"Do you really believe that once the settlers have earned money by turning the soil in the fall, they will want to stay and purchase their own land?" Jelle asked.

"You've seen the wagonloads heading to the Dakotas. They are coming with their families. Once the wagon bed is lifted off and the wife and children commence housekeeping in it, it will be difficult to pack up and move on. They will either return to their homesteads and use the same method to clear their land of grasshoppers, or they will purchase the newly cleared land from us. In the meantime, we will be able to sell the crops they plant and ship them to market on the railroad."

Jelle's eyes began to dance with the possibilities I outlined. "New settlers will need homes, barns, sheds, and a granary. All that building will undoubtedly require mortgages." At this point, I knew I had him hooked.

"When can we start?" I asked.

"Immediately," he answered. "I'll telegraph to Sioux City for barrels of coal tar."

"We'll also need plates of sheet iron about eight feet long by four feet wide."

"I'll get it ordered," Jelle said.

By early June, the growing grain was already something to be proud of, but a close inspection revealed the ground alive with grasshoppers. As soon as the materials arrived, Abraham and I enlisted the aid of a few other farmers to begin the task of clearing the first twenty acres of grasshoppers. Although the plan did not work smoothly and perfectly at first, it did after a few hours' practice. Elated with our initial success, we increased our efforts, and thus, we were able to cover the entire twenty acres in only a couple of days.

Abraham shook his head in disbelief. "I honestly didn't think this would work," he said. "The little pests have been destroyed without any appreciable injury to the growing crops."

Armed with the proof that our system would work, it was time to approach the railroad. Jelle spread the railroad map out on his desk. "I believe these two townships hold the greatest promise for our process," he said, pointing to the map. "The area is adjacent to the land we have already cleared and its proximity to the river will make it highly desirable for settlement once it's cleared of grasshoppers."

"We should move quickly," I said. "Once word gets out about our process for clearing the land, other investors will want in on it."

"I have a contact with the St. Paul & Sioux City Railroad headquartered in Chicago," Jelle said, thoughtfully. "I'll contact them to see if they are willing to make a deal." He picked up the bent piece of tin from his desk. "I'll need to speak to them in person to demonstrate how the process works."

Abraham nodded. "I'll start contacting some of the prominent members of the community about forming a Grasshopper Syndicate to help finance and manage the project."

Jelle grinned broadly and slapped me on the back. "I'll get the paperwork started and leave for Chicago as soon as I hear from the railroad. Just be ready to move the minute I cable you that the deal has gone through."

Jelle had scarcely been gone a week when he sent word that the railroad had jumped at the chance to unload what was otherwise worthless land. Once the land was purchased, Abraham went to work immediately marking off a square mile into 20-acre tracts. I intercepted the migrating settlers as they came in sight on their way to Dakota, or to anywhere beyond the grasshoppers, and before nightfall I had captured 12 of them, each with a contract to break 20 acres. Within six weeks I had over 2,000 acres turned over. A good many of these men, after completing their contracts, returned to their abandoned homesteads and broke 20 acres or more each for themselves. The news spread over the county like a prairie fire. These operations had been watched with great interest by neighboring farmers, and many of them returned to their homesteads and saved their crops by similar efforts.

With the grasshoppers under control, I turned my attention to my own farming operations in earnest. I sowed wheat on the eight acres that I had broken and cleared the previous fall. I also purchased a yoke of oxen and a plow as well as a cow. I continued turning the sod to create an additional field of 40 acres in which I planted corn and wheat. The homestead was taking shape and I was once again anticipating a successful harvest.

By mid-October of that year, the financial crisis had subsided, and it appeared that my dreams of prosperity in America were finally being realized. Once again, my thoughts turned to Catherine. I had not heard from her since she had written of her father's bank failure. I had kept the letter I had written to her during the blizzard all these months, waiting for the right moment to post it. Although I still lived in a sod hut on the prairie, I finally had the resources to begin construction on a frame house. Perhaps now I could finally ask her to join me. I just hoped she was still willing. I tucked the letter into my pocket and headed for the post office.

The postmaster was busy sorting mail when I arrived. He looked up when I came in. "Hank!" he said. "A letter just arrived for you from New York." He began rifling through the stacks of mail. "Ah! Here it is."

He handed me the letter and I immediately recognized the familiar slant of Catherine's handwriting. I tore it open and read with dismay what she had written. Catherine advised me that she would be staying in New York with her brother for the time being. Charles had taken over the family business after the bankruptcy and reorganized the firm with two new partners. He anticipated that he would be able to meet all his father's financial obligations within the year by using the proceeds from the silver mine in Utah. Unfortunately, they would have to close the bank in Philadelphia and consolidate all their business in the Chicago branch. She informed me that since she was unsure when she would return to Chicago, she had deposited the letters and the promissory note I had left with her in a bank vault in Chicago as I had requested. She left instructions on how to access the documents should I need to do so.

I read the letter over again trying to discern any hidden meaning, but her words were vague and held a note of finality that had not been there before. I touched the unsent letter in my pocket and was a sense of sadness and regret washed over me. I felt her slipping away from me and I was powerless to stop it.

17

During the next few months, my thoughts spiraled between foggy disbelief and the painful clarity that Catherine's feelings toward me had cooled. I was consumed by pain, disorganization, and confusion. At first, I refused to accept the obvious and clung stubbornly to the hope that our relationship could be salvaged. I wired her several times in New York, but I received no response. I felt as if I were balancing on the edge of an abyss. I had come to depend on Catherine's support during the difficult years. Without it, I had only myself to rely on.

Abraham noticed my morose behavior. "Why don't you come to Sunday services with the family," he asked. "It might do you good to socialize a bit."

Abraham believed that a church home was essential for the community's spiritual sustenance and social interaction. He had joined several other Dutch farmers to organize a congregation that became the First Reformed Church of Orange City. In the beginning, they worshipped in a log meetinghouse which also served as the schoolhouse until a permanent edifice could be constructed in town.

The thought of a church filled with pious believers filled me with dread. I had not prayed or thought about God since the days during the blizzard. "I don't think I'm ready for that yet," I said, evasively. "My father was a strict Calvinist who preached against the sins of modernism, but I have not thought much about the church since I left Gelderland. In fact, I'm not sure what I believe."

Abraham was not to be deterred. "I don't think you have to worry," he said. "While the church is still associated with the Dutch Reformed Church, we strive to strike a balance between accepting people the way they are and encouraging them to live by the Christian standards of fidelity, forgiveness and growth."

Still, I hesitated. Old feelings of bitterness and resentment resurfaced. I had blamed God for the tragedies I had faced in my life—the persecution of my family in Gelderland, Lainie's death, the grasshoppers, the blizzard—and Catherine's decision to stay in New York had only increased my feelings of abandonment. "I'm kind of angry at God right now," I said. "He seems determined to undermine my happiness at every turn."

Abraham nodded thoughtfully. "We have all experienced periods of doubt...including me. When we lost our first child, I didn't think I would ever be able to forgive God for taking him." He sighed heavily. "Nevertheless, I think that socializing with others might help take your mind off whatever it is that is troubling you."

"You sound like my father," I said.

Abraham grinned. "So, you'll come, then?"

"I'll come," I said, "but I'm not promising anything."

My appearance at church did not go unnoticed. It wasn't long before anxious mothers with eligible daughters of a marriageable age began to invite me to Sunday suppers. Henrietta Spencer and her daughter, Berta, were among the most persistent. Henrietta was a large woman with gap teeth and arms like tree trunks. She was married to Dwight Spencer, a meek little man who ran the mercantile house. With four daughters at home, Henrietta was desperate to find a suitable husband for her oldest daughter. Berta was an attractive girl with large breasts and an ample bottom. Her round face was accentuated by dark eyes and thick, full lips.

I accepted Henrietta's invitation to supper, hoping the diversion would take my mind off Catherine. The evening began innocently enough, however, I was soon reminded that young women experiencing their first sexual encounter were often over eager, and let their passions overtake their better judgement. After dinner, with her parent's blessings, we took a moonlight stroll. When the evening turned amorous, Berta's passion showed no restraint. After a particularly active session of kissing and fondling, she suddenly pulled up her skirts and thrust herself against me. "Take me," she panted, pulling my face into her breasts.

Although a willing young woman with large soft breasts was difficult to resist, thoughts of Catherine were never far from my mind. Reluctantly, I pushed her away. "I...can't," I said, breathlessly.

Her face displayed a mixture of hurt and anger. "Why not? Don't you want me?"

"Of course," I answered, pulling away. "But I have already given my heart to two different women who broke it into pieces. I don't think I will ever be strong enough to love again." I managed to skew my face into the most pathetic expression I could muster. "Don't you see? It would be unfair of me to take advantage of a woman in a vulnerable situation if I could not commit to giving her the lifetime of love she deserved. I hope you understand."

This response had the desired effect of protecting Berta's honor and awakening her maternal instincts. "You poor thing," she said, caressing my face. "Of course, I understand." Thereafter, she began to treat me as a broken soul who needed protection from other predatory females. They would cluck at me when I passed and whisper behind their hands, but for the most part, they curtailed their efforts to engage me in any romantic encounters.

To take my mind off my own unhappiness, I refocused my efforts on helping to expand the operations of the Grasshopper Syndicate. We continued to break up new land and sell out both new and cultivated lands as buyers appeared. With 13,000 acres now owned by the syndicate, of which about one-half was put under cultivation, and the establishment of two farm headquarters with buildings, Abraham soon found that he could give but casual personal attention to the oversight of these enterprises without neglecting his own land. He hired a capable foreman to establish three additional farms and oversee the cultivation of 4,000 acres. By the end of the year, this had been successfully carried through until all the land had been disposed of to the satisfaction and profit of the syndicate.

As his business improved, Jelle set up permanent residency in Orange City to oversee the operations here and leave his Wisconsin business in the capable hands of his manager there. He moved his office from the back of the mercantile building to a small building on Main Street. His new office soon became a gathering spot for local farmers and merchants seeking news of the railroad expansion through the area. He enjoyed holding court there in the afternoon, regaling his customers with the latest gossip and railroad news.

I wandered into Jelle's office one day when he was meeting with a client. I waited in the lobby until they finished their conversation. Jelle saw me as they came into the lobby. "Hank! I'm so glad you dropped by. I was just meeting with James Dubolt from the St. Paul Land Company. He is proposing the sale of some virgin land in the grasshopper district that was originally part of a land grant to build a line connecting to the Northwestern Pacific Railroad."

The man turned to look at me and his face went from placid to sinister in a matter of seconds. I felt myself recoil in horror. "This man is an impostor!" I exclaimed as soon as I could find my voice. "His name is not James Dubolt. It's Gregor Van Pelt!"

Jelle's face registered shock and surprise. "I don't understand..."

Realizing that his identity had been exposed, Gregor made no attempt to hide his disdain for me. "Yes, it's true," he admitted. "But sometimes changing one's name is essential if one is to start fresh. I'm sure Harke, I mean Hank, can understand that."

I bristled at the sound of my Dutch name coming from his foul mouth. "Unlike you, I didn't change my name to swindle anyone."

Jelle looked incredulously at Gregor and for a moment I saw a glimpse of the naïve young man I had met on the way to America. "You lied to me?" he asked him.

Gregor turned to Jelle. "I may have been accused of some underhandedness in the past," he said, "but I assure you that I have changed my ways along with my name. In fact, Hank and I have a mutual acquaintance from the old country. I'm sure he could vouch for me." He turned back to face me. "Perhaps Catherine mentioned that I was representing a Dutch investment firm in Arnhem. As luck would have it, the financial house her father referred me to was headed by a man named Dirk Van Huel. I believe you know him."

The mention of Dirk's name sent the blood rushing to my face. I struggled to control the beast within me. "Dirk is no friend of mine," I said, through clenched teeth. "And neither are you!"

Gregor raised his eyebrows in mock surprise. "From what Van Huel told me, I am not surprised." Then, he turned his attention to Jelle who had listened in dumbfounded silence. "It seems your friend, Hank, left a trail of death and personal destruction behind when he left the Netherlands."

Jelle came around from behind his desk. "Hank, what's he talking about?"

"Lies! I left my homeland because Dirk Van Huel blamed me for causing the death of his father and sister. It wasn't my fault, but he wouldn't listen! He vowed to make life miserable for me and my family. I thought I could escape his vengeance by emigrating to America, but it appears I was mistaken. He has reappeared in my life in the form of Gregor Van Pelt."

"I'm afraid you have it all wrong," Gregor said, smoothly. "I'm on my way to California. I was merely looking to dispose of some property in the area before I leave."

"Gregor Van Pelt is a ruthless crook," I said to Jelle. "He cheated Catherine out of her inheritance with this railroad scheme, and he'll cheat you as well. He is only here because he wants something from me." I turned to Gregor and spat out the words. "Well, I'm afraid you've made the trip in vain. I don't have it."

A flicker of doubt crossed Gregor's face. "What you did in the past is of no consequence to me," he said, dismissively. "However, I cannot speak for Catherine. Who knows how she will react to the news of her lover's dark past?"

Anger boiled in my brain. "You leave her out of this!" I yelled, advancing toward him.

"Calm down, everyone," Jelle said, stepping between us. "I'm sure there is a rational explanation for all this."

"He's right," Gregor said, gathering up the papers he and Jelle had been looking at. "There is no need for violence. I came here with an honest offer of a business opportunity, but it is obvious that I have wasted my time." He headed for the door. "Good day, gentlemen," he said.

"I'm sorry," Jelle said when he was gone. "I had no idea. He said his name was James Dubolt. It all sounded so legitimate."

With Gregor gone, all the anger drained away as quickly as it had arisen, and I sagged in relief. "It's not your fault," I said to Jelle. "He's an accomplished con man. Just be careful. He will do anything in his power to get what he wants, including eliminating anyone who gets in his way. I'm just glad that Catherine is safe in New York where he isn't likely to find her."

The Dutchman

Jelle reached into his desk drawer and produced the same small silver pistol he had showed me on the trip to Wisconsin. The sight of the pistol unnerved me. Although most settlers in the area carried a rifle as protection against wild animals and rattle snakes while they worked the fields, I had never carried a weapon myself. Jelle laid the gun on the desk in front of us.

"Don't worry about me," he said. "I've learned a few things about protecting myself from swindlers since we arrived in America."

18

Gregor disappeared shortly after our encounter in Jelle's office. Although I made a concerted effort to locate him, he had vanished as quickly as he had appeared. Jelle alerted other bankers in the area to avoid anyone claiming to represent the St. Paul Railroad or any land company associated with it. We discovered that several other bankers in the area had already been approached by Dubolt seeking to sell land in the heavily infested grasshopper area. It was obvious that Gregor may have changed his name, but not his unscrupulous business practices. I hoped that by exposing him, he had left the country for good. However, I harbored no illusions that I was through with him while he believed that I still had the promissory note.

With Gregor out of the picture for the time being, I returned my attention to the work of our Grasshopper Syndicate. Our efforts had not gone unnoticed by other investors in the area. The cartel in Sioux City had purchased many of the abandoned homesteads in the northern part of Sioux County during the initial grasshopper invasion. A representative had contacted Jelle to place their lands under his management for similar treatment against the grasshopper threat. The expansion of the business was more than one man could handle. He hired a clerk to assist with the development of reports and accounts to keep the system running smoothly.

Richard Hendrickson was an eager, capable young man, more at home interacting with his numbers and accounts than interacting with people. He wore a green visor over his close-cropped hair and garters on his sleeves. He seemed to thrive on the dusty atmosphere in Jelle's office among the myriad of files and papers that now littered the area.

We had just concluded another meeting of the Grasshopper Syndicate where we had finalized a decision to purchase two more townships along the railroad. Abraham gestured at the retreating syndicate members who were joking and joshing with each other as they left. "Everything appears to be going quite well; profits are up, and everyone seems happy with our efforts."

We were still congratulating ourselves on the success of our venture when Jelle came up beside us. His brow was knitted together in a grim expression. "I thought you would want to see this," he said, handing me an article from the Sioux City newspaper. "I didn't want to share it with you until after the meeting."

I took the paper and read the headline he pointed to: *Nation Mourns the Death of Joseph Weller, Financier.* The article stated that Weller had been found slumped over his desk in his Chicago office. He was survived by his son and daughter and the article gave an address in Chicago where mourners would be received. The room began to sway, and Jelle placed his hand on my shoulder to steady me. "Poor Catherine!" I exclaimed. "She must be beside herself with grief."

"I think you should go to her," Jelle said.

"I'm not sure I would be welcome. I have tried to reach her several times, but her last letter did not leave much hope for a reconciliation. It was pretty final."

"She is in mourning. She needs you."

I longed to comfort Catherine in her time of grief. But still, I hesitated, reluctant to intrude where I might not be welcome. "Catherine is a strong woman and I'm sure her brother must be with her. They've probably traveled together to Chicago to handle her father's affairs."

I handed Abraham the newspaper article and he read it over thoughtfully. "I agree with Jelle," he said. "In times like these, the emotions of dealing with the death of a loved one can be quite overwhelming. Sometimes the comfort of family is not enough."

"Besides," Jelle added, "Weller's bank has been a valued partner with the syndicate. It makes good business sense to maintain a relationship with the family."

"Jelle's right," Abraham said. "Regardless of the status of your personal relationship with Catherine, you should go and express condolences on behalf of the syndicate."

"I'd go myself," Jelle said, "but I've never actually met Catherine. I don't think it would be appropriate."

In the end, their consistent arguments wore down my defenses. "Alright," I said, at last. "If you think it's wise, I'll leave on the next train."

"I was planning to visit my uncle in Wisconsin and check on the business there," Jelle said, scratching his chin. "If you like, I can travel with you as far as Waupun. Then I'll meet up with you later in Chicago."

"There's no need for you to bother," I answered.

"It's no trouble," Jelle answered. "I do have some syndicate business in Chicago that requires my attention."

Before I could talk myself out of it, Jelle and I were on our way east across the familiar landscape of southern Minnesota and Wisconsin. The countryside had changed in the last few years. When I first set eyes on this land, it was little more than a naked prairie, almost as destitute of trees as of human inhabitants. However, during the years when the lands were being claimed and occupied by settlers, the railroad believed that the planting of trees on the barren land would bring additional growth and prosperity to the area. Understanding that beautifying the land would also increase rail travel, the railroad had begun transporting young trees, cuttings, and tree seeds to every station along the line free of charge. Now, groves of young trees surrounded comfortable farmhouses and shaded the parks and streets in the villages and cities. Even the familiar limestone buildings of Waupun seemed to have taken on a more permanent and stately appearance.

After a brief homecoming with Jelle's uncle at the depot, I traveled on to Chicago alone. The city had also changed in the ensuing years. Despite the Great Fire in 1871 that had destroyed the central business district, the city had grown exponentially, becoming the nation's rail center and the dominant midwestern center for manufacturing and commerce. Even the smell seemed more tolerable. Everywhere I looked there was evidence of massive reconstruction efforts using the newest materials and methods. Builders had developed the innovative use of steel framing to reclaim the soft swampy ground near the lake. Now tall masonry buildings reached skyward where old wooden structures once stood.

Despite the bittersweet memories it held, I had decided to stay at the Ambassador Hotel where I had met Catherine the last time we were together. Nathan was still behind the desk when I checked in and he greeted me warmly. "Mr. De Jong! It's so good to see you again. Have you come to see Miss Weller?"

"Yes," I answered. "I came to express my condolences to Miss Weller on the death of her father."

Nathan nodded sadly. "Yes, we are all quite shaken by the news," he said. "I can direct you to the home where they are staying if you like."

I had no difficulty locating the address Nathan gave me, but I still hesitated to approach. The curtains were drawn in mourning and the house looked cold and sad. The heavy oak door stood as a gloomy deterrent for intrusive visitors. I could not bring myself to knock on the door for fear that Catherine would slam it in my face. Instead, I paced up and down the street in front of the house, hoping to catch a glimpse of her. I had just about given up hope when a carriage pulled up in front of the house. A tall, handsome man in top hat and mourning clothes stepped out. He turned and extended his hand to help a beautiful woman whose coiled hair peeked out from her bonnet like ringlets of fire. She glanced in my direction and my heart leaped to my throat when our eyes met. Then she turned back to the man who lifted a small child of about two years old high into the air. The child squealed in delight before he set her down next to Catherine.

I was overcome with a sinking feeling in the pit of my stomach at the sight of them. In my own loneliness and self-imposed isolation, I had not considered that Catherine would marry and move on without me. As the family moved toward the door, Catherine stopped and spoke briefly to the man. He glanced in my direction before taking the child from her and moving on into the house. Catherine turned to face me. My mind told me to turn away, but my feet were rooted to the spot. She came toward me with a sort of half smile lighting up her face. Even in her mourning clothes, she was more beautiful than I remembered. "Are you going to come in or are you just going to wear out my sidewalk with your pacing?" she asked.

"Was it that obvious?"

Catherine's eyes crinkled into a smile. "You are hard to miss," she said. She gestured toward the front window of the house where a curtain suddenly fell back into place. "I'm sure Mrs. Jennings has been beside herself wondering when you would come to the door."

I felt myself flush with embarrassment. "I came to express my condolences to your family on the death of your father," I said. "I don't wish to intrude."

"Nonsense! Please come inside. At least let me offer you some refreshment."

She took my arm and I allowed her to lead me up the narrow stone path to the front door. Now that Catherine had arrived, the house looked less foreboding. The light gray exterior was accented in red and white trim and two ornate cupulas flanked a large front porch. Although much smaller than the house I had visited in Philadelphia, this house was still impressive compared to my small frame house on the prairie.

The gentleman and the child were seated in the parlor when we entered. Even though the house was draped in mourning, the room still looked bright and cheerful. The dark furniture had been covered in floral damask and there was little ornamentation to clutter the room.

The man stood and faced us as we entered the room. "Charles, I'd like you to meet Hank De Jong," Catherine said.

"Ah yes. Catherine has spoken of you," he said, extending his hand.

"Hank, this is my brother, Charles."

Once again, I found myself tongue-tied as reality overturned my assumptions. The child peeked shyly around him. "Lily," Catherine said, beckoning to her. "Come and meet Mr. De Jong."

The girl took a few hesitant steps forward. She had Catherine's auburn hair, but she peered curiously at me through eyes as black as coal. She held out a small doll toward me. "*Schatje*," she said, shyly.

I managed to find my voice. "Is that your dolly's name?"

She nodded and I took the doll she handed me. It was made of soft material, with yellow yarn for hair. She had black buttons for her eyes and nose and a lop-sided smile was sewn onto the face. "She's very pretty," I said, handing the doll back to her. "I can see why you call her your little treasure." The girl smiled broadly, and I noticed her smile was crooked like the face on the doll.

"Schatje goes with her wherever we go," Catherine said. "She even sleeps with her."

Charles cleared his throat and scooped the child into his arms "Perhaps, we should see if Mrs. Jennings needs any assistance with the tea," he said. Lily buried her head in his shoulder and stuck her thumb in her mouth.

"She is a lovely child," I said, as they left the room.

"Yes. I'm afraid Charles spoils her beyond reason and Father doted on her," she said, gazing after them. "Lily would often sit on the arm of his chair and he would make up stories, acting them out with Schatje. If I could hear their laughter, I had no need for tears. I cannot imagine what I would have done had she not been here."

Catherine turned her gaze to me, and I was once again at a loss for words. She motioned me to a chair and sat down across from me.

"She has your auburn hair," I said, when I could find my tongue again.

Catherine smiled and I caught my breath. There was a hint of sadness in her eyes, but she was still as beautiful as ever. The sun-kissed color of her hair had darkened over time and was now the color of burnished copper. It set off the chiseled features of her face. Her lips were still sensuous and inviting, but fine lines had started to form around the edges. "Yes," she said. "It's a family trait on my mother's side. Charles gets his dark looks from our father."

Another awkward moment passed between us. I cleared my throat. "I am truly sorry to hear of your father's passing," I said. "I know the two of you were very close."

When she spoke, her face conveyed the same strength and compassion that I had observed in the aftermath of the fire. "I came back to Chicago to care for Father several months ago when his health started to decline," she said. "Charles came a few weeks later."

"It must have been terribly difficult for you," I said.

Catherine nodded silently. Her eyes moistened and she looked away. When she returned her gaze to me, her eyes were dry and clear. "I'm afraid the bankruptcy took too heavy a toll on Father. Even though Charles has finally been able to satisfy most of the creditors, Father never fully recovered from the shame of it."

I hesitated to ask the question that was burning in my mind. "Will you be going back to New York with Charles after matters are taken care of here?"

She shook her head sadly. "No, Charles is planning to relocate here to be closer to the business. Now that the panic has subsided, there is more interest in expanding the line and promoting settlement in the northwest. Besides, New York is too noisy and congested for my taste."

"I could say the same of Chicago after so many years spent on the desolate plains of Iowa," I answered.

She smiled and my heart melted a little. She lowered her gaze to the hands folded neatly in her lap. "I received your messages telling me that you had been successful in stemming the grasshopper plague," she said. "But with Father so ill..." she let the words trail off.

"I quite understand," I said.

Catherine picked nervously at a loose thread on her sleeve. "Much has changed since we parted." she said, softly.

"I can see that," I answered. "But you're still as lovely as ever despite the difficulties you've been through."

"You're very kind," she answered, gracing me with another smile. "But you must fill me in on all that's happened with you since I saw you last."

Feeling myself on steadier ground, I launched into a description of how we had overcome the grasshopper plague. "We set up a syndicate with some of the large landowners in the area to handle the project. So far, things are working out quite well and we have been able to turn a profit on the land purchased from the railroad. I'm also anticipating a good harvest on my own property this year, and I've built a small wooden house." I paused, embarrassed by my rambling diatribe.

Catherine laughed softly. "My goodness!" she exclaimed. "You have been busy."

"I'm sorry to have gone on so about it." I said, sheepishly. "But what about you? Have you managed to recover from Gregor's betrayal?"

She paused and averted her eyes before continuing "When Father discovered that Gregor had swindled me out of Mother's inheritance, he hired a Pinkerton man to track him down, but

Gregor proved to be quite slippery. He was no sooner spotted in one city than he appeared in another. Shortly before Father died, the detective managed to find him and bring him back to Chicago."

The pronouncement startled me. Gregor had disappeared shortly after our confrontation in Jelle's office. When he left, he told us he was heading west to California. "I didn't know he was back in Chicago," I said.

"Charles has filed a lawsuit against him," she continued. "The judge has ordered him to meet with me to discuss a settlement. We have an appointment to meet tomorrow morning."

"Are you sure that's wise?" I asked. "I mean under the circumstances..."

Her eyes flared momentarily and there was a stubborn set to her jaw. "I know you think I'm foolish for pursuing this. But you must understand, Gregor took more from me than my inheritance, he also took my self-esteem and my honor. This is something I must see through to the end, whatever that may be. I cannot rest until I do."

I knew Catherine well enough to understand that once she made up her mind about something, there was no changing it, but still I was worried. "Gregor is still up to his old tricks," I said. "He showed up in Jelle's office a few months ago trying to sell some railroad land, under the name of James Dubolt. When he saw me, he renewed his threat to get the promissory note."

"You needn't worry," she said. "The note is safe where he can't get to it."

"It's not the safety of the note that I'm worried about."

"I assure you that I am quite cable of taking care of myself," she said, contritely.

"Of course!" I stammered. "I only urge you to be cautious. Emotions can often cloud reason, and Gregor can be quite ruthless. Will you at least promise me that you will not confront him alone?"

Catherine's shoulders relaxed, and the tension left her face. Her eyes softened and she reached out to touch my hand. For a moment, I caught a glimpse of the woman I had grown to love. "Please, try not to worry," she said. "If it will put your mind at ease, I promise not to go alone to meet with Gregor. If Charles is not available, I will ask Nathan to accompany me. He has remained a loyal friend to the family."

Charles returned with the tea. "Mrs. Jennings has taken Lily for her nap, so I'm afraid I will have to do the honors."

"I'll take care of it," Catherine said, reaching for the pot.

While she poured, Charles took a seat next to her. "I understand that you and Catherine met several years ago on the voyage over," he said.

"Yes. She was kind enough to help me with my English," I said, taking the teacup Catherine handed to me.

"Well, she must have been a good tutor. Your accent is barely detectable."

"Although I live in a Dutch community and my heritage is dear to me, I make it a point to speak English most of the time. America is my home now and I feel it's important to honor the customs of my new country."

Charles raised his cup to me. "Well said. So many immigrants seek out their own kind and never bother to learn the language and customs of America."

"Catherine wisely cautioned me against that same thing, and her words have stayed with me all this time."

"Hank was an excellent student and an extremely fast learner. One would think he had roots here before ever setting foot on American soil." Catherine's eyes twinkled mischievously, letting me in on the joke.

"I understand that you have been instrumental in stemming the grasshopper plague in that part of the country," Charles continued.

"We have formed a syndicate to address the problem. So far, our efforts have been quite successful, and settlers are beginning to return to the area."

"That's good news for the railroads, I'm sure," he said. "We've been concerned that the grasshoppers would move further north and affect the work we are doing on the Northwestern Pacific line. When it's finished, we will have a transcontinental route north through Canada to the Pacific that will open a whole new territory to settlement."

"Charles has reorganized Father's company and they are advancing the work that was put on hold during the panic years. He's taking a group of investors north in a few days to see the work that has already been completed."

"Your father must have been very proud to know that you are committed to continuing his legacy," I said.

"Yes," Catherine answered, with the slightest tinge of bitterness in her voice. "He was very proud of Charles."

Charles set his cup on the table. "I'm sorry to have to leave you so abruptly," he said, "but I have an urgent meeting downtown that demands my attention."

"I must be going as well," I said, rising.

"It was a pleasure meeting you," Charles said, extending his hand. "Catherine will see you out."

Catherine led me to the door after he had gone. "I'm glad you came," she said. "It's just that so much has changed since we parted. I'm still trying to sort things out."

"Do you think we will ever get back to where we were?" I asked, hopefully.

"Perhaps…in time." She gently touched the scar below my eye. She leaned in and her lips brushed softly against my cheek. I resisted the urge to pull her into my arms. I longed to hold her, to feel her skin next to mine, to taste the sweetness of her lips. I had reached out to Catherine in the hopes that we could rekindle our feelings for one another. The next move, if there was one, would be hers to make.

I was so lost in my own thoughts that I barely noticed the man who stepped out of the shadows behind me as I was leaving. His hat was pulled low over his eyes, and his collar was turned up against the early evening chill. He glanced up at the door from which I had taken my leave and stood for several seconds watching me before he turned and walked away in the opposite direction.

Jelle arrived in Chicago the next morning as I was having breakfast in my room. I poured him some coffee, but he didn't touch it. He was excited to share the news of his family in Wisconsin and how much the town of Alto had grown since he had departed over two years ago. I noticed that Jelle was sporting a new suit in the latest fashion. "Your uncle's business must be doing quite well from the looks of you," I said.

Jelle tugged at the sleeves of his new jacket. "The panic did impact his business, but things have picked up since then. I have no doubt that he will soon be back on his feet." he said. "But how was your visit with Catherine? Was she pleased to see you?"

"She didn't leave much hope of a reconciliation," I said, sadly. "I didn't stay long. Under the circumstances, it didn't seem appropriate to broach the subject of our relationship. Her brother was with her and a child that I assume was her niece."

"You mustn't give up hope. I'm sure she's still in mourning over the death of her father."

"I suppose you're right," I said. I took a drink of my coffee and let the dark liquid roll around my tongue before continuing. "She told me she had been in contact with Gregor. She seems determined to exact a settlement from him for cheating her out of her inheritance. I tried to talk her out of it, but she is a strong-willed woman and would not be deterred."

"Do you think she's in danger?" Jelle asked.

"I'm not sure," I answered. "I still don't trust him, but her mind was made up. She did, however, promise not to go alone." I finished my breakfast and we headed downstairs.

"I still have some papers to sign at the bank before we head back to Iowa," Jelle said. "I can meet you here later, if you like."

"That's fine," I answered. I stopped at the front desk on the way out to check for messages, hoping that Catherine might have reached out to me. I was surprised to find a young woman behind the counter instead of Nathan. "Where's Nathan?" I asked.

"He accompanied Miss Weller to a meeting early this morning. They should return any time now." She indicated the brocaded chairs lining the lobby. "You're welcome to wait if you like."

"No, thank you," I answered. "I will be leaving later this afternoon." I gave the girl my name and asked if there were any messages. She reached behind her to check the cubby holes for guest messages and handed me a note. "This was delivered by messenger a few minutes ago," she said.

I unfolded the note and felt a knot form in my stomach as I read the words written there.

You have something I want. Now I have something you want.
Another message will be delivered to the hotel later today giving you further

instructions for the exchange. Do not try to be a hero or Catherine will suffer the consequences.

Signed, G.V.P.

I folded the note with trembling hands. "When did this arrive?" I asked the girl. "Did you see who delivered it?"

She shrugged, helplessly. "I really didn't pay much attention. It was just a runner from the telegraph office."

I turned to Jelle in a panic. My words came in short gasps while I struggled to explain. "It's from Gregor," I stammered. "He is after the promissory note. He has taken Catherine hostage. I'm afraid her life may be in danger."

"Are you sure?" Jelle asked. I handed him the note without answering.

"Can you direct me to the nearest telegraph office?" I asked the girl behind the counter.

She gave me directions to the office a few blocks away. I left Jelle to keep watch in case another message was delivered and ran out the door. The streets were alive with early morning shoppers and businessmen hurrying to the first meeting of the day. I pushed my way through the crowds disregarding their protests. Shock and fear had grown to a burning anger in the pit of my stomach. My worst nightmare was coming true!

I arrived at the telegraph office red-faced and breathless. I pushed my way to the front of the line and shoved the note under the operator's nose. "Can you tell me who sent this?"

At first the man was irritated at my impatience, but seeing the alarm on my face, he quickly glanced over the telegram I handed him. "I remember this," he answered. "It was Nathan, the desk clerk at the hotel a few blocks from here. He looked wide-eyed and nervous when he came in. I asked him if anything was wrong, but he wouldn't say."

"Is there any way I can send a reply?"

"You can leave a message here in case he drops by again. But if you don't know where to send it, I'm afraid I can't be of much help."

Filled with hopelessness and despair, I grew more frightened and anxious by the minute. "This can't be happening again!" I thought. Instead of Lainie, Catherine's life was now in danger, and it was my fault! There had to be a way to stop this! I left the telegraph office and made my way back to the hotel, each step requiring a

Herculean effort. My vision blurred and I staggered into people who irritably pushed me aside. Several times, I nearly fell to my knees, but I managed to steady myself against the side of the buildings I passed.

Jelle met me at the door. "Any luck?" he asked.

I shook my head and collapsed into the nearest chair. "Gregor has sworn to do whatever it takes to get the note from me. Catherine is the only other person who knows how to access it"

"Where is it?" Jelle asked, sitting down beside me.

"Catherine secured it in the vault at the bank. It is obvious that Gregor will go to any lengths to get it." I rose unsteadily and started for the door. "Nothing is worth putting Catherine's life in danger! I'm going to retrieve the note from the bank so I will be ready to make the exchange when he contacts me again."

"I'll go with you." Jelle said, coming toward me. "We'll leave word where we can be reached if another message comes in."

I approached the desk where the girl was absently thumbing through a lady's journal. "I am expecting an important message," I said. I glanced at Jelle who was already waiting at the door. "This gentleman and I have some other business to attend to, but we will return shortly. If a messenger arrives, please detain him so I can send a reply."

The girl glanced at me with a disinterested look and nodded without comment. I hoped she understood the gravity of the situation, but I was reluctant to share anything more. When we returned several hours later, there was still no word from Gregor. Jelle and I took turns pacing the floor in the lobby in case a messenger arrived. But as the day wore on, my hopes grew dimmer by the moment.

19

By nightfall, we still had not heard from Gregor. Jelle urged me to get some rest while he took a shift in the lobby, but it was no use. Each time I closed my eyes, visions of Lainie face down in the river floated just behind my eyelids. But when I pulled her from the water, it was not Lainie, but Catherine whose cold dead eyes stared back at me. My mind whirled with the possibilities. Was Catherine alive or dead? And what of Nathan? The telegraph operator said he had sent the original message. Was he in on Gregor's scheme? Or was he merely a pawn, easily disposed of when he was no longer useful?

The message arrived later that evening by post instead of telegraph. I gasped when I tore open the letter, and a lock of copper-colored hair fell into my hands. I immediately recognized Catherine's feminine slanted handwriting. My heart caught in my throat as I read.

My Dearest Hank,

By now you know that I am in the hands of Gregor Van Pelt. There is so much I want to say to you, but Gregor has insisted that I write only the words he dictates. He wants me to assure you that I am alive and unharmed, but that you must follow these instructions carefully if you wish to see me alive again.

Place the letters and the promissory note in a saddlebag and take the eleven o'clock train this evening toward Aurora. Come alone and unarmed. It is about a two-hour journey from where you are to the Batavia Junction water stop. It is a small station with no accommodations nearby, and the area is easily visible from all directions, so it would not be in your best interest to try something foolish here. Get off there and wait for us. Do not waiver from these instructions or you will put my life in danger.

Yours, Catherine

Wordlessly, I handed the note to Jelle. He furrowed his brow and made several incomprehensible sounds as he read it over. Then he handed it back to me. "I'll go there immediately and wait for them," I said.

I started to rise, but he grabbed my arm restraining me. "Wait!" Jelle said, and the urgency in his voice stopped me in my tracks. "What's to prevent him from killing you both once he has the note?"

I turned to face him. "It's a chance I'll have to take."

"You're not thinking clearly. You must consider your response carefully to make sure that he releases Catherine safely."

"I'm giving him the note!" I exclaimed. "Nothing is worth risking Catherine's life."

"Be reasonable," Jelle pleaded. "You have no guarantees that she is still alive. You need some assurance that she is unharmed before you hand over the note."

I wrenched myself free from his grasp. "Catherine has been kidnapped because of me. I will not endanger her life further by disobeying his instructions."

"Perhaps we should call the authorities," he said.

"Don't be a fool! Their involvement would only make things worse."

"Then I'm coming with you," he said.

I shook my head. "The letter stipulates that I am to come alone if I want no harm to come to Catherine."

"The letter looks to be a woman's handwriting. Can you confirm that it is Catherine's?"

I nodded. "I would recognize it anywhere."

"Well, at least we know she was alive and well when this was written." Jelle paused, while he applied his logical mind to the situation. "Gregor seems a clever sort. He has to know that you will insist on seeing that she is still in good condition before you hand over the note."

"I will make sure of it."

He reached inside his coat and produced the small silver revolver he had shown me in his office. "Gregor will most certainly be armed," he said. "I know the note says to come unarmed, but this is easily concealed in a coat pocket. It will help to even the odds against you."

I shook my head. "I can't take that chance. Gregor is ruthless. If he thinks I am armed, he will not hesitate to kill for what he wants. My only hope for Catherine's safe release is to do as he says."

"Don't be foolish! He could still kill you both and take the documents."

I was not to be moved by his logic. Catherine's safety was of utmost concern. "I understand the risks, but it's a chance I'll have to take."

"I still think I should come with you."

"No, I need to do this on my own. If Gregor knows you are with me, he may turn his anger toward you. I can't risk putting you in danger as well."

But Jelle was adamant. "I insist on coming along as far as Lisle. I can change trains there and return to the hotel to await your return." Seeing that he was not to be deterred, I finally agreed to the plan.

We still had two more hours before the departure of the 11 o'clock train to Aurora. Jelle did his best to keep me occupied while we waited for the time to pass. I let him talk but made few comments in return. Finally, he fell silent and left me to my thoughts. I went over Gregor's instructions in my mind until I could recite them by heart. I wanted to ensure that the exchange went well and that no harm would come to Catherine in the process.

When Jelle spoke again, his voice was soft and pensive. "Do you remember when we first met on the ship out of Rotterdam?" he asked.

I could not help but smile. "You were very scared, as I recall."

"Yes, and you took me under your wing and stayed by me on the journey. You even kept me from making a bad decision when Lubbert tried to cheat me out of my money on our first night in America."

"You were pretty naïve," I chuckled.

"I don't think I ever properly thanked you for coming to my rescue when my money was stolen on the train in Philadelphia," Jelle said.

"Given the thriving nature of your business and our success with the Grasshopper Syndicate, I'd say that was a good investment."

"America has been good to me," he said. "I owe you for that. When you helped me after my money was stolen, I was able to save my uncle and his family from ruin. Not only is his business doing well, but I have also established a successful business of my own." He paused and there was no mistaking the compassion in his voice when he continued. "I just hope your situation turns out as well."

"I plan to do everything in my power to ensure that it does," I answered.

Jelle was silent for several minutes, as if searching for the right words. "There is something I've been meaning to ask you," he said. "When you confronted Gregor in my office, he accused you of some pretty terrible things in your former life. He mentioned a man named Van Huel," Jelle continued. "I took it upon myself to do some research of my own after he left. All I know is that he runs a financial house in Arnhem in the Netherlands that is heavily invested in the Des Moines Valley Railroad."

I felt a door slam shut in my mind. I had not shared that part of my past with anyone since coming to America. As far as anyone knew, I was simply another immigrant hoping to improve my economic prospects in America. Gregor had brought the past out of hiding and there was no escape but to face it head on. I closed my eyes and forced the images to the surface that I had tried so hard to suppress.

"I suppose I owe that to you," I said at last. I took a deep breath to gather my thoughts. "I came to America to escape the past, but it seems to have followed me and will not allow me any peace until I put it to rest." I had never put my feelings about the past into words, and I now found it difficult to know where to begin. "Dirk's father was a member of the wealthy ruling class in Gelderland," I began. "Dirk had ambitions to become the next Governor. When his father promised his sister, Lainie, to the Governor's nephew in marriage, it appeared that his future was set."

"But Lainie was in love with you?"

"Lainie and I were very much in love, but I could not provide her the life she was accustomed to. I tried to convince her that our only chance at happiness lay in emigration, but her father was in failing health and she refused to leave him."

Jelle shook his head. "The situation sounds hopeless."

"Lainie and I continued to sneak away together hoping that things would eventually work out for us. When she became pregnant, I thought I could finally convince her to come away with me. But it only hardened her resolve to go through with the arranged marriage."

"Did Dirk and her father know about the pregnancy?"

"No. It was still early, and she hadn't started to show yet. When her father discovered that we were still seeing each other, he confronted me, and we argued. I shoved him and he fell. When I realized what I had done, I was horrified. I ran away and left him lying there gasping for breath and clutching his chest. He died a short time later."

"It was surely an accident. You can't be blamed for that."

"He had been in failing health for some time. But Lainie and Dirk blamed me. Lanie refused to see me again and Dirk made sure of it."

"So, you never saw her again?" Jelle asked.

"On the day before she was to be married to the Governor's nephew, I waited outside her house until she finally came out," I continued. "We argued. I threatened to reveal our child's true birthright if she went through with the marriage. She told me that she loved me, but it was her father's last wish that she go through with the wedding. She had no choice."

"Is that why you left?"

I took a deep breath to gather my courage. "I told her she was being foolish. There was always a choice. I begged her to meet me that night so we could leave together." I shook my head to clear away the painful memory. "I waited until long after dark, but she never came. Later that night, a terrible storm caused the river to rise and flood the town. The next morning, when I discovered that she was missing, I joined the search to find her. I found her body tangled in the debris left by the storm not far from where we were to meet."

"That must have been terrible, but you can't blame yourself for the choice she made."

I choked back a sob. "Don't you see? I forced her to make a choice. She and our child would both be alive today if not for me."

Jelle placed his hand on my arm to comfort me, but I withdrew from him. "You've been carrying around this guilt for too long," he said. "It has kept you from finding your own happiness in life. You can never move forward until you let it go." Jelle's advice was well-meaning, but the past was deeply rooted and not easily left behind. Every setback and disappointment I had suffered since Lainie's death only served as a reminder of my guilt. And now it seemed as if the past was repeating itself. But I could not let that happen.

#

It was almost time to leave for the station. Although all my senses were heightened, I felt strangely calm. I needed to keep my wits about me if I were to outwit Gregor and bring Catherine home safely.

At last, it was time to go. I tucked the packet into the saddlebag and went directly to the station. While I waited anxiously for the train to pull into the station, Jelle loitered nearby and did his best to ignore me. When the train finally arrived, I boarded ahead of Jelle. He followed shortly thereafter to avoid the appearance of our traveling together. Once on board, I found a seat next to a window and placed my hat on the vacant seat next to me. He boarded a few minutes later.

"Is this seat taken?" he asked, pretending we were casual strangers. I said nothing, but I removed my hat so he could take the seat beside me. He opened a newspaper and appeared engrossed in reading while I gazed out my window into the darkness. The countryside passed in a blur of ominous black and gray shadows. Occasionally, a silver sliver of moonlight pierced the overcast sky causing the shadows to gyrate crazily as we passed. Soon, large droplets of rain began to land against the window and run in tearful rivulets down the pane. I closed my eyes and it was not long before the gentle sound of the rain and rhythmic click of the wheels on the rails lulled me into a troubled sleep.

When the day of Lainie's wedding arrived, I was depressed beyond belief. It had been raining for days, big heavy drops that pounded the ground and filled the rivers and canals to overflowing. Small rivers turned into raging torrents. Hurricane force winds raged over the Dutch coast funneling water through the narrow canals and flooding the lowlands. The spring tide was already perilously high and served to increase the force of the water even more. The peak high waters occurred during the night when most of the people were asleep. We were awakened in the early morning hours by the sound of church bells and people running door to door to alert us to the danger of the flood. We began frantically working to move livestock and equipment to higher ground.

By *midmorning, the skies had cleared, and we began surveying the damage. A newborn calf had been swept away in the flood waters and several goats were missing. Some of the outbuildings were damaged, but nothing that was beyond repair. Unfortunately, some of our neighbors had not fared as well. An entire family was lost when they tried to escape the rushing water in a small raft.*

Once I determined that we were all safe, Father and I made our way into town to see if we could assist with the clean-up there. That is when I heard that Lainie was missing. As news of her disappearance spread through the village, my first thought was that she had finally come to her senses and decided not to go through with the wedding. But hope turned to despair when I realized that she would surely have tried to contact me if that were the case.

Dirk snarled at me when I approached and offered to join in the search. "I wouldn't be surprised if you weren't behind this. You probably have her hidden away someplace and just want to throw us off the trail."

"I assure you I had nothing to do with Lainie's disappearance. I want nothing more than to see her safe and sound."

Dirk eyed me suspiciously. He surveyed the motley group of men and boys that had volunteered to help with the search. None of them looked up to the task. Every able-bodied man was already at work clearing the debris and could not be spared. "Alright, but I want you to stay close to me where I can keep an eye on you. And follow my directions or I'll have you arrested."

Dirk divided us into two groups. He assigned one group to go with Lainie's fiancé and search every building in the town. Dirk led the rest of the group on horseback to search the woodlands near the river. I fell in behind on foot with the rest of the search party. A nagging thought kept telling me that the effort was futile. Lainie would not have gone without leaving word for me. And there was only one place I could think of where she would have left a message.

As we approached the river, Dirk directed us to fan out and search along the banks for any sign of her. I headed to the large oak tree that had been our special spot. I half expected to find her there waiting for me. However, the river had breached its banks and the gentle stream that had orchestrated our lovemaking was now an angry torrent. It rushed along its banks dragging tree branches and debris in a mad dash downstream.

I searched along the banks of the river, but there was no sign of Lainie. Just as I was about to turn away, a golden shimmer of sunlight revealed something tangled in the debris where a log jam had developed. I tied my belt around a tree stump to anchor me and waded out as far as I could. Then I caught sight of flaxen hair floating amongst the branches.

"Over here!" I yelled, trying to get the attention of the searchers. "She's over here!"

The searchers arrived and we formed a human chain to reach Lainie. I disentangled her from the clogged branches and debris. I held her cold, lifeless body in my arms as the searchers pulled us to shore.

"Oh, God! Lainie! No!" I wailed.

Just then a hand touched my shoulder and I awoke with a start. "Hank," Jelle said. "Wake up. You were dreaming." I awoke with a start, disoriented and unsure of my surroundings. The jerk and the screech of the rails signaled that the train was coming to a stop. "This is where I get off," Jelle said. He gathered his things and moved into the aisle. His eyes clouded with concern. "Are you sure you don't want me to come with you?"

I shook myself fully awake. "I'll be fine," I answered, rising to shake his hand. Then in a louder voice lest someone was listening, "Godspeed you on your journey." He nodded solemnly and joined the other passengers disembarking at the station in Lisle.

20

The train ground to a halt at Batavia Junction with a groan and a sigh. An elderly couple exited ahead of me, holding onto each other for support. They hobbled off into the darkness leaving me alone on the platform. There was no sign of Gregor and Catherine. The rain had stopped, but dampness still hung heavy in the air. I sat down on a bench to wait. It seemed like an eternity passed before I finally heard Gregor's voice in the darkness.

"Do you have the note?" I started to turn and face the direction of his voice. "Don't turn around!" he ordered. "Let me see it."

I stood up and I held out the saddlebag. "It's all here. Just as you instructed," I said into the darkness.

"Take it out and show it to me."

I turned in the direction of his voice. "Let me see Catherine first."

Gregor emerged from the darkness, pushing Catherine before him. Her hands were tied behind her back and her hair hung loosely around her shoulders. She looked haggard and stressed. He shoved her forward and she fell onto the platform. I started to move toward her. "Don't!" she said. "He will not hesitate to kill you!"

Gregor moved forward and produced a pistol and held it to her head. "I would do as she says," he said.

I held up the saddlebag. "I've done as you requested. I've come alone and unarmed." I started to open my coat so that he could see that I carried no concealed weapons.

"Slowly!" he said. "And keep your hands where I can see them."

"You can see that I've kept my end of the bargain. Now let Catherine go." I held out the saddlebag, but he made no move to take it.

"Not so fast. Open it and show me the documents."

I removed the documents and held them up for him to see but made no move toward him.

"Bring them closer so I can see," he ordered.

"How do I know that you won't kill us both once you have what you want?"

He made a sound deep in his throat, somewhere between a chuckle and a guffaw. "I guess that's a chance you'll have to take." He cocked the pistol at Catherine's head, and she stared at me wide-eyed with fear.

A rustle of the bushes behind us diverted our attention momentarily. I saw the dark outline of a familiar shape and the glint of a silver pistol. "Jelle! No!" I screamed.

In one swift movement, Gregor turned in the direction of the sound and fired his pistol into the darkness. I heard Jelle moan and saw his body crash through the bushes onto the platform. The silver pistol slid out of reach in the darkness. Jelle's face registered a mixture of surprise and pain. A red stain began to spread across his chest.

Seeing Jelle mortally wounded ignited all the rage I had contained for so long: anger toward Dirk, anger toward Gregor, anger toward God. My fury was so great that it blocked all sense of reason. I dropped the saddlebag and hurled my body toward Gregor, knocking the pistol from his hand. It went skittering off into the bushes. He rolled aside and scrambled away from me. As he got to his feet, he grabbed the saddlebag I had dropped and tried to run.

I grabbed him again and landed a solid blow to the side of his jaw. He stumbled but managed to regain his footing. He reached inside his coat and produced a knife. He took several swipes at me without dropping the saddlebag, but I managed to sidestep them. His face blurred in front of me. The Beast was in control now and it wanted blood.

I grabbed his arm, and the knife grazed my cheek. I tasted the warm stickiness of blood as it dripped into the corners of my mouth. I held onto his arm as we tumbled to the platform. The saddlebag fell onto the tracks. In the distance I heard the long, low whistle of the Express on its way into Chicago with its load of commuters from Naperville.

While I wrestled with Gregor for the knife, I caught a glimpse of Catherine who had crawled away from us and now sat next to Jelle, her hands still tied behind her back. The image infuriated me even further. Gregor had reopened old wounds, and now they cried for revenge. I summoned all the strength I could muster and threw my body to the side knocking the knife from his hand.

But the effort had thrown me off balance and Gregor managed to slide away from me. The train whistled louder as the Express barreled toward us. I regained my balance and started toward him again. We were both unarmed, but I was larger. I was also fueled by emotion rather than greed. The saddlebag still lay on the tracks where it had fallen.

Gregor hesitated momentarily weighing his options. If he could grab the saddlebag and jump to the other side of the tracks before the train passed the station, it would allow him time to escape. He would have to time it perfectly so that the passing train would keep me from following him. There wasn't much time. The train was almost upon us. I could see the conductor leaning out of the cab waving us out of the way. Reason was slowly seeping back into my mind. I could read the determination in Gregor's eyes. "Don't do it!" I said.

Without a word, Gregor smiled thinly and jumped onto the track. But the platform was higher than he anticipated causing him to stumble when he landed. His recovery cost him precious seconds. He picked up the saddlebag and got to his feet just as the train reached him. The saddlebag erupted into the air. The papers scattered and disintegrated in the heat of the steam engine. I watched as the envelope containing the promissory note floated gently in lazy arcs before an errant spark set it aflame. The high-pitched scream of metal on metal filled the air as the train ground to a halt.

I turned away from the scene and hurried to where Jelle and Catherine lay. I untied Catherine's hands and she cradled Jelle's head in her lap. His eyes fluttered open when I spoke to him. "I told you not to come," I said, choking back my emotions.

He smiled weakly. His voice came with great effort and he had to pause often for breath. "I'm sorry," he gasped. "I just wanted to help."

"It was a stupid move," I said, trying to stem the flow of the red blotch that was spreading on his chest. But when I opened his shirt, it was evident that my efforts were in vain.

Jelle smiled weakly and his voice came in gasps. "For someone who is usually quite rational and self-assured,...I knew you were thinking with your heart and not your head...There was no way...Gregor would have allowed you and Catherine to walk away...I knew you were walking into a trap." He winced in pain and a trickle of blood formed at the corner of his mouth. His next words were barely above a whisper. "Besides, I owed you one." He closed his eyes and licked his lips, "I'm so thirsty," he said softly. Then he released his breath in one long exhale and said no more.

The sun was already casting its early morning shadows across the horizon by the time the authorities finished questioning us and the bodies had been removed. The engineer corroborated the fact that Gregor had jumped in front of the train at the last moment. He had not seen him shoot Jelle, but there seemed little doubt when the two guns were examined and Jelle's pistol had not been fired.

Catherine and I took the train back to Chicago as soon as we were released. We were exhausted and relieved when we were finally left alone to deal with our grief. We rode in silence most of the way. There was nothing left to say. Catherine's eyes were red and swollen, but she had finally exhausted her tears. I held Catherine's hands and tried to sort out my own feelings. Catherine had almost been killed and Jelle had given his life for us. I felt an overwhelming sense of guilt that I had once again caused the death of someone I cared about.

Catherine's voice interrupted my thoughts. "I'm sorry about the promissory note. Now you have nothing to link you to the Van Pelt claim."

I had barely thought of the note since the incident ended. Given everything that had happened, I wasn't sure how I felt about it. "It was just a piece of paper," I said. "I never thought of it as a link to family. I'm more upset about losing Jelle. He was more like family than anyone else in America."

"But your inheritance…" she began. "You have as much right to it as anyone else."

"My inheritance is more than a promise to repay a hundred-year old debt," I said, thoughtfully. "My inheritance is the freedom and independence that promise provided. If Washington had not received the aid he needed, his army would have perished. And this nation might never have come to be. The fact that I am here, and I can prosper as an independent landowner is my real inheritance."

"I never thought of it that way," Catherine answered. "I only thought of inheritance as something tangible like the money my mother left me."

"Don't you see?" I asked. "She left you more than money. She left you strength and an independent spirit. You were very brave to confront Gregor like you did."

"I don't think bravery had anything to do with it. It was just supposed to be a business meeting to discuss a settlement for my lawsuit. Looking back, I can see how foolish I was to think I could trust him…how many lives I put in danger." Her eyes glistened with tears. "And poor Nathan and Jelle! They only wanted to protect us and look at what happened." She began to sob again. I put my arms around her. I felt helpless. There was nothing I could do to ease her pain, and it only amplified my own grief.

I envied her ability to relieve her grief through tears. I had kept mine bottled up all these years, grieving in private. Talking openly about my pain only made it worse. I needed quiet space alone. But would she understand that?

By the time we arrived back at the station in Chicago, the morning sun was already high in the sky. It promised to be one of those bright Indian Summer days when the warm sun teased young lovers to enjoy the last picnic of the year. The trees wore the brilliant reds and golds of late autumn and there was just a hint of chill in the air. The sound of laughter mingled with the noise of the city and set my nerves on edge. Jelle's coffin lay draped in black far back in one of the train cars. And yet, life went on.

I shaded my eyes from the bright glare of the sun as I helped Catherine from the train. Charles Weller met us at the depot. He looked tired and haggard. His shoulders were stooped, and his eyes were lined with worry. Catherine rushed into his arms and dissolved into tears while I stood by helplessly.

"My darling sister," he said, stroking her hair. "I've been so worried. When they fished Nathan's body out of the river, I feared the worst."

"Poor Nathan," Catherine sobbed. "He tried to protect me, but Gregor was ruthless. If it had not been for Hank and Jelle, he might have killed me too."

Charles finally looked up to acknowledge my presence. "Jelle?" he asked, confusion clouding his eyes.

"My business partner," I answered, swallowing hard, "and my friend. He followed me against my wishes. But his intervention ultimately saved us both. Unfortunately, he did not survive. I'm accompanying his body to Wisconsin to be buried with his family." These last words were delivered with much effort.

Charles held out his hand to me. "Thank you for saving Catherine's life," he said. "I don't know how I can ever repay you. But you must at least let me provide you with a place to rest and something to eat before you continue your journey."

"I appreciate the offer, but I really must be on my way."

Catherine disentangled herself from her brother and gazed up at him through tearful eyes. "Charles, can you give us a few minutes?"

"Of course." He moved away to a discrete distance to allow us some privacy.

"When will I see you again?" Catherine asked me.

"I don't know. I have much to think about. I cannot help but feel a sense of responsibility for everything that has happened. My best friend is dead and the woman I love was nearly killed. Not to mention the loss of a perfectly innocent young man whose only crime was trying to help you."

"None of this was your fault. It was my own stubbornness that led me to confront Gregor and fall into his trap. I'm as guilty in this matter as anyone."

"But if I had never approached the Van Pelt's with the information about my heritage, none of this would have happened. There would have been no need for him to use you as ransom for the note."

"I put myself in harm's way," she argued. "I should never have agreed to meet with him. It was my father who initially insisted that I speak with Gregor about investing in his company. The Van Pelts had been clients for many years. He had no reason not to trust him."

"But when Gregor discovered that I cared about you, he saw an opportunity to use you to get the promissory note from me."

Catherine shook her head. "If it had not been me, it could just as easily have been Jelle. Didn't you say Gregor had recently met with Jelle to sell him some railroad land? He was probably planning yet another scheme to force you to give up the note."

"I hadn't thought of that."

Her soft gray eyes held a look of pleading. "Fate is a result of events beyond our control. We must not lose hope. Together we can help each other heal."

I took her hands and gazed into her eyes. How could we possibly find happiness together if we both carried this burden into the relationship? I could see nothing but sadness in our future. "I know you mean well," I said, "but I must have time to sort out my feelings on my own. And you must think of your own family. Charles needs you as well."

Catherine blinked away her tears. "I'm not sure I'm strong enough to deal with this on my own."

I wiped a tear from her eye. "You will find strength by leaning on each other. Besides, there is the child to think of. She needs you both now more than ever."

Catherine's eyes widened and she set her jaw in a stubborn line. "Is that why you're leaving me?" she asked. Her voice held a mixture of hurt and anger and she took a step away from me. "Because of the child?"

"Of course not!" I exclaimed. "Catherine, there is nothing I want more than for us to be together with children of our own, but you are still mourning the death of your father. Your emotions are raw. You need time to heal."

Tears formed at the corners of her eyes, but she blinked them away. "There is something I need to tell you...," she said softly, but the train's whistle interrupted her.

"I must go." I took her in my arms and kissed her. "It is my greatest hope that we can one day be together," I said. "But grief has no deadline. We will have to see what the future holds for us." The engineer blasted his whistle again, signaling the train's departure, and I stepped back onto the platform just as it began to move away.

She was still standing where I had left her as the train pulled away from the station. She was silhouetted against the sky with her hair blowing loosely around her face and rivers of tears flowing silently down her cheeks. I raised my hand in farewell, but she did not move. Charles came up behind her. He put his arms around her, and she allowed him to lead her away. It was not until she was completely out of sight that I allowed myself the comfort of my own tears.

PART III

True love does have the power to redeem, but only if we are ready for redemption. Love saves us only if we are ready to be saved. — bell hooks

21

I turned my grief inward during the long, lonely train ride to Wisconsin with Jelle's body. While the train rumbled on, I wallowed in loneliness and self-pity, trapped in my own unbreakable bubble. I glanced up briefly when a sad, old man, bent from years of care, boarded the train at one of the nondescript water stops along the way. He made his way slowly down the aisle and stopped next to me. I made a conscious effort not to make eye contact with him and to look as uninviting as possible. Nevertheless, I heard him speak in a soft voice, crackling with age. "Do you mind if I sit here?"

Without speaking, I moved aside the parcel I had placed on the seat to discourage such a request. He sat down heavily and sighed as if the act had taken every bit of his strength. "I don't get around as well as I used to," he said, through gasps of breath. Once again, I nodded without looking in his direction.

We rode in silence while the countryside streamed by in rivers of brown and gold. Father had preached that the dying leaves were all part of God's plan for rebirth and renewal, but I found no comfort in God's Grand Plan. I still believed that if I had done things differently, I could have not only prevented Jelle's death, but also kept Catherine out of danger. I could not accept that sometimes things happen that are completely outside of our control.

Finally, the old man spoke again. "What is it you're running from, young man?" he asked.

His question shocked me. "What makes you think I'm running?" I asked.

"You are alone and burdened with sadness," he said. "You are obviously running from whatever it is that caused it."

"I'm accompanying my friend's body to be buried in Wisconsin with his family," I answered, curtly. "I guess that gives me a right to feel sad."

The old man nodded. "The loss of a friend is certainly cause for sorrow," he said. "It exposes our vulnerability and makes us shy away from new relationships." When I didn't respond, he continued. "When I was a young man, I was anxious and afraid that any new relationship would end in another disheartening or stressful encounter. It was just easier to avoid it altogether." He paused as if the mere act of speaking had exhausted his energy reserves. After a few minutes of silence, he began again. "After a while, it became a self-fulfilling prophecy, a kind of vicious circle, and it caused me to be extremely lonely." He fell silent again and his breathing was hardly noticeable.

I glanced at him and his eyes fluttered open. "What did you do about it?" I asked. "About the loneliness?"

The old man smiled weakly and I noticed for the first time, his rheumy eyes, and liver-spotted hands. "I took a good hard look inside myself. I thought about all my strengths and limitations and I accepted them."

"But you were still alone," I said.

"Yes, but I was in control of how I felt about it," he said. "I even started to enjoy my own company." He turned to face me. "I learned that until you learn to love yourself, you can never truly love someone else."

He closed his eyes and leaned back in his seat. His breathing became deeper and more regular. He began to snore softly. I leaned back in my seat and watched as darkness embraced the land like an old friend. Since leaving my homeland, I had resisted the idea of relying on others, insisting on making my own way in America. When things did not go my way, I had only myself and God to blame. I had convinced myself that I was unworthy of anyone's friendship or love. However, Jelle had seen beyond my own self-loathing and found something in me that was worthy of his friendship and sacrifice. I just didn't know what it was.

≠

Mourners came from all around for Jelle's funeral. He was obviously well-known and loved by the people in the community. I tried to block out my own emotions and provide some degree of comfort to Jelle's family, but the strain of suppressing my own grief was almost too much to bear. I left shortly after the funeral with the excuse that I needed to return to Iowa to settle his affairs there.

I upgraded to a first-class compartment on the way back to Iowa so I could be alone, away from the noise and the intruding conversations of other passengers. I had no regrets about what had happened to Gregor. He was an evil man motivated by greed. But my chest tightened painfully when I thought of Catherine. She had nearly been killed! Although Catherine and I had left our relationship unresolved, I believed that her feelings for me were as deep as mine for her. I just could not bring myself to act on them until I could put Jelle's death behind me.

I arrived in Orange City to find that news of Jelle's death had preceded me. The whole town was in mourning. Abraham met me at the station. He clasped my hand and greeted me with compassion. "I am truly sorry to hear of Jelle's death," he said. "He was a good man and fine businessman. He was an asset to the community, and we will all miss him."

"He was a good and loyal friend," I added, swallowing the lump that rose in my throat. "He sacrificed his life to save ours."

Abraham nodded in understanding. "I know that you feel responsible for Jelle's death," he said. "But that's the thing about freewill. Every decision we make is a choice against something as much as it is a choice for something else. Jelle made a conscious choice to try to intervene to save your life. It was his right to do so. You mustn't take that away from him by assuming guilt for his choice."

Jelle had said as much to me when I shared my guilt over Lainie's death. "Sometimes I think that the universe is so unpredictable and chaotic that we have no control over our own fate." I said.

"Jelle's freewill led him to make the choice that ultimately determined his fate." Abraham answered. "We have control over the choices we make in life, but we are not free to choose the consequences."

"Perhaps you're right," I answered, "but that doesn't take away the guilt."

We arrived at Jelle's office to find it shuttered and dark. After a few seconds of hesitation, Abraham cleared his throat. "I'm afraid that Jelle's death has left us in a bit of a jam."

"What do you mean?"

"With the land now cleared of grasshoppers, many of the settlers who had been hired to clear the land are now eager to it Ifor their own homesteads. They have come to me asking about mortgages."

"We'll have to refer them to the bank in Sioux City until we can get things sorted out," I said.

"I'm afraid there's more," Abraham continued. "When news of Jelle's death reached the railroad company, they became concerned about the payments on the land the syndicate had purchased from them. They are sending a representative to audit our accounts. He should arrive in a few days."

"I'm sure Jelle left things in order and Richard has all the records up-to-date."

"Let's hope so," Abraham said. "I left the business of running the syndicate entirely in Jelle's hands while I worked with the teams to clear the land." He paused before continuing. "Nevertheless, I think we should plan to meet with Richard to go over things. The syndicate members are already anxious about Jelle's passing. We can't afford any surprises."

I nodded in agreement. "I'll plan to see him first thing in the morning."

The next morning, I stood in the doorway of Jelle's office for several minutes trying to erase the image of Jelle at his desk. The room smelled musty and everything was covered with dust. Papers were haphazardly scattered over his desk. It was obvious that it would take time to straighten everything out. I spent the remainder of the day with Jelle's clerk, Richard Hendrickson, sorting paperwork and trying to make sense of Jelle's scribbles. We were finally able to piece together enough information to see that Jelle had set up a separate account so that the payments he received for the sale of the land to settlers would go directly to the railroad. He had another account for the interest he collected and used to reinvest for the syndicate. It was a simple system, but everything seemed to be in order.

I called a meeting of the syndicate to inform them of the audit. Several of the members had mortgaged their own lands to help finance the operation. "Are you sure everything is in order," asked John Klein, one of the bankers from Sioux City and the self-appointed spokesman for the group. He was a pompous man with a round face and large jowls that wobbled back and forth when he spoke. Although his voice was not commanding, he spoke with a thoughtfulness that made others listen. His bank had invested heavily in the syndicate and held the majority of shares.

"Abraham and I have reviewed the documents with Richard, and he has assured me that when the auditor arrives, he will be ready for him," I answered.

"I hope you're right," added Eldon Sweeney. "I've staked my farm on the success of this venture. I can't afford to lose it." Sweeney was one of the largest landowners in Sioux County. He was not a tall man, but what he lacked in stature, he made up for in bravado. His voice often carried above the others and was quieted only by Abraham's calm logic. Sweeney prided himself on his common roots and usually arrived at syndicate meetings looking as if he had just come in from the fields. He had been influential in convincing the new settlers to remain and farm the land they had cleared for us. His reputation was at stake if things did not go as well as we hoped.

"I promise to do everything in my power to see that the auditor is satisfied." I said. "There is no need for anyone to worry."

Nevertheless, a rumble of concern rolled through those assembled. Abraham stepped forward. "You all know me," he began in his calm, clear voice. "I have as much invested in this operation as anyone here. I put my trust in Jelle's good judgement and his management skills. I continue to put my faith in the man I knew. I think all of you should as well."

Sweeney was not so easily convinced. He puffed up like an adder and boomed out in a threatening voice, "Well, it will fall on your head if there is a problem, so you had better hope that Jelle was as good as you say he was!"

"Now, Eldon," Klein said, in his sensible, reassuring voice. "Abraham is right. Until we hear otherwise, we must remain calm and trust that everything is as it should be."

"I promise to keep you all informed as things progress," I said. "This is not a setback; it's just growing pains."

The meeting ended on a cautious note. They had trusted Jelle to manage their affairs and they had no reason to doubt him now. There was nothing to do now but wait for the results. When everyone had gone, I turned to Abraham. "Do you really believe what you told the others?" I asked. "About trusting Jelle's judgement?"

"Absolutely," he answered.

Harold Stanford arrived a few weeks later. He was a small, bespectacled man dressed in a tweed suit and vest with a derby hat perched atop his head. He carried a case in one hand and a handkerchief in the other. He stopped on the platform and looked anxiously about. He blew his nose noisily into his handkerchief and nervously checked his pocket watch.

"Mr. Stanford?" I asked, approaching him.

"Yes," he answered, ignoring my outstretched palm. "What is this god-forsaken place?"

"Welcome to Orange City, Iowa. If you'll follow me, I'll let you drop your bags at the hotel and then we can proceed to the syndicate office."

I picked up the bags left by the conductor and started down the street with Stanford in tow. He sneezed several times before we arrived at the hotel. He checked in and left his bag to be taken up to his room; then he insisted on going directly to Jelle's office.

"Let's get on with it," he said. "The sooner I can clear this up, the sooner I can get back to civilization."

"I hope you're right," I answered. Clearly, this was not going to be a pleasant experience for either of us.

I introduced Stanford to Abraham and Richard, who stood by nervously with his green visor pulled low over his eyes. Stanford only sniffed in disgust. He kept his handkerchief over his nose and offered muffled comments as he poked about the office. He ran his finger over the dust covered furniture. "I don't know how anyone can work in this filth." He picked up a paper off the desk and tossed it aside. "And don't tell me this is supposed to pass for a filing system."

Abraham shoved his hands in his pockets and rocked back on his heels. Richard shifted uncomfortably. I quickly diverted Stanford's attention to the map on the wall depicting the work of the Grasshopper Syndicate. "The areas outlined on the map show the land we have already purchased from the railroad and cleared of grasshoppers. So far, we have successfully cleared two townships and much of it has already been sold back to the settlers for homesteading." I pointed to the large area of unsettled land outside of the outlined areas on the map. "You can see that there are ample possibilities for future settlement and growth in this area."

Stanford blew his nose noisily into his handkerchief; then he turned to Richard. "We'll begin first thing in the morning. I will need to see all the records for the purchase and sale of the land that the syndicate acquired from the railroad. I trust you will have everything ready for me by then."

Richard nodded and mumbled a reply that sounded like a whimper.

"He'll be ready," I said.

Stanford hastily departed, leaving us staring in disbelief. "What do you think?" Abraham asked, when he had gone.

"He's definitely a dandy and not much interested in what we're trying to do here. He sees his role as tidying up our mess and getting back to Chicago as quickly as possible."

Abraham shook his head sadly. "He's no Jelle, that's for sure. I just hope he's trustworthy."

I turned to Richard. "I guess we had better get organized." Abraham and I spent the remainder of the afternoon helping Richard gather the necessary paperwork to appease the audit. We even spent a few hours tidying up the office to alleviate as much of the incessant Iowa dust as possible.

The next morning when we arrived at Jelle's office, we found Stanford already at work with Richard bustling around like a nervous mother hen. He had been in on the ground floor of this organization, and naturally, felt a kind of maternal instinct toward protecting it from an outsider.

Stanford had removed his coat and rolled up his sleeves, but he still wore the vest and broad tie he had on when he arrived. His case was open on the desk and he was sorting through the mounds of paperwork Jelle had left behind "Well, it looks like your man kept adequate records. That should make the work go faster," he said, without looking up.

Over the next few months, Stanford and Richard settled into a workable routine. Stanford barked orders and Richard jumped to provide whatever paperwork he asked for. Stacks of papers and ledgers littered the desk and spilled over onto the floor. The two of them were engrossed in a world that only they appeared to understand. I often caught them hovering over a page of figures as if it contained the secrets of the holy grail, completely oblivious to anything going on around them.

It wasn't long before the news spread of another eligible bachelor in town. Henrietta Spencer and her daughter, Berta, came to call bearing a basketful of homemade bread and jam. Berta wasted no time, making her intentions known. She bent low over Stanford's desk to make sure he had a good view of her ample assets and batted her eyes coquettishly. When the inevitable invitation for Sunday supper arrived, Stanford was already sweating profusely.

"He's done for," I said to Abraham later.

Abraham smiled, knowingly. "Couldn't happen to a better man."

The cool autumn days morphed into winter and we noticed that Stanford had finally stopped his sniffling. His attitude had also changed dramatically. He was considerably more relaxed and even seemed to enjoy the holiday festivities that accompanied the season. I suspected that this change might have been due, in part, to his budding relationship with Berta Spencer.

It was mid-January by the time Abraham and I met with Stanford to review the initial results of the audit. A cold winter wind blew across the prairie and promised that winter was here to stay. "It looks like everything is in order at the present time," Stanford said, as he banked more wood into the stove in the corner of his office. "However, I did turn up something interesting in my review of the documents." He took his glasses off and rubbed the bridge of his nose. "Were you aware," he began, glancing up at me. "that Jelle signed papers to transfer his share of the syndicate to you in the event of his death?"

Abraham and I stared at each other in shock. "We had no idea," I said. "When did this happen?"

Stanford glanced down at some papers on his desk. "Apparently the papers were signed when he was in Chicago on the day before he died." Stanford looked up at me. "Hank, it appears that you are now the majority shareholder of the Grasshopper Syndicate."

We stared at each other for several seconds while the realization of Stanford's words dawned on us. "He must have done it when he went to the bank with me to retrieve the promissory note," I said at last. "He obviously knew that what he planned to do was extremely dangerous." My voice cracked with emotion as I uttered these last words.

"It's evident that he thought highly of you, to risk his life that way," Stanford said.

"This community has always brought out the best in people," Abraham said, "and Jelle was a good example of that."

Stanford nodded, "I'm beginning to see the truth in that," he said. "People have gone out of their way to tell me how much Jelle was admired and respected." Then he cleared his throat and leaned back in his chair. He laced his fingers together and stared at me. "The fact remains," he said to me. "Now that you are the primary shareholder, you have significant sway over the future direction of the company. I'm afraid that I have uncovered some areas that will need your immediate attention."

Abraham and I braced ourselves for bad news. "I have discovered some unsecured mortgages that are of great concern," Stanford continued. He shook his head. "Small independent banks like this one are not regulated. Several of these loans are at risk of defaulting. If the mortgages had gone through a federal bank, they would have been properly vetted and secured."

"Can you identify how many loans are at risk?" I asked.

"I can't be sure, of course. But it looks like Jelle approved about 30 mortgages to settlers who worked to clear the land for the syndicate. Of those it appears that roughly seven are already in arrears. Three of those have abandoned the land altogether, and the other four have yet to make a payment."

"Can we resell the abandoned claims to recoup our losses?" Abraham asked.

"Once the bank forecloses on them you should be able to recoup some of the losses. But the more immediate problem is related to your cash flow. Without those mortgage payments, I don't see how you will be able to meet your obligations to the railroad."

Abraham and I exchanged nervous glances. "What do you suggest we do?" I asked.

Stanford affected a disinterested air and turned away from us. "It's really none of my affair, but if I were you, I'd contact those settlers in arrears and let them know where you stand. They have three months to bring the payments up to date. If not, they will risk foreclosure."

"Perhaps we can work something out with them," Abraham said, hopefully.

Stanford peered at us over the top of his glasses. "I don't have to tell you that if you are unable to meet your obligations to the railroad, not only will the settlers who are behind on their mortgages lose their land, but the syndicate risks losing all the unsold land that has already been cleared. It will more than likely bankrupt you."

"Will you be reporting all this to the railroad?" I asked.

"It's my obligation to let them know if their investment is secure." Stanford responded.

"But…"

I quickly interjected. "Can you give me a couple more days before you notify them?"

"I had planned to send a wire this afternoon, but I guess a few more days wouldn't hurt. However, now that the audit is almost completed, I won't be able to hold them off much longer."

Abraham and I left the office with a sense of urgency. "We have to notify the syndicate," I said. "I'll put out the word immediately."

Abraham nodded. "We can meet at the community center tomorrow afternoon. In the meantime, I'll notify the four homesteaders of their situation."

Tension was high as the syndicate members filed into the room. They knew the audit was nearing completion, and their anxiety filled the air with the scent of sweat and stale tobacco. Chairs scraped against the wooden floors as the men took their seats and waited for me to speak. "I'm sure you have heard by now that the auditor has just about completed his review of the syndicate books." I began. A murmur of concern passed through the group. "The good news is that Jelle's records were all in order." An audible sigh of relief filled the air and the tension in the room eased considerably. "Jelle kept two accounts on behalf of the syndicate. One account was set up to deposit payments to the railroad for the sale and purchase of the government lands we cleared of grasshoppers and then sold back to the settlers. The other account was for the interest and profits paid directly to the syndicate. That all looks clean as far as we can tell."

"So why are we here?" John Klein asked. "You could have handled this update with a wire."

Abraham stepped forward and cleared his throat. "It seems that Jelle was using the syndicate profits to offer the settlers mortgages to stay and farm the land they cleared. Some of those loans are in arrears causing a problem with our cash flow. Without those mortgage payments, we will not be able to meet our obligations to the railroad."

There was an audible gasp throughout the room as the members grasped the gravity of the situation. "I told you we shouldn't have put our faith in Jelle!" Sweeney thundered, pointing his finger at me. "You vouched for him. You should have been keeping a closer eye on things!"

"We were counting on those payments to cover our loans from the railroad for the purchase of the land infested by grasshoppers," Klein said, nervously.

Abraham shook his head sadly. "I'm afraid so." The grumble of discontent rose to a fever pitch and Abraham raised his hand to quiet the men. "My faith in Jelle's decision remains steadfast," he said. "He would not have put the syndicate at risk if he believed we could not cover the loans to the railroad."

"Can we cover the debt from our reserves?" Klein asked.

This time it was my turn to shake my head. "We can cover some of it, but not all of it." Once again, the room erupted in noise.

"I knew it!" Sweeney yelled. "We should never have trusted him."

"What happens if the settlers default on their mortgages?" one of the men asked.

"Without those mortgage payments, the syndicate is at risk. Our profits could be garnished to cover the losses," Klein answered, quietly. "If that's not enough, the railroad will foreclose on the unsold land."

The room descended into silence as the men contemplated what was at stake. "What can we do?" another man asked.

"The first thing we need to do is find out just how much risk we are talking about," Abraham answered. "We need to know which loans are most at risk of defaulting. I have already contacted the homesteaders who are in arrears. They have indicated a willingness to cooperate if we can give them time to sell this year's harvest."

"Let's not panic until we have a clearer picture of what we're up against." I said. "In the meantime, we need to get Stanford to hold off notifying the railroad until we figure this out."

"How do you propose to do that?" Sweeney asked, his voice dripping with contempt.

"By offering him a job and a share of the syndicate profits," I answered. Another rumble of concern made its way around the room as the men questioned the merits of my solution. "Abraham and I have observed Stanford closely over the last few months. He has proven himself to be both fair-minded and knowledgeable. The syndicate needs a manager to replace Jelle, and I believe that Stanford would be a valuable advocate for us with the railroads."

"But how can we afford to hire him away from the railroad and still meet our financial obligations?" Klein asked, doubtfully.

"Jelle was my friend as well as my business partner. Before he died, he signed his share of the syndicate over to me in the event of his death. I propose offering Stanford that share if he will stay on and help manage our affairs."

"What makes you think he'll accept the offer?"

"Just leave that to me," I answered. "I think that Stanford has a good reason to want to stay here in Iowa. I believe he will negotiate with the railroads with our interests in mind, especially if he holds a share in the syndicate."

"Well, I'm not happy about this situation," Sweeney grumbled. "We don't know anything about Stanford. How do we know he's trustworthy?"

"I'm willing to turn over my controlling share of the syndicate to him," I answered. "So, I guess that shows how much trust I've put in him. If that is not enough for you, I'm willing to listen to another solution."

There were general nods of consent as the men considered their options. Then Klein spoke on behalf of the group. "Stanford appears to be our best hope at the moment," he said. "If you're willing to put up Jelle's share of the syndicate to keep him here, then I guess that's good enough."

"I'll speak to him tomorrow afternoon," I said. "I feel certain he will agree. He has already agreed to delay notifying the railroad of the situation to give us time to find a solution."

The meeting ended on a cautious, but positive note. I promised to keep them all apprised of the situation as it developed, and they promised to be patient while Abraham and I worked things out with Stanford.

"What do you think?" I asked Abraham when we were alone. "Can we make this work?"

"I hope so," Abraham said. "Jelle was naïve in a lot of ways, but he was a shrewd businessman. I do not believe he would have put the syndicate in jeopardy. He must have believed that the risk was worth the gamble."

22

Stanford had become a regular visitor at the Spencer home during his time in Orange City. He had ceased sniveling into his handkerchief and could often be caught smiling for no apparent reason. There were times when he left the office early and was not seen again until morning. When he returned, he looked relaxed and quite pleased with himself.

Shortly after the meeting with the syndicate, I cornered Henrietta Spencer as she was leaving church services with her daughters and asked to speak to her privately. "Did you know that Harold Stanford has almost completed his work for the Grasshopper Syndicate?" I asked. "I imagine he'll be returning to Chicago soon."

She raised her eyebrows in surprise. "I had no idea. I thought he would be here for some time."

"He could be leaving before the week is out. I thought you should know so you could prepare Berta. I know the two of them have become quite close and it could be quite a letdown for her."

"I will certainly do my best," she clucked. "He's coming for supper this evening." I smiled as she scurried away. A little part of me felt sorry for Stanford.

When I met Stanford in his office the next morning, he looked red-eyed and beaten. He had trouble concentrating on the simplest of tasks. "I assume you will be returning to Chicago as soon as you hear from the railroad," I said to him.

He nodded and stared vacantly off into space. "Yes," he said, "I should be able to wrap things up by next week."

"I'm sure Berta will be sorry to see you leave," I added. "I saw her leaving church yesterday. She was looking particularly fetching in a new bonnet."

"We've grown quite fond of each other in the past few months," he said. "I gave her the news last night."

"It must have been difficult," I said, mustering as much sympathy as I could. "I know how much you thought of her. How did she take it?"

Stanford dropped his head into his hands. "We had a terrible fight," he said, sadly. "She accused me of toying with her emotions and taking advantage of her feelings."

"Did you ask her to return to Chicago with you?"

"Yes, but she refuses to leave her family. We argued about it. She said she never wanted to see me again."

"Do you think she would feel differently if you were to stay here?" I asked, innocently.

He looked up at me with the eyes of a beaten pup. "And do what? I'm not cut out to be a farmer."

"Stay on here at the bank. With Jelle gone, we could use someone with your expertise to manage the affairs of the syndicate. We can't offer you much of a salary, but we can offer you Jelle's share of the syndicate. It's enough to support two people until this mortgage business gets straightened out."

"But Jelle left his share to you!" Stanford exclaimed.

"To do with as I please," I answered. I gestured around the office. "To be honest, I'm a farmer not a businessman. If the syndicate is to remain solvent and profitable for the investors, it needs an experienced manager. That's why I'm offering you the job."

Stanford's face lit up with hope. "You'd do that for me?"

"You would be doing us a favor. We need someone who understands the banking system and can reassure the railroad that this mortgage situation will soon be under control. I've already spoken to the syndicate directors and they have unanimously agreed to offer you the position."

I could see him turning over the possibilities in his mind. For a moment, I thought he might jump across the desk and embrace me, but he quickly regained his composure. "I'd like to talk to Berta first," he said.

"I understand completely," I said, smiling. "The syndicate is anxious for your response. I can keep an eye on things here if you want to go and talk to her now."

Stanford wasted no time arguing. He grabbed his hat and coat and bolted for the door. "Thanks," he called over his shoulder. "I hope to have an answer for you by tomorrow morning." He was gone before I had time to respond.

\#

By the time Abraham and I arrived in Stanford's office the next morning, he was already there. "There you are!" he called excitedly. He opened his desk and produced a bottle of whiskey and three glasses. "I know it's early, but I believe congratulations are in order."

"I take it you are accepting our offer," Abraham said.

"Not only am I accepting your offer," Stanford said, "but you are looking at a newly engaged man. Berta has agreed to be my wife!"

"That's wonderful news," I said, shaking his hand. He poured the whiskey and we drank to his good fortune. "But before we can celebrate properly, we need you to go to Chicago and talk to the railroad."

Stanford poured himself another shot. "What do you want me to say?"

"You need to buy us time to straighten things out here," Abraham answered. "If we can put them off until after next fall's harvest, I believe the farmers who are in arrears can meet their payments. This will cover most of the loan payment to the railroad. The syndicate reserves should cover the remainder until the foreclosed land can be resold."

Stanford ran his finger through his thinning hair. "It will take some convincing," he said, thoughtfully. "But the railroad executives have much to lose and little to gain by insisting on the loan repayment at this time. They might agree to extend the date for the loan payment until after the settlers have time to sell their harvest."

"I knew we could count on you," I said.

"There are a few stipulations," Stanford said, hesitantly. "If we extend the mortgage loans to the settlers, I will need to impose a penalty to cover the fees levied by the railroad. Jelle wrote the loans at a flat 10 percent interest, but I will need to charge them 12 to cover our costs."

"They won't be happy," Abraham said. "But faced with the prospect of losing everything they have worked so hard to achieve I think we can convince them to go along."

"Good!" he said. "I'll notify the railroad and book passage to Chicago first thing in the morning."

Stanford's wedding to Berta Spencer that spring was the social event of the year. The day dawned bright and clear. The air was crisp and scented with the aroma of wildflowers. The ceremony took place in the newly erected First Reformed Church building in Orange City. The ceremony was a simple affair. The bride was resplendent in a tightly corseted blue cotton gown made especially for the occasion. It featured a high neckline and ruffled hem trimmed in ribbon and lace. The groom looked uncomfortable in his black towncoat and vest. He continually tugged at his tie and mopped beads of sweat from his brow.

After the ceremony, the bride's family hosted a dinner at their home for the wedding party. Then the table was cleared away and the dancing commenced. I watched the revelers from the sidelines. My father would have frowned on such frivolity, but here in America, one celebrated even the smallest successes with abandon. And coming on the heels of the successful elimination of the grasshoppers, the entire community was in a mood for celebration. However, my own feelings were dampened by an overwhelming sense of loneliness.

I had received word from Catherine that she had decided to stay in Chicago after her father's funeral. With Charles's help, she was proceeding with a lawsuit against Gregor's estate to recoup the loss of her inheritance. The process promised to be long and drawn out, but she was determined to see it through. She asked how I was coping and expressed the hope that we would meet again soon. My love for Catherine had not diminished in the months we had been apart, but I had put off seeing her again for fear that it would ignite memories of Jelle's death. I was afraid our reunion could cause more pain than either of us could bear.

The revelry of the wedding party reached a fever pitch, and I stepped outside for a breath of fresh air to find Abraham similarly engaged. The air held a hint of moisture signaling the coming of another spring shower. "Not much for dancing, are you?" Abraham asked.

"I never learned," I admitted. "Father was a strict Calvinist and believed that dancing was the work of the devil."

Abraham smiled. "I remember well the sermons of my youth, filled with dire predictions of burning in hell for our sinful behaviors."

"Weren't you afraid?"

"Terrified," he admitted. "Then I came to believe that if dancing was all it took to cast your lot with the devil, I might as well enjoy myself while I still could." He chuckled to himself. "Besides, I believe in a God of forgiveness. If God could forgive the sins of murderers and adulterers, he could certainly forgive me for dancing."

"If only we could forgive ourselves and easily as God forgives us," I mused.

"We all make mistakes," he said. "But sometimes we judge ourselves too harshly and punish ourselves for things beyond our control. Instead, we must learn from our mistakes, so we don't repeat them."

"You sound as if you speak from experience."

"I've made my share of mistakes," Abraham said. "My biggest mistake resulted in the death of our first child. I was obsessed with staking a claim in the west. I insisted on pushing westward although Emma was heavy with child. As winter approached, we built a sod hut on the prairie far from civilization and settled in to prepare for the birth. When she experienced complications, I left her alone in the soddie while I rode for help. By the time I returned, it was all over. She was covered in blood, holding our dead child in her arms." His voice caught in his throat. "Emma never blamed me, and in time, I was able to forgive myself. But the memory still causes me great pain. I don't think that will ever go away."

"And yet, look at what you have accomplished," I said. "You have a large family and a successful farming operation. You are revered as one of the founding fathers of the community."

"I never asked for any of it," Abraham answered. "I thought only of providing a comfortable life for my family. The rest came as a result of hard work and sacrifice." The sound of voices and laughter grew louder as the music inside ceased and revelers made their way outside for fresh air. Tiny droplets of rain began to fall, creating a tinny symphony as it hit the roof and slid to the ground.

"I believe that now would be a good time to hit the refreshment line," Abraham said.

We moved back into the cozy warmth of the house. The aroma of fresh flowers mingled with the soft glow of candlelight creating a romantic atmosphere for the festivities. The band struck up a waltz and Abraham's wife sought him out in the crowd. Emma's face was aglow with the excitement of the evening. She had a new dress that accentuated the color of her eyes and she looked happier than I had ever seen her. "Where have you been?" she asked him. "You owe me the next dance."

Abraham winked at me. "It would be my honor…as long as you don't mind my stepping all over your feet in the process." They walked off arm-in-arm, their heads bent together conspiratorially.

It was time for the bride and groom to make their exit. They would be spending their first night upstairs in her parent's home. As the bride was spirited away by the women to prepare for the big night, Stanford was treated to several rounds of drinks and a great deal of ribbing by the men. When, at last, it was time from him to ascend to the bridal chamber, he was carried aloft on the shoulders of the men amid a chorus of hoots and cheers. It was a joyous occasion, and no one noticed that outside, the wind had increased, and the gentle shower had become a downpour.

23

Optimism ran high that summer. The grasshoppers had generally left the country without depositing eggs. Those who did appear were less in numbers and were easily handled. The Grasshopper Syndicate, under Stanford's careful management, continued its operations, breaking up new land every year, and selling out both new and cultivated lands, as buyers appeared. His efforts returned to each man all the capital he had invested, with interest and a handsome dividend of profits. The town of Orange City had also grown from its humble beginnings. It was now a thriving community with stores, hotels, and even a theater for hosting traveling minstrel shows.

At the edge of town, the framing was almost complete for the grand new house Stanford was building for his bride. Stanford's demeanor had changed in the few months since his marriage to Berta. Gone was the jaunty spring to his step. In its place was a tired, bent overworked little man. He could often be seen scurrying along behind Berta and her mother lugging home the latest purchases for the new house. The lights in his office often burned late into the night while he poured over his files and ledgers.

"I see your new house is starting to take shape," I said to Stanford one afternoon. "Berta and her mother have been telling everyone in town how grand it will be."

Stanford shook his head sadly. "That house will be the ruin of me," he said. "Berta and her mother have already added another wing to it."

"Can't you put a stop to it?" I asked.

Stanford shook his head sadly. "I promised her a new house when we got married. Sometimes I think it was the only reason she agreed to marry me."

The situation seemed to call for me to say something encouraging, but I had no idea what that was. It was not my place to comment on another man's marital situation, no matter what I thought about it. Instead, I shifted from foot to foot, and tried to look sympathetic until he spoke again.

Finally, he looked up at me with his mournful eyes. "I'm afraid I made a terrible mistake," he said, at last. "This past winter when I went to Chicago to negotiate for the syndicate, I was so excited about becoming a partner and marrying Berta that I wasn't thinking straight. I was so eager to please her, I let it rule my decision-making. The future looked limitless."

"What did you do?"

"I ran into a man who was selling 100-acre tracts of land in central Iowa that had been owned by the Des Moines Valley Land Company. He claimed that the company was building a line north from Des Moines that would connect to the St. Paul and Sioux City Railroad in Minnesota. However, the railroad had defaulted during the Panic of 1873 and was under reorganization, so the construction of the road had been delayed. He was selling the land at a severely depressed value." The mention of the company name sent shivers down my spine. This was the same company that Gregor had been associated with when he swindled Catherine out of her inheritance.

"I'm familiar with the company," I said, hesitantly. "I didn't know it was still in existence."

"The railroad went under during the panic and has since been absorbed by another company, but the land company is still operated by a Dutch investment company in Arnhem," Stanford continued. "People are clamoring for railroads at any price. I knew that the value of the land would increase tremendously once the railroad was finally completed," Stanford paused as if to gather enough courage to continue. "It sounded like an amazing opportunity to turn a quick profit so I could build Berta the house of her dreams... so I bought it."

"Where would you get that kind of money?" I asked.

Stanford looked at me sheepishly. "I put my share of the Grasshopper Syndicate up as collateral on the loan."

"You what?" I exclaimed.

"I know. I know. It was a stupid thing to do. But like I said, I was not thinking straight."

I collapsed into the nearest chair as the weight of his words descended on me. "So, if you default on the loan, this company could assume your share of the syndicate?"

Stanford nodded morosely. "I'm afraid so."

"Is that a possibility…that you could default?" I asked.

"So far, I have been able to make the interest payments with my share of the syndicate profits," he said. "But the expenses for the new house…"

I could see where this was going. "Do you have anyone interested in buying the property?"

Stanford's voice caught in his throat. "I'm afraid not. A Canadian company was interested, but the deal fell through." He struggled to contain his emotions. I turned away to allow him time to regain control and saw Abraham crossing the street toward the office.

"What's wrong?" Abraham asked, when he saw our faces.

"I'm ruined!" Stanford cried. "I'm about to lose everything I've worked for...the house, my job, everything! Berta will kill me!"

"Hold on," Abraham said with his characteristic calm. "Why don't you start at the beginning of the story."

While Stanford recounted the story, I walked across the room to study the map tacked to the wall. It showed all the syndicate lands as well as the lands still available along the railroad. There had to be a solution to this problem. I just could not see it.

"And that's not the worst of it," Stanford wailed, as he came to the end of his story. "The railroad bonds that the Dutch company issued for the defunct line were secured by a mortgage on the land. But since the security turned out to be of little value, the company has been forced to exchange the bonds for any remaining railroad land." Stanford sniffled and wiped his nose on his sleeve. "Because I still owe on the land I purchased, the company has called for the loan to be paid in full or forfeit my rights to it."

"Can't you put them off until you sell the land?" Abraham asked.

Stanford shook his head. "I've tried, but they have threatened to come after all my assets if I default, including my share of the Grasshopper Syndicate." Stanford sank deeper into his chair and sunk his head into his hands. "I just didn't see this coming," he moaned. "The prospectus looked solid and the company is well-respected in Holland."

"How much money are we talking about?" I asked.

"I have managed to sell off some of the land to farmers in the area, but I still owe almost $2,000 on the loan. The company has given me just 30 days to come up with the money. There is no way I can raise that kind of money and meet the deadline!"

I studied the map tacked to the wall. The land in question was located near Webster City in Iowa just north of the Dubuque and Sioux City Line that connected Sioux City to Chicago. I knew from my days in Pella, that Sandford's land included some of the most fertile land in the area. An idea began to take shape in my mind. It was a long shot, but perhaps...

"Are you willing to absorb your losses and sell the land for what you owe?" I asked.

"I don't see that I have much choice," Stanford answered. "I would willingly give up any hope of making a profit off the land just to be free of this burden of debt. But the fact remains that I don't have a ready buyer."

"What if you sold the land to the syndicate?" I asked. "With the land's proximity to the railroad, I am certain that if we can hold onto it until the economy is fully recovered, we could resell the land to farmers in the area wishing to expand their operations. We can offer it to the farmers with a promise of a low interest loan from the bank here."

"You would need to get the approval of the syndicate to move forward with such a purchase," Abraham said. "We may need to hold on to the land for several years before it would turn a profit. I'm not sure that the members would want to commit their profits to such a risky venture."

"What if I provide the syndicate with a loan to buy the property?" I asked. "Then we wouldn't have to dip into syndicate profits."

"Where would you get that kind of money?" Abraham asked.

"Years ago, just after we arrived in America, I loaned Jelle some money to reach his family in Wisconsin," I said. "When he sold his uncle's land to the railroad, he paid me back at a generous interest rate. I deposited the money in a bank in Chicago, and I have left most of it untouched. I'm sure there is enough there to cover Stanford's debt."

"Why not purchase the land yourself?" Stanford asked.

"I have all I can handle with my own claim," I answered. "I don't have time to manage any more. If the syndicate owns the land, I will not only collect interest on the loan, we will all share in the profits when the land is sold."

Abraham scratched his chin thoughtfully. "If we can satisfy Stanford's debt, we may be able to survive this without sacrificing any syndicate shares." He turned to Stanford. "You will need to inform the syndicate of the situation. They have a right to know that the membership is at risk."

A look of fear and dread passed over Stanford's face. When he spoke, his voice was barely above a whisper. "I know," he said. "I've been putting it off for fear they will decide to fire me. My salary at the bank is the only thing keeping me afloat right now, and Berta and her mother spend it as fast as I can earn it. If I lose this job, I will be ruined!" There was no mistaking the desperation in his voice as he uttered these last words.

"Abraham and I will stand by you," I said. "But you must confront the situation. It will be much worse for you if you don't."

Stanford reluctantly agreed to address the syndicate at a special meeting. Abraham and I left him to draw up the paperwork for the proposal while we notified the members. "Do you think the syndicate will agree to your plan? Abraham asked, when we were alone.

"I don't know," I answered, "but everyone loses if we allow an outside company to gain a share of the Grasshopper Syndicate. Once they get in, they will begin buying out the other shareholders until we have lost control. If we allow this company to gain control of the syndicate, they could negotiate with the railroad to increase their own profits even though the community may suffer. There is already talk of an alternate route around Orange City that will divert settlement in the area and cause us to travel further to bring our goods to market. We can't stand by and allow Stanford's mistake to ruin everything we have worked so hard for."

Abraham shook his head. "I still believe the syndicate will want Stanford's head. I don't envy his position."

\#

The members of the syndicate assembled for an emergency meeting with an attitude of impatience. They huddled together in small groups, talking in low growling voices. Occasionally, one of the men would stray from the pack, but he would soon be drawn back in. They were like wolves sensing a fresh kill. I had no doubt they would tear Stanford to pieces and take me down with him if this did not go well. Abraham and I stood apart from them and waited anxiously. Finally, the groups separated, and the men took their seats.

"What is the meaning of this?" Klein asked. "I thought everything was going well. Has something happened?"

As the chairman of the group, I took my place behind the table at the front of the room and called for order. "I called you all together because I have just been informed of a situation that could ultimately affect us all."

"That sounds serious," one of the men said.

"I'm afraid, it could be," I answered. "We have relied on the good faith and intentions of the syndicate shareholders to keep us all informed and involved in any decisions that could alter or otherwise interfere with the work of the syndicate," I began. "But we have never set down in writing the process for doing so. Nor have we outlined any rules or stipulations for transferring shares outside of the original membership."

"What are you getting at," Sweeney asked, impatiently.

I cleared my throat and glanced at Stanford who was sweating profusely and looking as if he might be sick.

"Without these rules in place, we have had a situation arise where one of our members may have inadvertently made a decision that could affect us all."

The air in the room turned hostile, and Abraham stepped forward. "I assure you," he said. "This individual did not act with malice, but with innocence in this matter."

"Who is it?" Sweeney demanded, looking menacingly around the room.

Stanford rose hesitantly to his feet. "I was the one," he said, his voice shaking with fear. "I did it. I used my share of the syndicate to secure a personal loan."

A torrent of anxiety flooded the room as the men considered the implications of this news. Finally, Klein spoke up. "Let's not overreact," he said. "I don't see this as a problem unless the loan goes into default."

"What happens then?" one of the men asked.

"Then the shares could be used to settle the debt," Klein answered.

The grumbles of discontent grew louder, and Sweeney's voice rose above the din. "I wasn't in favor of putting Stanford in charge in the first place. He doesn't understand how we do things out here." The men began to mumble in agreement and the tension in the room increased.

Soon others joined in to voice their concerns about Stanford's judgement. "How can we trust someone to manage our affairs who puts our organization at risk?"

I raised my hand to silence the crowd. "Hold on!" I said, spreading out the map on the table. "I have a proposal that may not only solve this dilemma, but in the long run, bring additional profits to the syndicate."

The men gathered around the table while I laid out my proposal for the syndicate to purchase the land in question. "Why wouldn't you just purchase the land yourself instead of loaning the syndicate the money to purchase it?" Klein asked.

"I have a personal reason for wanting to do this," I began. "The money I intend to use comes from a loan I made to Jelle many years ago. It seems only fitting that it should be used to rescue the company he fought so hard to establish."

The room descended into silence as each man remembered their friend and colleague. "Jelle would have wanted the money to be used this way," Abraham said, quietly. "I can't think of a better way to honor his memory."

Stanford stepped forward hesitantly. "I have drafted a preliminary proposal for your review," he said, presenting a copy of the document. "The document states that I will transfer the deed for the property to the syndicate, and in exchange, they will assume the responsibility for satisfying the loan against it. If you agree, Hank has agreed to accompany me to Chicago to negotiate with the company on our behalf."

"I'll need time to review this," Klein said.

Abraham cleared his throat. "I'm afraid time is of the essence," he said. "Stanford's loan goes into default in 30 days."

"That's not much time!" Sweeney exclaimed.

Abraham continued calmly. "If the negotiation goes well, as I'm sure it will, we can purchase the land for much less that it is currently worth, and still satisfy the loan. We may need to hold the land until the economy is fully recovered, but our profits will increase tenfold."

"I'm not sure what choice we have," Klein said. He turned to Stanford. "You had better read the proposal to us so we can make a decision."

They spent the next hour refining the language and adjusting the proposal until they reached a satisfying agreement. "I'm ready to sign off on it," Klein said, at last. The others nodded and one by one, they stepped up to add their names to the document.

"I want to assure you all," Stanford began in a voice slightly stronger than before. "I take full responsibility for this situation. That is why I have agreed to sell the land to the syndicate for only the amount required to cover my obligation. I assure you that I will take special care to ensure that nothing like this happens in the future."

"For your sake, you'd better hope so!" Sweeney grumbled. The unspoken threat was not lost on Stanford who was visibly shaken by the words.

"There is nothing to be done about the situation now," Klein sighed "But to avoid something like this in the future, I believe we must develop a procedure for the transfer and use of syndicate shares. Should someone unscrupulous gain a controlling share of the syndicate, it could bring about our ruin."

There were general nods of agreement all around as the group gave in to the logic of Klein's words. I took control of the situation again. I put Abraham and John Klein in charge of a committee to formulate the new guidelines and draw up a proposal to present to the members. Stanford and I promised to keep them informed of our progress in our negotiations with the land company.

The whole ordeal had taken every bit of Stanford's nerve. As soon as everyone had gone, he collapsed into a chair, shaking uncontrollably. "I didn't think I would survive this meeting," he said. "When Klein demanded answers, I really thought he would have my hide!"

"It all worked out this time," Abraham said, sternly. "But if things don't go as planned, I cannot guarantee that the next meeting will go as well."

When everyone had gone, Abraham fixed me with his steady gaze. "Didn't you tell me once that this was the company that defrauded Catherine out of her inheritance?" he asked.

"Yes" I said." But the railroad did complete its line from Keokuk all the way to Des Moines. I'm just not sure how much the land company was aware of and whether they were behind Gregor's scheme."

"Do you think you can trust them to negotiate in good faith?"

"If the company is legitimate, and they are as desperate to settle as Stanford says, then hopefully we can come to an agreement that will be to the benefit of us all."

Abraham clasped me on the shoulder. "For everybody's sake, I hope you're right," he said.

24

Stanford and I spoke little as we began our journey to Chicago. Stanford chewed nervously on his fingernails, an irritating habit that had only gotten worse since his marriage to Berta. We had gone over the details of our plan until we could recite them in our sleep; however, there was no way to know what we might encounter from the other side. If the negotiations did not go well, not only would Stanford lose everything, but the syndicate itself could be in jeopardy.

The nearer we got to Chicago, the more anxious I became. This was my first trip back to Chicago since Jelle's death. I paced the aisles of the train car during the day, and tossed and turned in my bunk at night. I had a dual purpose for this trip and there was reason to believe that both could go terribly wrong. It had been almost a year since Catherine and I had parted, but my feelings for her were as strong as ever. I hoped that enough time had passed for us both to come to grips with our grief over Jelle's death. It was my fervent desire and that we could renew our relationship. I only hoped she felt the same. But no matter how desperately I wanted to see Catherine, my first obligation was to Stanford and the syndicate. If this deal didn't go through, I stood to lose more than my initial investment.

I touched my jacket where the silver pistol rested in the holster under my arm. I had never carried a gun on my travels before, but this time I was not taking any chances. Although Gregor was no longer a threat, the events of my last visit were still vivid in my mind. I was still haunted by Catherine's stricken face as she held Jelle's head in her arms when he died.

I had notified Charles Weller that I would be coming to Chicago to withdraw the funds from my account. The brick and stone building had survived the fire intact with only a few scorch marks left as a reminder. Although the bank no longer bore Joseph Weller's name, the clocklike workings of a financial institution remained intact. The building hummed with the general buzz of activity signaling that the business had recovered from the panic and was back on its feet. Charles came from his office to greet me.

"Hank!" he said, extending his hand. "I've been expecting you." He ushered me into his office and motioned me to a chair. Charles reached inside a drawer on his desk and handed me an envelope. "I have closed your account with us," he said, "and provided the money in cash as you requested." He leaned back in his chair. "Now, can you tell me what this is all about?"

"I'm afraid I can't go into details," I answered. "But I'm here with a business partner to negotiate a land deal."

Charles regarded me silently for a few minutes before responding. "Well, I hope it goes well and that we can all celebrate this evening. Catherine and I have settled the lawsuit over Gregor's estate. I know she is anxious to fill you in on all the details."

"I hope that this will allow her to finally put the whole distasteful episode behind her," I said. I made a few polite inquiries about Catherine's health hoping to get a clue about her feelings toward me, but Charles appeared oblivious to my intent. Eventually, I gave up and rose to make my exit. "Please give Catherine my regards," I said, "and tell her that I look forward to hearing all about the settlement when we meet this evening." In truth, the thought of seeing Catherine again filled me with apprehension. I was still unsure whether we had a future together.

I rejoined Stanford who was waiting outside. "This should settle things with the railroad," I said, handing him the packet of money. "Then you should be free and clear." I had signed the loan contract with the syndicate up before we left, so the only thing left to do was meet with the railroad representative and pay off Stanford's debt.

"I can't thank you enough," Stanford said, taking the packet from me. "We are to meet with representatives of the land company at the office of the Des Moines Valley Land Company located in the Marquette Building," he said. "It's only a few blocks from here, so I think we can walk."

I glanced at his face which had taken on a paler shade of gray. "Are you sure you're ready for this?" I asked.

"As ready as I'll ever be," he answered.

The Marquette Building was one of the most profitable skyscrapers built in Chicago after the Great Fire. It was created as a collection of first-class office spaces whose primary purpose was to fatten the pockets of real estate investors taking a gamble on an up-and-coming urban center. The building's rich terracotta ornamentation, decorative bronze reliefs and sparkling Tiffany mosaics were designed to woo prospective tenants and their clients with dreams of riches beyond imagination.

Stanford and I rode the elevator to the tenth floor and entered the door marked Des Moines Valley Land Company. The woman at the reception desk greeted us brusquely and asked us to take a seat while she announced our arrival. She returned in a few moments and led us into an adjoining office.

The office was as ornately over-decorated as the hotel lobby. An old Paterson Colt revolver was on prominent display in its cradle on the desk. A man was standing at the window with his back to us when we entered. The blood drained from my face when Dirk Van Huel turned and faced us. He was older and somewhat thicker than I remembered, but there was no mistaking the contempt in his eyes and the curl of his lips. "Harke De Jong," he said, with a smile that still contained traces of the old sneer. "Or is it Hank now? It's been a long time."

"Hello, Dirk," I said.

Stanford looked at me with his mouth agape. "I didn't realize you two were acquainted," he said.

"Hank and I go way back," Dirk said. "You could say that we practically grew up together."

"Why didn't you tell me?" Stanford asked me.

"I wasn't aware that he would be here," I answered, eyeing Dirk warily. "We knew each other a long time ago. I'm sure we've both changed since then."

"Please sit down," Dirk said. He gestured to a small bar set up nearby. "I can see that I have taken you by surprise. Would you like a drink before we discuss the business at hand?"

"No, thank you," I said, taking the seat he indicated. I felt the reassuring press of Jelle's revolver next to my ribs.

"Well, then, let's get right to it, shall we?" Dirk sat across from us, enjoying his position of authority, and waited for us to begin.

I gathered my wits about me and produced the signed copy of the proposal Stanford had prepared for the syndicate. "I am here representing a syndicate of landowners who have purchased land from Mr. Stanford to develop for agricultural purposes. We are here to negotiate a transfer of the deed and satisfy the loan against it.

Dirk shifted his weight in the chair and leaned toward me. "Mr. Stanford should have read the contract more carefully. There is a clause that prohibits the sale of the property to a third party without the express approval of the Des Moines Valley Land Company."

I struggled to control my emotions. "And you won't agree to the sale?"

"I didn't say that," Dirk responded. "I'm sure we can come to an agreement if my company is fairly compensated in the deal."

"What do you consider to be fair compensation," Stanford asked.

"My company would need an additional $2,500 to release Mr. Stanford from his contract."

"That's robbery!" I exclaimed. "The land is not worth that much."

Dirk continued to smile. "It is now."

"You do not have any interest in developing the land," I hissed. "Your railroad is defunct. You need the money from this sale to satisfy your creditors!"

"I'm sure I can locate others who would be willing to clear the land for agriculture," Dirk said.

"That could take years," I answered. "Years that you do not have. Your creditors will not wait that long."

"The fact remains that the land cannot be sold with the company's approval," Dirk said, rising from his chair. "You have my offer."

I felt the blood rise to my face s I rose to face him. "You are only doing this because I'm involved!" I exclaimed. "You were quite eager to sign until then."

"You flatter yourself," he said. "But then you always did believe you were good enough to play in my league."

I started toward him. "You have had it in for me ever since Lainie's death! That's why you sent Van Pelt to find me in Iowa."

Dirk's eyes narrowed and his lips turned up in a sneer. "I didn't even know about your connection to the Van Pelts until Gregor mentioned it to me. He came to me with a proposal to set up a branch of the company in Chicago selling railroad bonds. It sounded like a promising venture at the time, but when I discovered that he was swindling me out of my share, I confronted him. That's when he told me of your interest in Catherine Weller and the possibility of obtaining Washington's promissory note. I agreed to back off for a share of the settlement." Van Huel advanced toward me menacingly. "But you took care of that, didn't you? I won't let you ruin me again!"

"That promissory note had been in my family for generations. I had letters to prove it was gifted to my great-grandmother from Jacob Van Pelt."

"That's very touching," Dirk sneered. "But that note should have gone to Van Pelt's heirs."

"I am an heir," I said. "Jacob Van Pelt was my great-grandfather."

"That's preposterous!" Dirk scoffed.

"I had the letters to prove it, but they were destroyed along with the note when Gregor died."

"So you say," Dirk said, advancing toward me. "How do I know what was actually destroyed that night? You could have kept the original documents for yourself."

"I wanted no claim to that inheritance," I answered. "I offered to hand over the documents to Gregor in exchange for some land he owned in Pennsylvania, but he wanted more than that. When I refused to hand over the note and the letters authenticating it, he vowed to do whatever it took to take them from me."

"So, you killed him to keep him from collecting his rightful inheritance?" Dirk asked. "I guess that makes you a thief **and** a murderer!" He took a few steps toward me. "Not only did you steal my business partner's rightful inheritance, you are also responsible for the deaths of my father and my sister!"

Stanford had witnessed this whole exchange with wide eyes and mouth agape. "Is this true?" he asked, backing away from me.

"He's lying!" I exclaimed. A small vein began to pulse in my brain, and I clenched my fists. Years of suppressed anger propelled me forward and I punched him squarely in the face. Dirk reeled back and blood began spurting from his nose. He wiped it away and sneered at me. "I have a witness that you came into my office and attacked me," he said pointing at Stanford, who had backed himself into a corner. Dirk grabbed the revolver from its perch on the desk and pointed it at me. "I am perfectly within my rights to defend myself."

"That old gun hasn't seen action since the Indian Wars," I laughed. "I doubt if it will even fire."

Dirk cocked the lever. "Shall we find out?" he said.

I started toward him again.

"Don't!" Stanford cried out.

"That's right," Dirk said, his voice dripping with contempt. "As I recall, Harke was never one to stand up to a fight."

I held my ground and stared at him scornfully. "Do you intend to shoot me in cold blood?" I asked.

"There's no need for that," he said, lowering the gun. "Unless you can come up with enough cash to satisfy my demand, I plan to foreclose on Stanford's land and take over his share of your precious syndicate."

"I can't let that happen," I said, reaching inside my jacket pocket.

"Hold it," Dirk said, raising his gun.

I slowly withdrew my hand and tossed a paper onto the desk. "The syndicate has also taken precautions against such a hostile takeover. This charter document states that in the event of any sale or transfer of syndicate shares without the express approval of the membership, the new owner shall forfeit all voting rights and shall not be eligible to share in any profits gained through the expansion or reorganization of the syndicate holdings beyond the date of sale. If you insist on following through with your plan, we will simply reorganize the syndicate and your shares will be worthless."

Dirk raised his pistol and came toward me. "You think you're so clever," he said, through gritted teeth. "I'm tired of your interference. I want you out of my life for good!"

"There is nothing I would like more than that," I answered. "But if you kill me, my shares will go to one of the other syndicate members, giving them the majority. They can make sure that your shares are worthless."

"Stanford had no right to sell the land without my approval. The sale is void!" he shouted.

"I guess we'll have to let the courts and creditors decide that," I said.

A sudden movement from Stanford, who was cowering in the corner of the room, caused Dirk to turn his attention in that direction. The distraction gave me the opportunity to withdraw Jelle's pistol from my pocket. Dirk turned back toward me and I heard the click of his gun being cocked. I raised my pistol to face him.

"It looks like we have a standoff," he said. "I wonder which one of us will back down first. Given your history, I'm betting that you will."

"Not this time, Dirk," I answered. "I'm way past being intimidated by you. My guess is that you are not nearly as brave without your goons to back you up."

"Intimidation was not my only weapon against you," Dirk said, leveling his pistol toward me. "As I recall, you sometimes allowed all that restrained anger to explode into violence. Like the time you attacked my father."

"He attacked me. I merely defended myself."

"Then perhaps you could be goaded into another reckless act that would require me to defend myself against you."

"I don't think so."

Dirk smiled wickedly and waved his pistol, taunting me. "What if I told you that Lainie didn't drown that night? What if I told you that I overheard the two of you arguing? When I heard that she was pregnant with your child I became incensed. Van der Donk would have called off the wedding himself rather than suffer the humiliation of marrying a woman who was already pregnant with another man's child. It would have brought tremendous shame on our family. I couldn't have that. There was only one other option. I killed her myself. I carried her body down to the river in the rain and dumped it."

"That's why you allowed me to assist with the search!" I exclaimed. "And why you sent me to the river. You wanted me to be the one to find her!"

"And you were more than willing to assume the guilt for her death. The rest was easy."

The anger surged through my veins and clouded my vision. Old memories rose to the surface. Old feelings coursed through my brain. Images of Lainie floating among the reeds of the swollen river. Images of Jelle's pale face as the life drained away from him. The room spun in colors of red and black. I felt my finger on the trigger and heard the gunshot and then there was only darkness.

25

I awoke with a searing light burning behind my eyelids. I turned my head away and gasped when a sharp stab of pain in my chest nearly took my breath away. My mouth tasted of dry sand and I ran my tongue over my lips. Gradually, the pain in my chest subsided enough for me to blink open my eyes and the shadows in the room began to take shape.

"Welcome back." Catherine's voice was soft and soothing. Her face was bathed in light just as it had been when I found her at the church after the fire.

I raised my head to look around the room. "What happened?" I asked. "Where am I?"

"You've been shot," she said. "We moved you to the hotel while the police investigated. Stanford is with them now." I winced against the pain and lay back against the pillows. "You need to rest," Catherine said. "The doctor said you were lucky. A few inches to the left and the bullet would have hit your heart."

"Where's Dirk?" I asked through the pain.

"I'm afraid he didn't make it," she said.

I tried to raise myself up on my elbows, but the pain was too great, and I collapsed back onto the bed. "I didn't mean for it to end this way," I gasped.

"Stanford told us about the meeting with Van Huel," Catherine said. "He said Dirk threatened you and accused you of being responsible for the death of his father and his sister."

I closed my eyes against a new round of pain. "It wasn't my fault," I said, clenching my teeth against the pain. "He was the one who did it."

"Stanford also told us that Van Huel had been Gregor's business partner," she said. "He said Dirk was in on the railroad swindle from the beginning and knew about the promissory note you held."

"They were both motivated by greed. They chose to pursue their own agenda at the expense of others." Tears formed at the corners of my eyes and I blinked them away." So many people suffered because of the selfish and spiteful actions of those two men." I closed my eyes and lay still for several minutes trying to resurrect the memory of my final meeting with Van Huel. Dirk's words flooded through my memory. "All these years…," I said, "I thought it was my fault that Lainie died, but Dirk was the one who killed her."

"Who's Lainie?"

"Dirk's sister. We were in love once, but she was promised to the Governor's nephew. When she refused to go through with it, he killed her and blamed me."

"And you've been carrying this guilt for all these years?" Catherine asked.

"I was the one who found her body. Dirk planned it that way. He knew I would feel guilty and that he could use it against me. He wanted to punish me for ruining his political future."

Catherine patted my hand to sooth me. "It's over now," she said. "You need to put it behind you and focus on getting better."

The door opened quietly, and Stanford stepped into the room. "How are you?" he asked.

"I'll live," I answered. "I'm sorry things turned out the way they did."

"There's no need to worry," he said. "I've been talking with Charles about the purchase of the railroad land. He has reviewed the contract and believes that Dirk was not acting in the best interests of the land company. He has agreed to negotiate with them on our behalf. He's meeting with the board of directors now."

"But Dirk said…" I began.

Catherine placed her fingers over my lips to stop me from protesting. "Apparently, Dirk was acting without the full consent of the board. Charles thinks they can come to an agreeable solution. Now get some rest. I will be right here when you wake up. I still have something I need to discuss with you as soon as you are better." She leaned forward and kissed me on the lips. I closed my eyes and surrendered to the sweet oblivion of sleep.

#

Within a few days, I had regained enough strength to be able to get myself out of bed and get dressed. Charles and Stanford had been able to negotiate an acceptable agreement with the railroad and we agreed that Stanford would return to Iowa to inform the syndicate. I planned to follow in a few days, but first, I had some unfinished business to take care of.

I arrived at the Weller home with a bouquet of flowers. Catherine greeted me at the door with Lily in tow. Catherine wore a dress of pale lavender with a trailing skirt trimmed with pleated ruffles and ribbons. Her hair was braided and piled into a high crown on her head. "You look wonderful!" I said.

Catherine smiled to accept my compliment and her gray eyes danced with delight. She took the flowers and kissed me on the cheek. "Lily, do you remember Mr. De Jong?" she asked the girl.

"Lily and I met several years ago, so she is to be forgiven if she doesn't remember." I stooped to her level as far as my injury would allow. "How is Schatje?" I asked. Lily smiled and held out her doll to me. It was somewhat worse for wear. One of the button eyes was missing, but the crooked smile was still evident. "It looks like she's been well-loved," I said.

Catherine laughed. "Schatje is rarely out of her sight. She even has a special place at the table."

Mrs. Jennings arrived, and Catherine handed her the bouquet of flowers. "Will you put these in water for me?" she asked.

Mrs. Jennings' face lit up at the sight of me. "Aren't you the young man who rescued Catherine from that horrible Van Pelt man?" She grabbed my hand in her free hand and pumped it up and down. I tried not to wince from the pain. "I can't thank you enough for what you did."

"It was the least I could do under the circumstances," I answered, pulling my hand away.

Catherine turned her attention to the child who was clinging to her skirts. "Lily, why don't you go see if you can help Mrs. Jennings with the final preparations for dinner." Then turning to Mrs. Jennings, "And would you ask Charles to join us in the drawing room?"

I followed her into the room where I had met with her after her father's death. The somber mourning bands covering the portraits were gone now and the curtains were pulled back, flooding the room with light. It was hard to believe that this same room had been the scene of such sadness a little over a year ago. "May I offer you a drink?" Catherine asked.

"Whiskey, if you have it," I answered.

I studied the gentle curve of her neck while she clinked the ice into the glasses. "That's Charles's preference as well," she said. Charles entered the room and she handed us both a glass. She poured herself a small glass of sherry and turned toward us. "To your successful recovery," she said, raising her glass.

We tipped our glasses. The amber liquid burned my throat, but I welcomed its calming influence. "Charles and I have been very busy since I saw you last," she said.

Yes," Charles answered, "Why don't we sit down? I'll let Catherine fill you in. I'm just here to lend my support."

I took a seat across from Catherine and Charles remained standing nearby. I waited a moment while Catherine gathered her thoughts. "You were wise to insist on giving our emotions time to heal from the trauma of Jelle's death," Catherine said. "It gave me time to focus on other issues." She glanced at Charles who smiled in encouragement. "As you know, Charles has helped me to file a lien against some property Gregor owned in northwest Iowa as payment for the money he swindled from me. We have been working on the settlement all winter long and the judge has finally awarded me the title to the property!"

"That's wonderful news," I said, "But I don't see how that involves me."

"The land is located in the heart of the grasshopper district, near Sheldon, Iowa. Do you know the area?"

"I know it well," I said. "It is about 30 miles north of Orange City, not far from my own land. I believe the area was part of the original St. Paul and Sioux City land grant. Gregor came to Jelle trying to sell the land to the syndicate. I thought it was another one of his fraudulent schemes."

"He apparently purchased the land from a beleaguered homesteader during the grasshopper plague at a sharply reduced price," Charles said. "He still held the deed to it when he died."

"I plan to come west to inspect the property and I was hoping you could accompany me," Catherine continued. "Your knowledge of the area and its agricultural potential would be of great assistance to me in deciding what to do with the property. I would go alone, but Charles is adamantly against it. Unfortunately, he is committed to another business excursion through the northwest that will take several months, and I was hoping to make the journey before the weather turns cold."

"I would consider it a great favor if you agree," Charles interjected.

Relief flooded through me. "Of course!" I exclaimed. "Nothing would make me happier."

Catherine clapped her hands and her broad smile made the room even brighter. "It's all set then!" she exclaimed. "I know you are anxious to return to Iowa, so I can be ready to leave at a moment's notice."

"I was hoping to leave in a couple of days," I said. "Will that give you enough time to pack?"

Charles laughed. "She's been packed for days," he said. "She's just been waiting for me to give my blessings for her to go. Now that it is all settled, I suggest we retire to the dining room. Mrs. Jennings will skin us alive if her dinner is ruined. She's been slaving over it all day."

After dinner, Catherine and I went for a stroll in the garden. We were greeted by a rich tapestry of yellow, purple, and blue, and the sweet scent of flowering crabapples. "I'm glad you were able to salvage something from your mother's inheritance," I said.

We were silent for several minutes, listening to the rustling sound of the wind through the trees and letting the moment wash over us. Catherine turned to look at me. "Do you ever regret losing the promissory note?" she asked.

I thought about her question for several minutes before answering. The promissory note had changed the course of my life. It had altered my perception of who I was. Pursuing its promise had brought about pain and suffering and put lives in danger. I was glad to be rid of it. "My father used to preach against the sin of covetousness," I said, at last. "The promissory note made me desire something that had never really been mine. Losing it has finally set me free."

She reached out and ran her fingers down my jaw, pausing to caress the scar on my cheek. Her touch caused shock waves to ripple through my body. The closeness of her excited my senses. She leaned toward me and I pulled her close. She came to me eagerly. Her lips were moist, sweet, and inviting. I held her close listening to her gentle breathing and feeling the beating of her heart next to mine. "I don't think I can ever let you go again," I whispered, stroking her hair.

She nuzzled against me. "There is something I need to tell you," she said, quietly. She pulled away from me and gazed at me intently.

"What is it?" I asked.

"Lily is not my niece."

"I had assumed..." I began.

"I know," she said. "I didn't correct you because I wasn't sure how you would react."

Slowly the realization dawned on me...the crooked smile, the dark eyes that stared at me so intently. Still, I was reluctant to believe what was now so obvious. "What are you saying?"

"Lily is your child."

Hearing the words out loud had the effect of stopping time in its tracks. The world began to spin, and for a moment, everything went black. I felt Catherine's hand on mine and heard her voice as if it were suspended in space. "Hank? Are you alright?"

"Why didn't you tell me?"

"I tried to, but you left me at the station before I had a chance."

"Leaving you was the hardest thing I have ever done in my life. I was consumed with guilt and shame over Jelle's death and the danger I had put you in."

"There was no need to feel guilty. It was my own obsession with Gregor that led me into his trap. If anyone should feel guilty, it should be me for causing the death of both Nathan and Jelle."

My emotions battled for control of my thinking. "I should have stayed with you. It was selfish of me to put my own emotional turmoil ahead of yours."

"I don't deny that I hated to see you leave, but I also understood that you needed to return to Iowa...to the land you had come to love. It was the only place where you could begin to heal. Besides, I wasn't alone. I had Lily."

"I would never have left if I had known."

"I didn't want to trap you into staying. You had to want to stay on your own."

I tried to process what she was telling me. It was as if the earth had suddenly changed its rotation and nothing was the same as it had been. My mind was reeling with the possibilities. I had a daughter! I had a family. I brushed a stray hair from her face and kissed her tenderly.

She smiled and took my hand leading me deeper into the garden. "Come on," she said, "I want to show you something."

We walked toward a line of trees at the western edge of the property that bordered a small stream. Clusters of violets bloomed in sunlit patches along the edge of the bank.

Catherine knelt and picked a small cluster; then she gently pushed it into the stream. "This is for Jelle," she said, watching it float away. "I never had a chance to say a proper goodbye."

I put my arm around her waist and pulled her close. "He was a loyal friend," I said, when I could trust my voice to speak. "I have never known anyone quite like him."

Catherine turned to face me. "Everything that was good in Jelle, he passed on to you. He will live on in your heart along with the other memories you hold dear."

I picked another cluster of violets from the bank and set it adrift. "And this one is for Lainie," I said. "May she rest in peace."

I felt a profound sense of release as we stood together watching the violets float out of sight. I was finally letting go of things that were out of my control. As my past floated away, I realized that now my life had the space to create new beginnings. With Catherine by my side, the future looked bright and full of opportunities.

Epilogue

Catherine and I were married early Sunday morning on July 4, 1876 at Abraham's home. Her brother, Charles, had arrived for the occasion with Lily and Mrs. Jennings. After church we all headed to town for the festivities. It was the first centennial celebration of signing of the Declaration of Independence and everyone in the community turned out. There were three-legged races and sack races in the morning for the children, followed by a parade. Colorful floats had been constructed on wagon beds and the bridles of the horses were decorated with bright flowers. Catherine and I rode atop one of the floats with Lily by our side and threw sweets to the children on the sidelines. The floats were followed by a marching band made up of locals playing whatever musical instrument they could find. The parade ended at a small park at the end of the town's main street where a bandstand had been erected amidst a grove of young trees.

Local politicians took advantage of the public platform to deliver fiery political speeches to anyone who would listen. One speaker invited anyone who was heavy laden in other lands to come and find freedom and liberty on our shores. Another challenged England to a fight and berated the King, calling him a skunk and causing ripples of laughter to flow through the crowd.

"We can thank Jacob Van Pelt for the freedom we are enjoying today," I said to Catherine. "If he had not provided assistance to Washington's army at Valley Forge, we might still be under the King's rule."

"We owe him and those like him a debt of gratitude," she said, nudging me forward. "I think you should do the honors."

Several others joined in to encourage me to speak and I reluctantly found myself being pushed forward toward the stage. I looked out over my friends and neighbors and felt a profound sense of gratitude. These people had banded together to form a common brotherhood dedicated to embracing the promise of American independence while still preserving our own national heritage. Abraham and his wife beamed and applauded loudly as I stepped forward. Berta Stanford cradled her new baby while her husband looked on proudly. In the distance, the long low moan of the train whistle signaled another arrival. From my vantage point, a clear view of the town spread out before me. There was the mercantile run by Berta's father. embracing the promise of American independence Several other new businesses lined the street on either side. Across the street was an imposing two-story stone building where Jelle's bank had once stood. The building housed Stanford's new bank which was now one of the premier financial institutions in the area.

My attention was drawn to a young girl with a lilting laugh at the far edge of the crowd. She flashed a bright smile and tossed her golden curls at an admiring group of young men. She caught my eye momentarily and smiled as if in recognition, and for a moment, time stood still. She gave an almost imperceptible nod and quickly turned back to her admirers. Just then Catherine and Lily pushed their way to the front of the stage and smiled up at me with encouragement. I glanced back at the spot where the girl had been, but she had disappeared.

A hush fell over the crowd while they waited for me to speak. I stepped forward hesitantly, unsure of what to say. "On this special day, I would like to offer a word of thanks to all those who made this day possible," I began with a faltering voice. "Many of us gathered here today are immigrants. Some of us came seeking religious and economic freedom, and others of us came to escape a past that threatened to destroy our futures. It is never easy to leave an old life behind, but we saw America as a chance for new beginnings. We knew it would be difficult, but we also knew it would be worth the effort if we worked hard and persevered."

I glanced down at Catherine's smiling face and was filled with a new sense of purpose and pride. I felt my voice gain strength and power as I continued. "We know that our struggles are not over, but a journey like this can only succeed with the help of others who extend the hand of friendship and help us along the way." A general hum of approval coursed through those assembled and several of them nodded in agreement. "However, we must always remember that without the foresight of this country's founding fathers, we would not have all the rights and privileges we enjoy today. We may never know the names or the personal sacrifices of all those who are responsible for this freedom. This heritage is ours by choice and by adoption. May we never regard it lightly!" I sought out Catherine in the crowd and was surprised to see her dabbing at her eyes. "May we ever be grateful to those unsung heroes who in years past have labored and loved in order that we might have something to inherit and pass on to our children. They have given us the power to choose, and therein lies our freedom."

The crowd broke into loud applause when I finished. Abraham pumped my hand enthusiastically and several others slapped me on the back as I left the stage. The band was already starting to take its place on the bandstand as Catherine and I made our way through the crowd with Lily between us. I thought again of the golden-haired girl I had seen earlier. For one fleeting moment we had shared a common bond, but her smile had set me free. It had been almost ten years since I had left my homeland to escape the memories that lay buried there, but I had continued to keep one foot in the past. It was time to let go. Time to release the hurt and fear. I squeezed Catherine's hand and she smiled at me as if she had read my thoughts. The energy it had taken me to hang onto the past had held me back too long. It was time to embrace the future.

ACKNOWLEDGMENTS

I owe a sincere vote of thanks to the people who provided support and insight into the writing of this book. To my editors, Stella Port and Ann Hamer, I offer my sincere appreciation for your sharp-eyed comments and guidance in bringing this work to completion. Thanks also to my extremely talented and patient cover designer, Alexander von Ness whose creativity has brought the heart of all my stories to life. Thanks also to all those who volunteered to read and critique this book at various stages of completion. Your comments and suggestions provided valuable input towards improving the final product.

And finally, this work would not have been completed without the love and support of all my friends and family who kept encouraging me when the motivation to write had all but died. To my husband, Ken, you are the love of my life and my rock. Thank you for always being in my corner.

A Note on Sources

While I have attempted to maintain the integrity of the historical events and places mentions in this novel, I acknowledge that some liberty has been taken to support the plot and setting. I consulted a variety of sources during the writing of this book. Chief among those were "A Dutch Immigrants Success Story: E.J.G. Bloemendaal's Sojournes and Settlement in Northwest Iowa," by Brian W. Beltman, (State Historical Society of Iowa, Volume 62, Spring 2003.), and "History of the St. Paul & Sioux City Railroad, 1864-1881" by Gen. Judson W. Bishop, (Library of Congress, April 13, 1903) both of which are available online as are various descriptions of the Great Chicago Fire. The former supplied first-hand knowledge of Dutch immigration and settlement in Iowa. The latter provided insight into the building of the railroad and the solution to the grasshopper plague of 1873.

Information on Dutch railroad investments including the Des Moines Valley Railroad was gleaned from *Slow Train to Paradise: How Dutch Investment Helped Build American Railroads*, by Augustus J. Veenendaal., Jr. (Stanford University Press, 1996). Other sources providing background on American railroad expansion during the Gilded Age include *Railroaded: The Transcontinentals and the Making of Modern America* by Richard White (W.W. Norton & Company, New York, 2011) and *The Great American Railroad War: How Ambrose Biere and Frank Norris Took on the Notorious Central Pacific Railroad* by Dennis Drabelle, (St. Martin's Press, New York, 2012).

Although the story of Jacob Van Pelt is based on a historical family account of Jacob DeHaven as documented in the *New York Times*, May 27, 1990, the story of an illegitimate heir is solely a product of the author's imagination.